# Mistress of Music

## Grace's Story

# Mistress of Music

## Grace's Story

Ladies of Independent Means Trilogy, Book 2

# EVELYN RICHARDSON

CAVEL
PRESS

Kenmore, WA

A Camel Press book published by Epicenter Press

Epicenter Press
6524 NE 181st St.
Suite 2
Kenmore, WA 98028

For more information go to:
www.Camelpress.com
www.Coffeetownpress.com
www.Epicenterpress.com
www.evelynrichardson.net



This is a work of fiction. Names, characters, places, brands, media, and incidents are either the product of the author's imagination or are used fictitiously.

Cover design by Scott Book
Interior design by Melissa Vail Coffman

Mistress of Music: Grace's Story
Copyright © 2022 by Evelyn Richardson

ISBN: 978-1-94207-844-9 (Trade Paper)
ISBN: 978-1-94207-845-6 (eBook)

Library of Congress Control Number: 2022932666

Printed in the United States of America

*To two wonderful colleagues/friends, and superb
librarians, who have supported me through thick and thin:
Jane Eastman and Cathie Ghorbani*

# ACKNOWLEDGMENTS

I AM FOREVER GRATEFUL FOR THE FRIENDSHIP and support of Kristin Ramsdell (former romance reviewer for *Library Journal)* and author of (among others) *Romance Fiction: a Guide to the Genre* and John Charles, *Booklist* reviewer, and co-author of (among others) *Romance Today: and A to Z Guide of Contemporary American Romance Writers*. What would I do without your inspiration and encouragement? And to Melinda Helfer of *Romantic Times* to whom I shall always be grateful for advising me to torture my characters as much as possible. You are missed.

# CHAPTER 1

The music washed over her like a benediction as Grace, oblivious to the candles in enormous crystal chandeliers gleaming on the sumptuous white and gold surroundings gave herself up to the beauty of the moment. The time was hers to lose herself in the magical notes of *Die Zauberflote* and forget everything else. She drew a deep breath as the world receded and music took over. Music had always been her joy, her companion, her solace, and the Philharmonic Society concerts in the Argyll Rooms, her one indulgence. Here, she could be herself again, and here, unlike the opera, where the ladies from Mrs. Gerrard's select establishment went to see and be seen, she could relax and enjoy—as once upon a time she had relaxed and enjoyed the music filling their happy little home in Oxford. She closed her eyes and pictured her mother and father together on the piano bench playing four-handed, as they smiled tenderly at one another and their daughter playing on the floor beside them.

"... wishes to make your acquaintance." Her companion's voice brought Grace back to reality with a start. She had been so lost in memories and the music that she hadn't even realized the concert was over or that the nice-looking young man standing respectfully at Mrs. Taylor's elbow was regarding Grace with a deferential earnestness more in keeping with one of her father's students than with any of the men she had encountered since coming to London.

"As I was *saying*," Mrs. Taylor gave her a significant look, "Lord Farnsworth begs an introduction, Miss Owen."

"Oh . . . er . . . yes. I am honored, my lord." Completely forgetting her courtesan's ways, Grace slipped back into the manners of her childhood.

"No, it is *I* who am honored, and delighted to discover a fellow musician in this crush. I *am* correct in thinking you are a musician? No one in the audience except you seemed to notice the few slips here and there in what was otherwise an excellent performance. On the whole, however, I thought Miss Frith did a most creditable job, though I could see you wince when her duet partner hesitated a fraction of a second too long."

Grace really looked at him this time. He was not only a deferential, but a very observant young man indeed—an unusual combination in a society where men cultivated an air of enervated boredom to an extraordinary degree. You appear to be a mind-reader, my lord."

"I also noticed you looking at music the other day in Chappell's," he admitted with a self-deprecating smile.

"Ah, then I take that back about the mind-reader, but you are correct, I *did* notice the hesitation." *And I also would have sung more powerfully than Miss Frith*, Grace added to herself. *Will sing more powerfully than Miss Frith . . . when I give my own benefit concert,* she amended.

"Then you must be a singer. I, too, am a musician, but, as a devotee of the organ I am not so finely attuned to vocal music."

"The organ?"

"I only admit that to someone who can appreciate musical passion as surely you must. My family would rather I spend my time on anything else, and as for composing, they think that a dreadful waste of my time," he admitted sheepishly.

How odd that someone who, from his title and the somber richness of his clothing, would seem to have all the advantages in the world, felt as thwarted as she in following his dream.

The crowd began to close in on them as they proceeded towards the door and Lord Farnsworth again addressed himself to Mrs. Taylor. "This crush is hardly conducive to conversation, but I should like very much to continue it if it is possible for me to call on Miss Owen?"

"Miss Owen, is very much engaged at the moment. As a student of Signor Lanza she must spend her time on her music."

Even Grace was taken aback at her companion's fierce expression and forbidding tone.

"Oh. I see. I *do* beg your pardon. I hope I am not too impertinent. It is just so rare that I find anyone I can talk to that . . . that . . ."

"Perhaps we may encounter you here again at another concert, my lord." Grace was no proof against the disappointment in his brown eyes or the hopeful expression that lit up his long bony face. She favored him with an encouraging smile as Mrs. Taylor hustled her out to Mrs. Gerrard's elegant carriage.

"Now what on earth possessed you to encourage that young man when you *know* Mrs. Gerrard would tell you he is utterly unsuitable—a nice young man like that in our establishment? How could you think such a thing?"

"Mrs. Gerrard's has nothing to do with this," Grace protested. "I know Helen's standards—only those who have *the town bronze, the taste, the fashion, and the blunt.* I would not be a party to luring an innocent into our place, I assure you, but I see nothing wrong with giving him a bit of intelligent conversation at a concert every now and then."

"There will be the devil to pay." Mrs. Taylor sighed gloomily. "If he doesn't fall in love with you immediately, which he very likely will, then you will fall in love with him and you *know* what Mrs. Gerrard will have to say to that."

"I am not such a fool. Neither Helen nor I has any use for love—not that such a thing even exists. It is merely a weakness, a self-indulgent dream that people use as an excuse to gratify their own vanity while claiming to be devoted to someone else's." Grace knew. She had seen her parents, two fools for love if there ever were. Yes, it had made for a happy home when her mother was alive, and absolute desolation after her death. Her father had been so dependent on his wife for his happiness that he lost all interest in life after she was gone, barely awaking from his drunken stupor from the moment she was laid in her grave until the moment he was laid in his. Oh, Grace knew all about love, and she also knew better than to have anything to do with it. But she would not mind having a friend, especially one who clearly knew about music.

Friends were far more precious and rare than lovers, more devoted and reliable than family, and Grace had never had any until she had come to London and lost everything—home, family, self-respect—everything but the clothes on her back; and then, oddly enough, Mrs. Gerrard's had given it all back plus friendship.

How impossible life had been that day her father had died, so loaded with debt that their landlord could not throw her out on the street fast enough. It was the ultimate betrayal by a man who was only allowed to keep his job in the theater's orchestra because his daughter was forced to endure the loathsome attentions of the theater's manager who was also quick to rid himself of her once her father was gone.

In spite of her words, Grace did suffer an attack of conscience later that evening as she entered Mrs. Gerrard's drawing room where Helen, her face enigmatic as usual, presided over the card table, and Dora regaled a group in the corner with one of her saucy stories. The card players and Dora's coterie were top-of-the-trees men of fashion, of impeccable lineage and dizzying sophistication; Lord Farnsworth, with his earnest intellectual enthusiasm, would be eaten alive in such a crowd. No, Mrs. Gerrard's was no place for him, even if Grace Owen called it home.

"Miss Owen," a cheerful voice interrupted these cynical thoughts as Freddy, Marquess of Wrothingham, bounded over to greet her. Freddy, who had initially patronized the establishment after seeing his future sister-in-law at the opera and visiting her in order to discover the secrets of her dress design and stayed to advise on all matters artistic, was another innocent, but since his interests had everything to do with the redecoration of their establishment and nothing to do with its inhabitants, with the exception of a suggestion or two as to the most becoming cut or color or the latest in trimmings for their gowns, no one thought anything about his being there. In fact, Freddy, having become something of an adopted brother to them all when he helped their dearest Juliette achieve her dream of becoming a fashionable modiste, and now mother of his young nephew, was more comfortable at Mrs. Gerrard's than he was with his supposed peers at the gaming tables of White's, the dance floor at Almack's, or watching the magnificent parade of horseflesh at Tattersall's. Freddy, heir to the Duke of Roxburgh, had eventually been responsible for introducing his entire family to the ladies at Mrs. Gerrard's: his brother Major Lord Adrian Claverton, who had married Juliette, his brother the Reverend Lord John Claverton, who escaped St George's Hanover Square as often as he could to offer them spiritual counsel, and his sister Lady Georgiana, who had finally been convinced to adopt a presentable wardrobe by patronizing Juliette's shop. "I do hope you will indulge us with a song or too—nothing too elaborate," he lowered his voice confidentially, "I know you can easily hit the high F in *Der Holle Rache kocht in meinem Herzen*, but this crowd will be more entertained by popular airs than a challenging aria from *The Magic Flute*"

Freddy had been gently leading her to the pianoforte as he spoke, and now he pointed proudly to some sheets of music on it. "Try this new song by Dibdin. You will find it a trifle easy, and the sentiments are not very original, but the connection of the words with Mr. Whitaker's melody is very well done and easily appreciated." He nodded toward the rest of the drawing room's inhabitants.

Freddy was right, as usual, where matters of taste were concerned, and soon Dora's little group had turned to listen, applaud, and ask for more. Winking at Grace, the Marquess lifted up the music of *Now Isn't It A Pity* to reveal more music beneath—Gentle *Zephyrs*. No, it wasn't Mozart and it wasn't challenging, but the room had fallen silent as Grace felt the power of her voice pulling them to her. Would she have the same effect on stage at the opera? Could she capture their attention, make them feel the beauty, give them a moment of magic, lift the audience out of themselves to receive the gifts that music gave her?

Freddy, her loyal admirer always made her feel as though she could, made her feel that she could equal—even eclipse—Catalani herself, and Freddy, who had attended nearly every one of the celebrated singer's performances would know.

What would Lord Farnsworth think? Freddy was kindness itself, and he wanted to help her realize her dream, but Grace needed the opinion of someone—a musician—who didn't know her story, who only knew her music, someone, not a teacher who was being paid to maximize her range, improve her breathing, and increase her power of projection. She pictured again the fire of enthusiasm in Lord Farnsworth's otherwise gentle brown eyes and the tautness of his hands as he spoke of his music. He, despite his obvious youth and fresh country innocence, would be the perfect person

# CHAPTER 2

"I TELL YOU, UNCLE MAX, SHE IS the first woman I have encountered in London worth speaking to," Randall responded just a touch defensively in response to his uncle's notable lack of enthusiasm over his new acquaintance.

"At a concert?" Lord Maximilian Hawkesbury didn't know why he should be surprised. He shouldn't have expected Hubert's son and heir to be any less of a slow-top than Hubert, Marquess of Swanton was. And a bluestocking who attended concerts during the London Season was still more interesting than Randall's mother, Almeria, who was not only plain as pikestaff, but much given to good works which were, next to an enormous dowry, not to put too fine a point on it, her only claims to fame. The Marquess and Marchioness of Swanton had little style, and less grace, not to mention absolutely *no* interest in the *ton* which was why Max had been pressed into service to guide their son through its dangerous waters. Rustics they might be, but Hubert and Almeria knew their duty. In order for the Hawkesburys to continue, an heir to their heir was required. For that one needed a suitable wife, and suitable wives were only to be found in London at the height of the Season, hence the presence of Max, pulled reluctantly back into the bosom of a family he'd done his best to avoid for the past decade or so.

"Should be just your sort of thing, old fellow; this marriage business requires a delicate diplomatic touch," Hubert had nodded with ponderous humor as he had broached the subject one evening during Max's obligatory annual visit to Swanton Abbey. "All that gallivanting around Europe, hobnobbing with those dandified Frenchies ought to have taught you a thing or two. Surely after negotiating a peace with that lot, arranging a suitable alliance for Randall should be the merest nothing." Hubert pursed his lips in the face of

Max's thunderous silence. "And it is not as though you have done anything for the family lately."

*Or at all*, Max thought. And that was not by accident. The pursuit of glory in a military career had been less than appealing to an intelligent young man longing to see the world, but the opportunity to put as much distance between himself, his clinging mother, sanctimonious elder brother, and loose screw of a father had almost enticed Max into joining the cavalry until a chance meeting with Lord Castlereagh, a fellow Cantabridgean who was desperately searching for a brilliant young man to help him as he assumed the presidency of the Board of Control for Indian Affairs, had eventually plunged Max into foreign affairs, sending him to places as far distant, and not necessarily less dangerous, than he would have gone as a cavalry officer; however, they were more challenging to his intellect and more satisfying to his insatiable desire to learn.

It was these last two characteristics that had set him apart from most of his fellow men as well as his family. Sporting-mad friends simply could not grasp that when Max joined them at Newmarket, he was just as interested in the mathematics of the betting as in the horses themselves, and those whose fencing and pugilistic skills he outshone at Angelo's and Gentleman Jackson's were not the least bit comforted to be told that his success was owing more to his understanding of anatomy and physics than physical capabilities. Most females, on the other hand, were more than ready to attest to the outstanding perfection of his physique, from the broad shoulders to the narrow waist and powerful long legs.

There was one person, however, besides Castlereagh, who not only appreciated Max's intellectual acumen, but shared it, another *black sheep* of the family, as Max's mother liked to call him when bemoaning her younger son's lack of filial devotion, Max's Uncle Richard, his father's only brother, who had shamed the family forever by going into trade. Uncle Richard, who had only briefly met his nephew at his father's funeral during Max's last year at Cambridge, had struck up a conversation with him at the family gathering afterwards, largely to avoid having to speak to anyone else, had recognized in his nephew a kindred questioning spirit. In no time at all, he had found himself explaining the intricacies of finance, funds, consols, and other securities to an unexpectedly intrigued and knowledgeable listener, and both of them had surprised themselves by passing the time far more agreeably than either one could have imagined.

Neither one of them had, had much time to pursue the relationship except with an occasional letter or when Max, in the course of his diplomatic duties and a growing awareness of the objectives of foreign powers, would send his uncle informative articles from foreign newspapers that might prove useful in the prediction of prices or markets.

The fact that Uncle Richard had become fabulously wealthy had done nothing to improve his reputation in the eyes of the rest of the family and it had caused a good deal of annoyance when he head left his entire fortune to his nephew after his untimely demise in a balloon ascension gone horribly wrong, which explained Max's presence in London at this particular moment.

It was not that Max wanted to be in London—boring, hopelessly rigid, dully homogenous place that it was. In fact, he would have preferred almost anywhere else—Paris, naturally—but even St. Petersburg, or Venice or Rome would have been livelier, or at least less tedious and predictable than London at the height of the Season. But he owed it to his uncle to settle his affairs as he would have wished them, and he could only do so by managing them in person and in London. A man like Uncle Richard deserved no less.

So here was Max, marooned with a nephew who, though intelligent enough to be interesting, was not. Like his father, Randall, tended toward the ponderous, and what could be more ponderous than devotion to music, not to mention, the organ. "Perhaps you will see her at Almack's?" In Max's opinion dancing and gossiping at the holy temple of the *ton* was not high on the list of entertainment, but it was certainly more enlivening than a concert, and absolutely obligatory for a young man in search of a wife, or a young man whose parents wanted him to be in search of a wife. And not all the women at Almack's were young. Some of them were bound to be dashing matrons with complaisant husbands who did not care how much they amused themselves with a worldly stranger, as long as they were discreet.

Max was definitely a stranger to the *ton* which he had avoided like the plague even in his salad days, not so much because he found its rituals irritating and devoid of interest (though he did), but because his mother worshipped at its gathering places and was likely to press him into service as an escort, on the rare occasion she was without some slavish doddering courtier, or to push him into the arms of every eligible heiress regardless of age, attributes or appearance, in other words, to embarrass him in most cases and irritate him in all of them. Now, however, he was older and wiser and had discovered that brutal honesty, applied in the most public places, kept her away—that, and his connection with trade, which he never failed to mention whenever she forced her demanding presence on him.

Yes, a spritely young matron with appetites left unsatisfied by an inattentive spouse would be just the diversion Max needed to endure the rigors of the Season. It was a pity that Englishwomen never seemed as clever or witty as their coquettish continental sisters. It would be too much to ask for both sensual and mental stimulation here in England, but a man could dream.

". . . besides, not likely to be at Almack's from what her companion said," Randall pressed on.

"Not at Almack's? What sort of young woman would not be at Almack's?" Lord, he sounded as bad as his mother, or every other town tabby, but Max was no fool, and only a fool would have ignored this suspicious bit of information.

"As I said, she seems very strictly brought up, indulging in only the most educational and improving pursuits, like the Philharmonic Society. I gather they live very quietly and do not go about much which I, for one, admire." Randall's jaw lifted ever so slightly.

"Well, your parents won't. They will admire a well brought-up young woman who includes Almack's in her social pursuits and who is on excellent terms with several, if not all, of its patronesses. The attention of the Earl of Farnsworth is not to be wasted on a nobody."

Randall's jaw jutted even more defiantly. "I do not need a social butterfly if I am to devote my life to the organ. What I *will* need is a wife who understands music and is equally devoted to it. Anyone who has been accepted as a student by Gesualdo Lanza is the very essence of devotion to music. Signor Lanza's time is too precious for him to waste on anyone except the very best musicians, and that means not only the most talented, but also the hardest working. Perhaps, when we become better acquainted, I might ask Miss Owen if I could attend one of her lessons."

Max raised an incredulous eyebrow. This was serious indeed. Up until now, Randall had not evinced the least spark of interest in a bevy of eligible young ladies the *ton's* matchmaking mamas had thrust at him. Actually, Max didn't blame him—insipid milk-and-water misses every one of them, but even though Max was looking for something a good deal livelier and more sophisticated for himself, he would have thought these indistinguishably proper young damsels would have been just the thing for his sober young nephew. Apparently not. "And how are you to become better acquainted if she never goes out?" Max asked, not that he cared, but conversation, especially idle conversation with Randall was difficult, so, presented with an opportunity, he seized it like the skilled diplomat he was.

"Oh I expect I shall talk to her at the next Philharmonic Society concert."

And that, to all intents and purposes, was that. Certainly Randall appeared to be confident enough of the next encounter that Max did not waste a second thought on it. As long as he did not have to suffer the company of ape-leaders and bluestockings at a musical program not enlivened by opera dancers, he was more than satisfied. Then, feeling slightly guilty for such an unfamilial attitude, unspoken though it was, he offered to accompany his nephew to the opera.

"Oh, that's very kind of you, Uncle, but my taste runs to rather more serious music."

"More serious than Mozart? Surely you will not dismiss *Don Giovanni* as being frivolous."

A singularly sweet smile transformed Randall's relentlessly earnest countenance. "Why, thank you, Uncle Max, I do believe I would enjoy that."

And Max, oddly warmed by that smile, realized that he would too, and took himself to task for being so quick to label what he thought was dullness in a nephew when it could simply be shyness or a lack of confidence. After all, it did take a fair amount of fortitude to pursue one's interests in the face of family disapproval. Max could certainly appreciate that.

# CHAPTER 3

**B**ᴜᴛ ᴡʜᴀᴛ Rᴀɴᴅᴀʟʟ ʜᴀᴅ ᴛʀᴜʟʏ ᴇɴᴊᴏʏᴇᴅ was Grace's lesson with Signor Lanza to which he had ultimately been invited. Enjoyed was rather a tame word for his rapturous silence as she finished the last of her week's exercises and turned to her teacher for her next assignment.

Against her better judgment, and *definitely* against Mrs. Taylor's, Grace had given in to her longing to know what a real musician thought of her singing and invited Lord Farnsworth to attend her lesson. Freddy, enthusiast though he was, could not compare as a critic to someone who was actually studying for his degree in music from Oxford.

Randall was more than willing to admit that while his courses of study taught him a great deal about composition, they did not teach him much about execution which he had learned from the organist at his college chapel and any others he could interest in sharing their skills with him, but this still gave him better insight than Freddy into the challenges Grace sought for herself.

"I hope you will forgive my bemusement the other day," Randall apologized to Grace at the Philharmonic Society's concert later that week, "I am never one for clever conversation, and it takes me some time to articulate my opinions, but I was most struck by the range and clarity of your voice. More important, though, was your interpretation, the tempo, the pauses, the emphasis on certain notes. You have a natural instinct for what I struggle to learn from my teachers. You are fortunately indeed," he added wistfully, "simply to be born with all that talent and the innate knowledge that I have yet to acquire. But," he brightened, "my professors assure me that I do have the capability. In the meantime, they are exceedingly generous with their time and their knowledge."

*How could I not have the instinct when music was all my parents could spare their time for—that and each other?* Grace wondered. She longed to ask Randall if he'd heard of her father, if Thaddeus Owen was still known at the university, now, after time had softened the final unfortunate years, if he were re-membered as the brilliant musician and composer he had been, or the pathetic drunk who had skulked off to London with his young daughter under a cloud of disapproval. But even Grace, who had taught herself to face anything in life, could not face the answer he might give her.

"Thank you for that. It means so much to me to have an opinion from someone who is not only knowledgeable, but objective. Signor Lanza is expert enough, but naturally, he wants me to continue lessons so I shall *never* be good enough for him."

Randall, though he never noticed such things, thought he had never seen anything so beautiful as Grace Owen at this moment, her brilliant blue eyes sparkling with tears of gratitude, while the perfectly shaped lips twisted into a ruefully appealing smile, and it occurred to him that Miss Owen was not only a superb musician, she was a most attractive woman.

Grace's conscience smote her as she saw this realization dawn on him. "Oh dear, I am carrying on like a jaw-me-dead when we really should be going." Gathering up her shawl, she took Mrs. Taylor's arm and hurried toward the door.

"A jaw-me-dead? And when have *you* ever been missish?" Mrs. Taylor was not the least taken in by this little performance, which even Grace knew was weak. Now you *are* in the basket, my dear, for that young man is besotted, even though he isn't aware of it yet."

"I know. I know. I shouldn't have . . . but I *did* so want to know if I were really and truly good and . . ." Grace's voice trailed off as a host of unfamiliar emotions washed over her: guilt for taking advantage of innocence, longing for professional recognition, hope that her dream was not a complete and utter delusion, and confusion—she who was never confused about anything—not after that one awful life-changing moment when the manager of the Sans Pareil Theater had taken her over his desk and threatened her father's job unless she gave him what he wanted. Since then she had focused single-mindedly on their survival, not necessarily successfully, until Helen and her establishment had saved her and she had begun to erase that awful helplessness at the hands of the lecherous Smedley by making men pay to be victims of their own desires. But not Randall. She could not do that to that sweet boy. He, and his apprecia-tion for her talent were for her future, validating her dreams and obliterating her past.

Olivia Childs, the actress and singer who had sent the destitute and home-less Grace to Helen had also gotten her the introduction to Signor Lanza who never would have given her a second glance if she hadn't been very good. On the other hand, Olivia was a friend and mentor and Signor Lanza *was* being paid handsomely for his time, so, in an odd sort of way, Randall was the first musician whose approval really meant something, and it scared her because now it meant she had to do something about this validation, something more than just taking music lessons and entertaining anyone who happened to be in Mrs. Gerrard's drawing room and dreaming of bringing music to rapt audiences.

But how to start?

That was answered the moment the carriage deposited her in front of Mrs. Gerrard's impressive entrance on St. James' Square after her lessons followed by a drive in the park and errands. Grace heard the laughter and conversation spilling down from the drawing room as she paused in the black and white marble hall. The laughter grew louder as Dora, smiling up at him, led a rakish looking gentleman to the elegant curved staircase. "If your presence is required by one of the patronesses, then you must at least put in an appearance at Almack's." Her smile broadened, "I don't blame her for commanding your attention, but it's her loss; we're so much more amusing here."

"That you are, Miss Dora, that you are, but, *needs must when the devil drives.* Besides, an obligatory appearance on a regular basis lulls them all into complacency so they ignore how and where I enjoy my other amusements, and enjoy them, I do." He was about to plant a kiss on the lush red lips, but was stopped cold by Fenwick's basilisk stare.

Mrs. Gerrard's butler knew that the success of the business carried on upstairs depended on the strictest propriety being maintained on the more public ground floor. Mrs. Gerrard had entrusted the respectability of her establishment to his discriminating presence and he guarded it with the devoted authority of a grateful man saved from ruin by an alert compassionate woman who had recognized in the drunken sot lying in a doorway the former butler of an illustrious house whose name he had never revealed despite being illtreated at the hands of an ungrateful heir. From the moment she had brought him to St. James' Square, Helen Gerrard had possessed Fenwick's total, dignified, and undying devotion.

Giving Lord Williston a final wink as the butler closed the door behind him, Dora waited for Grace on the landing. "You do not look as though you are ready to go in there." She nodded toward the brilliantly lit drawing room. "Come upstairs for a moment before you face them."

Sinking into the chair in Dora's chamber, Grace smiled gratefully. "Thank you. You are right. I need a moment to compose myself No . . . I need to think."

Dora sat quietly waiting, and that was what Grace liked best about her, about all the women at Mrs. Gerrard's. Each one had her painful story to tell, and each one knew the comfort of telling it to someone who really listened. Even if it didn't solve anything, talking helped to organize one's thoughts and, more rare and precious than anything, it helped soothe the ache inside to be understood at last by someone else who had been cast off and ignored by society—worse than that, by humanity itself. "In a way, it is a good thing," Grace began, "Lord Farnsworth told me this evening how much he admires my singing . . . not just admires it, but knows it is good. I know, I know, Freddy admires it as well, and he is a dear—a very knowledgeable dear, a connoisseur even—but he is not a trained musician. Lord Farnsworth is a trained musician."

"And so are you."

"Well, I hope I am, but . . ."

Dora shook her head in disgust. "You sound like a silly girl when you say *Lord Farnsworth is a trained musician*," she mimicked Grace's awed tones. "Don't be so bird-witted. He is no more a trained musician than you are—less, actually, for I'll wager he was not playing the pianoforte with his mother at the age of three. The only difference is that he is a man and he is an earl, but he is *not*, he *cannot* be a better musician than you are. It is time to start trusting in your own talent."

"I do, but . . . it's just . . ."

"It's just that if you acknowledge it to yourself, then you have to do something about it, make a life with it the way Juliette is making a life with her shop."

"Juliette is making more than *a life with her shop*." Grace tried not to sound wistful. Even though they all were happy for their former colleague, they missed Juliette's vivaciousness and energy. "She has a home with her husband and her little boy."

"True, but she had her shop first." Dora was insistent.

"And she did it all on her own. Lord Farnsworth came to my lesson because, because . . . he enjoyed my company."

"And when he got there, his enjoyment of your company turned to admiration for your musical skill. You will succeed on your own too. Do *not* tell me that an inhabitant of Mrs. Gerrard's is worrying about capitalizing on a man's genuine appreciation of her and her talent!"

"Well . . . I know it seems odd when we charge so much for our *companionship*, but Lord Farnsworth is so young and innocent I feel guilty about taking advantage of his interest in me. Money given in return for our favors somehow seems so much more straightforward."

"And Mrs. Gerrard's is known as much for its honesty as its exclusivity, but remember, Grace, that even though Juliette would not let Freddy set her up in her shop the first time he offered, and most of the money for her shop came from her earnings here, she did work a perfectly businesslike arrangement with him for the rest when his sister needed a modiste. Just you wait, the right moment and the right circumstances will arise and you will claim your dream just as Juliette did. Besides, your father was a musician, did he not think you were good?"

The emptiness in Grace's eyes tore at Dora's heart. "Father never had the time or the interest to listen to me, even before mother died, and after . . ." her voice trailed off, then she rose. "I should go down to the drawing room now." She paused in the doorway, "Thank you. I feel better," then she grinned, "I knew you would have a bracing effect on me."

"I always do."

# Chapter 4

But the bracing effect was nowhere to be seen in Mrs. Gerrard's box at the opera the next evening. It was *Don Giovanni*, one of Grace's favorites, and it was a struggle to entertain the men crowding around them when the music was so glorious. It was even more difficult to stifle her frustration at Camporese's lackluster performance as Donna Anna. Where Grace would have risked it all, putting her heart and voice into the character and the music, the soprano walked tamely around the stage, playing it safe with every demanding note. And yet, the few members of the audience who were actually listening to this tepid rendition, were enraptured. Grace knew she was better than this passionless creature who stood there as though she were reciting a lesson instead of singing, but how, and when was she ever going to be able to prove herself? It did seem rather impossible when she had only been with Signor Lanza a short time, and all the noted singers had spent years studying at the great opera houses on the Continent, and were foreigners besides. No one wanted to hear an English woman, except for possibly Mrs. Billington, singing opera.

You are far too pensive, fair one," Sir George Neville draped his considerable length on the chair next to her. "Surely you are not listening to the music?"

Giving herself a mental shake Grace tilted her head, flashing a provocative smile, "Now why would I do that when you are around?"

"Why indeed," he reached for her hand and drew it to his lips, languidly trailing kisses up her gloved hand to the bare skin inside her elbow."

As the glossy dark head bent over her arm, Grace caught Dora looking at her. It was the briefest of glances, the barest perceptible nod of her head, but she felt her friend's encouragement, could almost hear her saying, *Of course you can do this, Grace!* That was all it took, for the moment anyway. Of course she could do it—one step at a time down the path toward her dream. And putting the action on stage out of her mind, Grace gave herself up to the real reason she was at the opera, to enslave the regular customers and to evaluate those eager attendants hopeful of being admitted through the discreet portals of London's most elegant and exclusive seraglio.

She was not the only one focusing attention on the occupants of Mrs. Gerrard's box. Directly across from them, another member of the audience happened to glance up from the stage. "It's Miss Owen!" Randall nudged his uncle's shoulder. "Look, over to the right, in the blue."

*And she is absolutely ravishing,* was Max's first thought, *and utterly wasted on Randall.* Then he realized where she was, *what* she was. "Ah . . ."

"So delightful to see you again, my lord . . . an age since we spent so many enchanting hours together in Paris," a tinkling voice that would not be ignored put all thoughts of Randall's mysterious Miss Owen right out of Max's head. Lady Caroline Daventry. Damn and blast! He had thought her safely stuck in Paris. Would that young miss never leave him alone?

"Lady Caroline, Lady Daventry," Max bowed to the shadowy figure hovering behind her determinedly smiling daughter. "This is unfor . . . an unexpected pleasure. I had thought Lord Daventry was hard at work on the reduction of the army of occupation and the indemnity payments."

"Oh he is," his daughter responded blithely, "you know Papa, always at work, but Mama and I needed a little gaiety so we are here for the Season."

As if Paris were not considered the gayest capital in the world, currently inhabited by many more important members of the *ton,* Max thought. "A pity, I should have enjoyed talking with him." Fortunately, everyone in the box was oblivious to the ironic tone he did not bother to hide. "But here, where are my manners, let me introduce you to my nephew." *And that will settle that.* Max edging away from the eager young lady to pay his respects to her mother, congratulated himself on directing both Lady Caroline's and Randall's attention to less dangerous pursuits, for Randall, well brought-up young man that he was, could not pointedly ignore the young lady as his uncle had just done, and Lady Caroline could not verbally lay claim to Max while he was being polite to her mother.

For the rest of the opera, Max devoted his attention to Lady Daventry who was more than happy to catalogue their social calendar in excruciating detail while her daughter, her enthusiasm considerably diminished, conversed in a desultory way with Randall.

There was no escaping helping the Daventry females to their carriage, but in the press of waiting vehicles, Max caught sight of Mrs. Gerrard's carriage— there was no mistaking Botticelli's *Birth of Venus* emblazoned on its panels— and even though its potential occupants were nowhere in sight, Max grimly resolved to pay a call in St. James' Square at the very first opportunity.

While it was true that Mrs. Gerrard's was known as much for its exclusivity as its dazzling and charming inhabitants, Max had few qualms about being admitted to this august sanctum. Its proprietress was known for being better informed on the first families of the *ton* and the exact state of their finances than Debrett's, and there was no doubt that someone as well-connected, both socially and politically as Lord Maximilian Hawkesbury would be welcomed with open arms, especially since he was also exceedingly plump in the pocket. Helen Gerrard, hardheaded businesswoman that she was, knew more about the finances of the Upper Ten Thousand than she did about their family trees, which was considerable.

Feeling in need of a walk to clear his head after the complicated evening, Max dismissed the carriage after depositing his nephew at his lodgings in Half Moon Street and began the walk back to his own chambers at Albany, a walk which, without going a great deal out of his way, just happened to take him past the brilliantly lit windows of a discreetly elegant building in St. James' Square. Mrs. Gerrard's carriage was nowhere in sight, and there was nothing about the classical Portland stone façade to distinguish it from any other building whose noble inhabitants were entertaining that evening, but Max knew the difference. The difference was family fortunes lost, fathers who ignored their wives or children, owners of estates whose rents were never enough to pay for the rapacious demands of inhabitants of establishments such as this, estates whose tenants were impoverished and whose buildings fell into disrepair.

Oh yes, Max, and Hubert, and their sister, Henrietta, knew all about such things. The burden had fallen on Hubert to marry Almeria, who made up in an enormous dowry all that she lacked in wit, charm, or beauty. Henrietta had been left entirely to her own devices, and Max had been stuck with the Dowager Marchioness whose unrelenting demands for money, attention, and admiration had driven him to the Continent and into the arms of women who were safely married, safely discreet, and safely detached from any sort of emotional needs except idle diversion.

Drawing a deep breath of soft spring air, he quickened his pace, leaving the square and its dangerous denizens behind for a glass of brandy in his own chambers, and the papers and dispatches awaiting his perusal. Tomorrow he would tackle the problem at hand and eliminate it—no negotiating or diplomacy this time. Tomorrow Miss Owen would cease to exist, for Randall at least.

# Chapter 5

Oddly enough, Miss Owen had come to exactly the same conclusion as Lord Maximilian Hawkesbury, and before he had even sat down to his breakfast, she had arranged to run into the unsuspecting Randall in front of Signor Lanza's lodgings. It was fortunate, she thought, that she had given in to her selfish desire for his encouragement and told him the days and the times of her lessons, knowing full well this would insure the prompt attendance of such a serious young man.

And there he was, hovering outside the doorway as Mrs. Gerrard's carriage pulled up.

"Miss Owen." Somewhat taken aback by the sumptuousness of the equipage, Randall hurried over to help her down as the footman opened the door.

He was even more taken aback when she invited him inside and tapped on the roof of the carriage.

Grace waited to speak until they had pulled back into traffic. The confusion in his eyes tore at her heart, but she had to do it. Even at the risk of shocking this decent young man, she had to tell him the truth about herself. She had to stop taking advantage of his innocence.

"My lord," she paused. It was a rare thing, after thousands of convivial evenings at Mrs. Gerrard's and tons of thousands of charmingly flirtatious conversations with men of the highest rank and utmost sophistication, to find herself at a loss for words. "My lord, I am not what you think I am."

"Oh but you are. You are a musician, a brilliant musician. I have heard you. There is no way to falsify such true natural talent."

Bless the lad, he really was too dear. And warmed to tears by his genuine admiration, she smiled tremulously as she patted his hand. "Thank you for that.

I *hope* I am a musician. I pray that I am, but I am also something else. I am not the proper young miss you might think I am."

A blank look told her, as she had already guessed, that she was going to have to be brutally honest. "I, er, *live* at Mrs. Gerrard's, a place dedicated to the . . . er *followers* of Venus."

"Ah yes, I saw the crest on the carriage door."

He really was an innocent. "Men come there, my lord to *be* with women."

He nodded, waiting expectantly for her to continue.

"Men like you, my lord, should *not be* with women like me."

"Why ever not?"

"Men *pay* to be with me." She held up her hand to stop the words she knew were coming next. "And men like you, my lord, decent young men, innocent young men, should *not* be paying to be with me. They should not *be* with me at all."

Comprehension dawned. "I see." He nodded slowly, seriously. "But I like you. You are the first interesting, intelligent woman I have met."

Frustration struggled with a heady gratification. "I am supposed to be interesting and intelligent, but I am not any of the things you should be seeking in a woman—excellent breeding, a spotless reputation, an ancient, honorable family, accomplishments that will make her an excellent wife and mother," though there were few families in England as ancient and honorable as Grace's mother's who had cast their daughter into oblivion the moment she married her music teacher, also from a well-known family that refused to acknowledge a son who had rejected his expected military career to become a music professor.

The look in his eyes tore at her heart. "I like you too, my lord. I treasure your friendship, and I especially treasure your musical opinion, but, let me make it abundantly clear that I am not any of those things. Don't be so downcast. It is the way of the world. I accept it, and I care too much about you to let you come to any harm by acting foolishly. Now, give me your hand, and let us part as friends. Believe me, it is the kindest thing for both of us."

"Very well then," he sighed, then flashed her a smile, "but when you are famous I will come to every one of your performances and I will continue to admire your talents as loudly and publicly as I can."

She chuckled and gave his hand an extra squeeze. "That I will allow. You are a very good young man, Lord Farnsworth, and I wish you all the best."

Grace might have smiled as she left Randall, but she was not smiling later as she sank down in the chair by the cheery fire in her bed chamber, a luxury her father had never been able to afford.

"You told him." Helen, enigmatic as ever, materialized in the doorway, the sympathy in her green eyes at odds with her ironic smile.

"Yes I did. I know it was for the best, but . . . but I shall miss him."

"Yes, but you know the human heart is an unreliably dangerous instrument and love does not exist except as a convenient excuse for poets."

"I did not love him; I just enjoyed his company, being able to talk to someone as . . . as a colleague."

The green eyes softened. "Poor Grace. Losing a friend is far worse than losing a lover. Lovers are easily replaced; friends, not so easily." She laid a gentle hand on her protégé's shoulder. "Come, there is no antidote for sorrow and loss like work. Show me all that Signor Lanza has taught you and then have a look at the drawings Freddy has made for re-decorating the drawing room."

In a flash Grace saw something else in those eyes, usually so cynical and enigmatic, and then it was gone, but it was enough to make her realize that Helen's re-decorating project was more than replacing curtains and upholstery. She was following her own advice and plunging into work—she and Freddy. And then Grace saw it. They both missed Juliette too, Juliette whose creative energy had inspired everyone. First it was her designs for gowns that brought out the best of their features and personalities, making them see in themselves all that they could be. Then it was the sumptuous materials, making them feel special and elegant even though the rest of the world might scorn them. And then it was Juliette's shop. Everyone had pitched in, from the footman's daughter, Alice who helped out with the needlework, to Grace and Dora who'd cleaned and polished, to Freddy's sister, Lady Georgiana who kept appearing with disused items from the Claverton House lumber room and who had brought Maison Juliette its first aristocratic customers, to Freddy himself who had designed the elegant looking glass that dominated the shop.

Now, of course, they had the added joy of Juliette's baby boy, Auguste, but he spent most of his time with his parents at Ashbourne Hall where his father bred and raised horses that were already beginning to be talked about among knowledgeable men of the turf.

Yes, losing a friend, even to the happiest of circumstances, was difficult, and even though Juliette visited her shop regularly to deliver designs and instructions and to consult with Alice, it was not the same as having her here at Mrs. Gerrard's, a constant confidante, sister of the heart, and dreamer of ambitious dreams.

Helen was right. It was time to throw themselves into work. Grace rose to lead them to the drawing room downstairs where she took her place at the pianoforte. Work was control, work was expressing one's true self, not the self the world saw, or thought it saw, and work brought independence.

"I cannot promise to take back the wrongs that have been done to you or help you win retribution against those who made you suffer," Helen had told Grace upon her arrival at Helen's establishment, "but I can make you wealthy and independent, I can give you control over your own life by paying you more than most men dream of making in their lifetimes, and by helping you invest your earnings wisely. And," she added cynically, "I have no doubt I will give you a greater and better choice of partner than any of the husband-hunting mamas who haunt Almack's and the assembly rooms all over England looking for the highest-born and wealthiest peers for their daughters, no matter their age, infirmities, deformities, or imbecilities."

Helen had been as good as her word. In the few short years Grace had been at Mrs. Gerrard's, she had more money invested in the consols than her father could ever have imagined, almost as much as her maternal grandfather, Lord Fairfax, had set aside for his daughter's dowry until she had enraged him to the point of cutting her off without a penny when she had married her pianoforte teacher. Grace now lived in greater luxury than she ever could have envisioned in her young life. As far as the men went, they were far less importunate, far more witty and sophisticated than any she had previously encountered, and a surprising number of them, in fact almost all of them, came to Mrs. Gerrard's for conversation and companionship as much as for anything else that went on in the establishment's luxurious bedchambers. As for that, it was no different than having her parents arrange a sensible marriage, and her freedom gave her more power than most wives ever dreamed of having over their husbands.

Grace shook the cobwebs from her brain and returned to the aria from *Don Giovanni* she had been humming to herself before Helen appeared. Hah! She sang it far more skillfully and easily than Camporese despite the opera singer's continental training—at least she thought she did. If only she could ask Randall. He would know, and he would tell her the truth, for surely, if he had not already attended *Don Giovanni* yet, he would, despite his more serious predilections. Music was music, after all, and how else would a serious musician amuse himself on the nights there was no Philharmonic Society concert except at the opera? Then, giving herself a mental shake. Grace put Lord Farnsworth out of her mind for once and for all.

# CHAPTER 6

OR, SHE THOUGHT SHE HAD, but Randall's uncle had other ideas. "There is a gentleman asking for you, Miss Grace," Rose announced the next afternoon as Grace, just having returned from a drive in the park, was removing her hat and pelisse before settling down to look through some new music Signor Lanza had given her.

"Oh?" She smiled at the maid hovering in the doorway. Rose, whose story was the same as everyone else's at Mrs. Gerrard's except that she lacked the beauty, wit, and sophistication to be one of Helen's *ladies*, insisted on treating them all as though they were the grandest ladies in the land and she their fortunate servant in spite of their insistence that she was part of their sisterhood.

"Yes, a Lord Maximilian Hawkesbury here to see you, and Mr. Sandys said to warn you that he didn't look best pleased."

Tom Sandys, the head footman at Mrs. Gerrard's and retired batman now that Major Lord Adrian Claverton's soldiering days were over, had a soft spot for all of the inhabitants of the establishment, especially Dora who had looked out for his daughter, Alice, during the terrible days her father and his master were involved in the ultimate confrontation with the Corsican monster.

*Not looking best pleased* was a mild description for the haughty, measuring stare that practically nailed Grace to the wall as she entered the drawing room. Gray eyes as cold as chips of ice under dark lowered brows on either side of a high-bridged nose bored into hers. High cheekbones, a clenched jaw, and lips set in a determined line did nothing to soften the intensity of what, even the most optimistic of observers would have called a glare.

"My lord." Mentally thanking Helen for her example of consistently poised composure, Grace gestured serenely to a chair on one side of the fireplace as she sank gracefully into the one opposite. Lord the man was arresting, despite his ominous expression. It wasn't just the long legs or broad shoulders that he disposed equally gracefully in the designated chair, it was the suppressed energy, the sense of purpose that radiated from him. Grace couldn't ever remember meeting a man quite like that, and she had met more than enough men in the past few years to last her a lifetime.

*Very clever* was Max's first thought as he surveyed the dark-haired woman across from him. He knew he looked murderous. He *meant* to look murderous. It was a look that had never failed to send petty foreign functionaries scurrying to do his bidding, yet this woman was unruffled as though she were offering tea to a maiden aunt. Never mind her stunning beauty—dark blue eyes set under slender black brows looked straight back at him, tranquilly with an unflinching self-possession he had never seen before in a woman.

"You have the advantage of me, my lord." The voice was compelling, low and musical. Of course it was compelling; she was a singer, and a splendid one according to Randall. His nephew, earnest musician that he was, would not be deceived about such a serious subject.

"You are acquainted with my nephew, Lord Farnsworth."

Not a muscle moved in the exquisitely sculpted face. No hint of conscious color stained the flawless white skin.

"I am."

"Well, unacquaint yourself with him." It was a crude statement, utterly lacking in his usual finesse, but, damn it all, she unnerved him.

"I think not."

It was an equally blunt response, but the languid tone of her voice robbed it of the crudeness of his, putting him at a disadvantage. How to recover? Gritting his teeth, Max summoned up his most winning social smile, the one that had conquered hearts from St Petersburg to Paris, from dowagers to demure misses. "Perhaps I misspoke. I am simply concerned for my nephew who, as you have no doubt surmised, is an excellent young man, but an unsophisticated innocent. I, on the other hand ," he leaned toward her, hoping desperately that the smile reached his eyes, "am not. I can appreciate all this," Max deepened his smile as he gestured at her admiringly, "all this, in a way he simply cannot." Good Lord, what was he doing? Had this woman so discomposed him that he could think of nothing more effective than offering himself in Randall's place? What had happened to the man who had negotiated treaties with diplomacy's toughest adversaries, the man who had not even flinched under Metternich's withering gaze? "And I, Miss Owen, am a far wealthier prize than Lord Farnsworth."

"I think not," she repeated, rising, glorious like the Venus emblazoned on the panels of the establishment's carriage. "You do not appeal to me. Here we choose our men, not the other way around. Perhaps Dora will find you to her liking I shall send her down."

And with that, she left, without a backward glance, glossy dark head held high as she glided from the room.

Not appeal to her? Max had never *not appealed* to a woman in his entire life. The arrogance of the chit! But damn, she was magnificent. She had quite taken his breath away, and the proud flash of her blue eyes before she turned her elegant back on him forced reluctant admiration in him. This was a woman who knew herself, who knew what she wanted, just the way Lord Maximilian Hawkesbury knew himself and what he wanted.

"My lord?" A dark-haired young lady with a wide saucy smile and sparkling brown eyes bounced into the room, or at least she appeared to bounce, radiating vitality and high spirits, from the rose-colored slippers to the matching rose ribbons loosely threaded through rich brown curls.

Max knew what he wanted, and it was not this. He wanted to turn his back and stalk out of the room, but he could not find it in himself to be so rude in the face of such good humor. "You are Miss Dora, I take it."

"Yes, my lord, and I . . ."

"I appreciate your coming down, but if you will excuse me, I have a rather pressing engagement." This woman, at least, seemed to find him attractive enough to look sorry at his departure.

The sparkle vanished from her eyes and her nose wrinkled in frustration or resignation, but she responded cheerily enough. "I am sorry to hear that, my lord. Perhaps another time?"

*Not until hell freezes over.* "We shall see." The barest of noncommittal smiles, a minimal bow, and he was gone, striding down the curved staircase, past the imposing butler, and out into the invigorating spring air.

What had just happened in there and why did Lord Maximilian Hawkesbury feel as though he had come off second-best in his encounters with both women? And worse than that, why was his curiosity piqued by what his good sense told him were very skillful, though undeniably attractive bloodsuckers?

"Uncle Max." The voice came from out of the blue, and it took Max some moments to disengage himself enough from his fit of abstraction to realize that he was in Bond Street and the person hailing him was Randall exiting the doorway of Chappell's, looking as self-conscious as if his uncle had run into him leaving Mrs. Gerrard's instead of the venerable music publisher. Randall, the indirect cause of Max's uncomfortable reflections. Well, he would be the indirect cause no longer. Max was going to nip the entire thing in the bud. "Randall, how fortunate we should meet. I thought, perhaps, that after our evening at the opera you might consider me sufficiently musically educated that I might join you at the next Philharmonic Society concert."

"The Philharmonic Society?"

"Yes. And perhaps I might make the acquaintance of your Miss Owen." Max thought he had spoken blandly enough, but his nephew looked troubled.

"She won't be there."

"Such devotee of music as you say she is?"

"She won't be there because she says it would not be good for my reputation to be seen with her."

All the years of Max's diplomatic training vanished. He could think of nothing to say, no response at all, not even the most trivial of banalities. He stared dumbly at his nephew.

"She says that I am too innocent to be seen with someone like her, and she told me what she is . . . a, a Cyprian."

Max had no idea that Randall even knew such women existed, much less what they were called.

"I told her I didn't care, that I simply enjoyed talking with her. I don't mind paying if it gives me the opportunity to enjoy a good conversation . . . a true conversation," he added, forestalling any possibility of a cynical response from his worldly uncle.

"Well then . . ." Max struggled to gather his wits from the chaos that threatened to overwhelm them, "perhaps we might enjoy the Philharmonic Society concert together without Miss Owen's company." Had he lost his mind? First he'd been bested by two demi-reps, and now he was agreeing to join his nephew at what surely was the world's most boring entertainment, if it even deserved the name.

"I would like that." Randall's troubled expression vanished. "But if you will excuse me, sir, I am late for a music lesson with Sir George Smart who has kindly consented to hear me play and perhaps share some of his musical expertise."

Randall was off like a shot, leaving his uncle standing like a fool in the middle of Bond Street, a fool suffering from an attack of guilty conscience.

Until this moment, Max had not been aware that he had any conscience to speak of—morals, yes; values and ideals, yes, but a conscience? Surely not. But now he *did* have one and it was telling him that he had behaved badly—not intentionally so—but badly, just the same. Who knew that a woman from Mrs. Gerrard's would turn out to be the soul of honor? The soul of honor with the pride to match. She had not deigned to explain herself when he had so baldly ordered her to leave his nephew alone. In fact, she had not argued or interacted with him at all; she had simply dismissed him. She had been magnificent. And that made Max feel even worse. He had rarely met a woman he admired, much less told her so. He couldn't ever remember wanting to apologize to one, and now he wanted nothing more than to go back to Grace Owen and do both—admire her and apologize to her, and not necessarily in that order.

The more he thought about it, the more apologetic he felt. It was a rare woman, a unique woman, who turned down one wealthy peer, but Grace Owen, in a very short space of time had turned down two. This was highly unusual behavior for an Incomparable, much less one of Helen Gerrard's *ladies*.

# Chapter 7

AT THAT VERY MOMENT, one of Helen Gerrard's ladies was learning a great deal more about Lord Maximilian Hawkesbury. "I was surprised to hear that Hawkesbury called on you." Helen looked up from the accounts she had been perusing. She had invited Grace into her office to discuss the bill for the tuning of the drawing room pianoforte and the possibility of purchasing a second instrument for the parlor that doubled as their schoolroom in order to give those who wanted to practice unlimited access, the one in the drawing room being dedicated to the use of those who had already mastered the instrument sufficiently to perform in public. "And even more surprised to learn he deigned to cross the threshold of this den of iniquity." A corner of her mouth lifted in an ironic smile.

"Well . . . it was not precisely a social call."

"Oh, I am certain of that." The emerald eyes gleamed. "A man whose father squandered the family fortune, not to mention all his time and attention, on women who inhabited establishments far inferior to this one is not likely to seek out people like us unless forced to by extenuating circumstances."

"He came to ask, er, demand I cease all interaction with his nephew."

"But I thought you had already . . ."

"I had. I explained to Lord Farnsworth the other day why we could not be friends." In spite of her best efforts, Grace could not hide the wistful note in her voice.

The green eyes softened, and the ironic smile warmed into kindness, "It was for the best, you know, no matter how difficult it was." Helen nibbled the end of the pencil she had been fiddling with. "But you could not see your way to sharing that useful bit of information with his uncle, I gather."

"No."

"One has one's pride." Helen chuckled, then sobered. "And sometimes that is all one has, but at least one has that."

"He offered himself in his nephew's place."

"Did he now? You must have made quite an impression."

"I sent him Dora, as he did not appeal to me."

"What? You could not stomach being ordered around by an arrogant opinionated diplomat, despite his being rich as Croesus and extremely attractive? How intriguing."

And that was what was so wonderful about Helen, Grace thought, not for the first time. She not only understood her ladies as well or better than they understood themselves, but she gave them her total and unreserved support.

"Oh, there you are, Grace." Dora popped her head in the doorway. "Clarissa is waiting for her pianoforte lesson."

"Gracious, the time! I am coming." Grace smiled gratefully at Helen and hurried to the drawing room. What she was giving Clarissa was more than pianoforte lessons; she was giving the girl back some of her old self, the self that had been a refined, gently educated solicitor's daughter in Bath before her father had died and her mother had thrown her out when she caught her fighting off the unwanted attentions of her new stepfather. Despite her manifold accomplishments and her exhaustive searching, Clarissa, who lacked references, had not been able to secure a position as a governess, and Helen, who had been in a similar position herself many years ago before a generous man had made her his mistress and left her a fortune, had found her moments before she was about to cast herself into the Thames. As she had with so many despairing women before, Helen brought Clarissa back to food, a warm fire, elegant surroundings and the sympathetic friendship of Mrs. Gerrard's ladies, and Clarissa had slowly recovered.

Every once in a while, however, the longing for lost lives would overcome them, and then it was the little things, like the music lessons they once had, that softened the sharp bite of longing for what could no longer be. Clarissa was not the only one who was soothed by the lesson. As Grace sat next to her on the pianoforte bench, she too was taken back to happier days in the family parlor in Oxford, her father sitting next to her mother, explaining, encouraging, interpreting, as only he could, and her mother, who was in fact the more technically superior player, breathing life into his compositions.

After Grace had left her, Helen sat for some time staring at nothing. The floor-to-ceiling shelves lining the room held all the books she had ever wanted—mathematical texts and treatises that not even most professors at Cambridge or Oxford were fortunate enough to own—but the rows of volumes were a blur, a muted background to thoughts that were not as orderly and predictable as mathematical theorems and equations . . . and certainly not so pleasant.

In the middle of her desk lay a letter from the agent for the owner of the freehold on which her establishment sat threatening eviction for irregularities on her lease, a lease that had been willed to her by Samuel Ward, her mentor, as she now thought of him, rather than the protector whose mistress she had become after he had sought her out several times at an establishment far less elegant and sophisticated than this one. Samuel, a City man whose wife refused to acknowledge the family connection with the thriving business that kept her in greater style and comfort than most women in the *haut ton*, had been lonely, not to put too fine a point on it. No one in his family—not his sons or daughters, and definitely not his wife—wanted to hear anything about the business that was his passion and their lifeblood. Helen, on the other hand, had been fascinated by every little detail and, with her quick mathematical mind, had sometimes been able to discover things in his accounts that even Samuel didn't see.

Relishing the comfort of having *someone to come home to* who would discuss his day and listen to his problems, Samuel had offered Helen her own establishment, a charmingly discreet house in Marylebone, and when he had died, he had left her, in addition to a fortune, an investment in her future, the ninety-nine year leasehold he had purchased on a mansion in St. James' Square that eventually became Mrs. Gerrard's. Yes, Helen could have rented it out and lived elsewhere in luxury for the rest of her days, but she wanted more than that; she wanted to take back her life, a life that had been filled with purpose, even if it had only been teaching two little girls until their father raped her and their mother tossed her out without a reference.

Samuel Ward had given her, her independence and means, and she wanted to put it to good use rescuing poor unfortunates like herself, providing shelter and a living whose earnings far exceeded the wildest dreams of most of the clergy and even many respectable merchants. She also provided them with the tools to make their own way in the world—education in the practical arts of account-keeping, needlework, and household management, as well as the more ornamental: music, French, dancing, Italian, and drawing, every skill that the most finished Incomparable could lay claim to. All of this was with the aim of making them mistresses of their own fates, forces to be reckoned with in the larger world as Juliette had become. Now, *someone* was trying to take that away from her. Well, she, Helen Gerrard, would not let them. No more harm was going to come to her ladies while she could still draw breath.

"I pity the poor tradesman whose bill has just invoked your wrath." Dora popped her head around the corner again. Then, seeing the trouble in

Helen's eyes, she slipped into the chair in front of the desk, cocking her head sympathetically.

"The owner of the freehold," Helen sighed, "seems to want to get rid of us."

"But that's impossible! You have the leasehold for ninety-nine years."

"Which apparently has some irregularities," Helen responded dryly. She chided herself for even letting that much slip. Her ladies had suffered enough; they didn't need to share her worries. But Dora, daughter of a once prosperous innkeeper, though lacking Helen's scholarly education, possessed a fount of practical business knowledge and experience the hard way by suffering a hundred economic and private indignities at the hands of her father's rapacious creditor, and Helen could not help confiding in her.

"Offer him more money."

"What?"

"Lay out the blunt. The establishment makes plenty of it, and no one is so plump in the pocket they can't use more, even someone who owns a freehold in St. James' Square, whoever that is."

"I wish I *knew* who it was, but every contact has been through an agent, and I sincerely doubt that someone important enough to own a freehold in St. James' Square would be persuaded by an offer of money."

"You would be surprised. It doesn't take much to find oneself under the hatches." Dora didn't even bother to hide the cynicism in her voice. "I know, even those *came over with the Conqueror* fellows with estates all over the place are often mortgaged to the hilt and spend every penny trying to keep up appearances. And there's no harm in trying." She flashed an encouraging smile as she rose and laid a sheaf of bills in front of Helen. "The linen draper's. You asked me to look them over and they are all in order."

"Thank you." Helen picked up a pen and a clean sheet of paper. "I do appre . . ."

"I know." A wink and Dora was gone. As the one who had been at Mrs. Gerrard's the longest, she was more aware than the others how tightly the proprietress held herself in check, remaining coolly detached, eternally calm, and saying very little, but Dora knew how much it had cost Helen to admit her misgivings, and how grateful she was to be able to do so.

As usual, Dora's instincts were correct. Less than a week later, Helen called her in to report that the future of Mrs. Gerrard's was secure, for the moment at least. "How could you guess?" Helen looked at her in amazement.

"How could you not?" Dora teased her. "You, who know everything about everyone in this city. How many of them are truly what they appear to be?"

And in a richly paneled library, not very many streets away, much the same question was being asked in an incredulous tone. "How *could* you allow yourself to be paid off like a common tradesman! What has come over you? Have you no pride at all?"

"Pride is only for those who can afford it. For those of us who cannot, it is a luxury to be dispensed with . . . as you would do well to remember."

"Disgusting." The brutal click of the door as it closed behind the visitor was more eloquent than words.

# CHAPTER 8

Pride was also causing Lord Maximilian Hawkesbury to spend an uncomfortable few days with himself until he was free to call again on the redoubtable Miss Owen. On the one hand, he had always prided himself on a forthright honesty that demanded he admit when he was in the wrong, earning him the trust of diplomats from Paris to St. Petersburg, and he knew he was in the wrong where Grace Owen was concerned. On the other hand, he had sworn on his father's grave never to have anything to do with the bloodsucking creatures that had drained his father's attention and inheritance away from his wife and family. Miss Owen did not deny her membership in that questionable sorority. And on the other hand—he was fast running out of hands—he had always possessed a talent for recognizing genuine honor and decency in someone, no matter what the rank or circumstances—another skill that had won him the confidence of human beings in lands whose languages and cultures were vastly different from his own, and made it possible for him to be successful where others more blinded by notions of propriety and ceremony failed completely.

So, at the first available opportunity he presented himself to the venerable Fenwick at Mrs. Gerrard's.

"I shall see if Miss Owen is at home, if you will just wait here, my lord," the butler responded with all the stateliness of one who had been requested to arrange a royal audience, but before he could take a step, liquid notes of music, pure and sweet drifted down the stairway. "I know that my Redeemer liveth." For the tiniest fraction of a second, Fenwick's glacial countenance seemed to soften with what almost appeared to be parental pride, but it was gone in an instant, the lines of his face returning to the rigidly proper before Max could be sure of his impression.

"I appreciate your assistance, but there is no need as Miss Owen is clearly at home." Max summoned what he hoped was a conspiratorial smile. "I would rather not interrupt her, and it would give me great pleasure to listen without distracting her."

"Very well, sir." The butler's dignified expression did not change, but Max thought he detected a note of approval in his voice.

The music flowed around him as he slowly made his way up the stairs, beckoning, inspiring, and somehow wrenching at his heart—a heart that was immune to most things, like feminine tears, languishing looks, or seductive smiles.

Holding his breath to savor the moment of pure beauty, the song of an unfettered soul, he paused in the doorway of the room.

"And though worms destroy this body . . ." The music stopped

Grace's spirit had soared with her song, a song, she especially needed after being subjected to the cold supercilious stares and haughty head-tossings of two ladies in Bond Street who, if they had been as well-bred as they pretended to be, would not have recognized Mrs. Gerrard's carriage in the first place. Grace knew what she was. She had come to accept it, but it still hurt when those who were as respectable as she had once been refused even to acknowledge her existence, and she needed this song to restore her after it.

But as she drew breath for ". . . yet in my flesh shall I see God" she suddenly felt as though she were not alone, and then a shadow flickered in the pianoforte's glossy surface. Snatching her hands from the keys, she turned to discover the broad-shouldered body of Lord Maximilian Hawkesbury propped against the door jamb, an unreadable expression clouding his dark gray eyes.

"I apologize," he whispered

"You what?" Arrogant men like Lord Maximilian were usually not even aware of the feelings of anyone, much less someone like Grace, and they certainly never apologized for offending them.

He shrugged away from the doorway and strolled over to the pianoforte. Grace rose. She was not about to let him tower over her, and, for once in her life, she was glad of her height because she could look him square in the eye.

"I misjudged you. I did not accord you the chance, or the objectivity to explain to me that my nephew is simply your friend . . . your friend, and," the hint of a wry smile tugged at the corner of his mouth, "I gather, an esteemed colleague. And . . . I am sorry I did . . . misjudge you, I mean."

Life, not to mention Helen Gerrard, had taught Grace never to be at a loss for words, and certainly to retain one's aplomb at all costs, but she felt all possibility of speech, not to mention aplomb, slipping rapidly away.

Max, on the other hand, felt his returning as her silence grew longer and longer. Good! Finally he had gained back some of the advantage he had lost the moment he met Grace Owen.

"Yes he *is* an esteemed colleague." Grace drew a steadying breath. "Something one rarely encounters in life."

"Particularly in yours, I should imagine."

The tone was ironic, cynical even, but the gray eyes that looked steadily into hers were full of a surprising understanding and, yes, sympathy. A quiver of some unidentifiable sensation sliced through her, and for some unknown and completely inexplicable reason, Grace felt drawn to the man. Why, she could not imagine, but somewhere deep in her soul she knew she could trust him.

"And having heard just the briefest example of your talent, it is quite obvious to me, ignorant as I am of all things musical, why my nephew, who is seriousness itself, particularly where his music is concerned, is so impressed with yours." Max felt the wariness in her tensely erect posture, the guarded expression in her eyes, and suddenly, more than anything in the world, he wanted her to let down that guard and feel comfortable with him, just to be herself—as she was with Randall.

"Thank you, my lord." Grace felt herself relax ever so slightly. The man was actually trying to put her at ease. It was rather flattering. Usually it was the task of the denizens of Mrs. Gerrard's to put everyone else at their ease.

And then it was Max's turn to be at a loss for words. Now that he thought of it, in every situation in which he usually found himself there was some mutual topic of conversation—diplomatic issues, shared friends, political gossip, or, if nothing else, complimenting a woman on her beauty or fashion. He had never had trouble conversing with women before—quite the opposite in fact. And this woman *was* beautiful, with deep intelligent blue eyes, white skin, and delicately sculpted lips. But this woman did not want to be admired; she wanted to be understood, respected, and how he sensed that, Max had no idea.

"You are wondering why, if I am serious enough about my music to appreciate your nephew's conversation, why I . . . why I . . . am here, at Mrs. Gerrard's. Again, she looked him fearlessly straight in the eye.

"Well . . ." Even someone who appreciated plain dealing as much as Max found her brutal honesty unnerving—unnerving, but intriguing.

Grace sat back down on the pianoforte bench, gesturing to a chair opposite, and Max understood. This was to be an explanation, not an appeal for sympathy or intimacy, or even friendship. She wanted to explain herself to him, and he felt oddly proud that she cared enough about his opinion to do so, though why she should after he had acted so gracelessly, he could not fathom.

Neither could Grace, but there was just something about the man, a lack of smoothness or flirtatiousness that set him apart form even the most unusual or intriguing of her admirers. He seemed to be a man who owned his own soul, who followed his own interests, who answered only to himself.

And so she found herself describing, in the most matter-of-fact way, the passion between a headstrong aristocratic young woman and her music master, their marriage, the disowning by both their families, the years of her father's glory as a composer and a music professor at Oxford, her mother's death, and his despair, the drinking, the loss of one position after another until only the theater owner's obsession with his daughter kept him employed, and lastly, the final rescue, the circumstance—quickly glossed over—by Helen Gerrard.

He listened to it all, absorbing the sordid details—the humiliation, the rage, the determination—with an intensity that was palpable. When she was finished there was silence, but she could tell he understood, really understood. There was nothing to say. What sort of conversation did one have after such a revelation? Even Grace, adept as she had become at engaging in banter with the dullest of men or finding a common topic with the most awkward and inarticulate of Mrs. Gerrard's patrons, could not dredge up a single word.

The ormolu clock on the mantel struck the hour. Grace jumped up from the bench like a startled rabbit. "My lesson! You must excuse me, my lord."

"Lesson? But you were just practicing."

"Not *my* lesson, not a music lesson, the class lesson, a French lesson."

"Class?" Max echoed stupidly. He had been moved by her story, angered at it, frustrated by it, but not rendered completely stupid, he thought, but now she was making no sense at all.

Grace could not help smiling just a little at his bewilderment. It was always gratifying to see a tall, powerful, obviously intelligent man at a loss for words. "Yes. Now that Juliette is married, I have taken over the French lessons as well as those on the pianoforte, and Italian, for those who wish it."

Max did not look much enlightened by this explanation.

"Helen is determined to give us all as thorough and complete an education as any well brought-up young lady so that when we become financially independent we will be equipped to go out in the world. In addition to the usual geography and history, she teaches Latin and mathematics, though Dora is the one who instructs us in household accounts. So, you see, I must excuse myself." A slightly apologetic inclination of her head, and she was off.

But Max did not see it at all. He felt as though the world had been turned on its head. Things he thought he knew were not at all what they seemed—a lowering thought for a man who had always considered himself to be not only fully aware of the petty assumptions of the *ton*, but above them. And now, he had been proven wrong himself . . . or certainly misguided, and proven wrong by a beautiful, talented, and, yes, courageous young woman who had not only outmaneuvered him, but caught his interest in a way no one, especially a woman, ever had, and she had done it without even intending to do so.

# Chapter 9

A FEW DAYS LATER A WOMAN, quite the opposite of Grace Owen, a woman Max had avoided for most of his adult life despite keeping her in decided comfort, if not the ostentatious luxury she craved, in a slim house in Hill Street, ran him to ground in Bond Street as he was exiting Gentleman Jackson's. "Max. How fortunate! I did not know you were in town since you haven't responded to any of my letters."

"Mother." Caught, Max tried not to sigh. It was his own fault. He should have been paying more attention, but he had been going over the recent pugilistic bout in his mind, figuring out how he could have done better and, unlike the other times he had managed to catch sight of the Dowager Marchioness of Swanton in time to avoid her, now he was fairly caught.

"Your presence is excellently well timed. You may escort me to Maison Juliette." Max's mother's brows rose at his blank look. "Do not tell me you haven't heard of it? Why, her designs are quite *le dernier cri* and it is said she can do wonders with any face or figure."

"Which you hardly need, mother."

"Nonsense, you silly boy." Utterly oblivious to the ironic tone, she tightened her viselike grip on his arm and led him off down the pavement, giving him no chance to escape.

Max's mother had always been a frivolous woman, but her devotion to fashion and its constantly changing definition of what it took to be truly *a la mode* had become an absolute mania once her husband, having insured the succession to the title, left her for the arms of one fashionable impure after another.

Maison Juliette's bow window, outlined by a swag of green silk and lit by a crystal chandelier whose light was reflected by an unusually handsome looking glass, was discreetly elegant, as was the customer who looked up from the folio of fashion plates she was perusing. Grace! What was she doing here, and how happy he was to see her.

"Please tell the proprietress that the Dowager Marchioness of Swanton is here," Max's mother announced to the girl who greeted them.

"She is engaged at the moment, my lady, but it is her custom to call on her patrons in their homes to consult with them first before she designs the particular costumes they desire so that they may discuss them at a later date. If you will let me know your direction I will make sure she calls on you. In the meantime I shall be happy to show you some of her previous designs and, of course, materials."

"I am quite capable of looking at them myself," the Marchioness snapped as she glanced disdainfully at Grace. "What sort of person runs such a ramshackle place as to require an appointment?"

"My sister-in-law, Lady Adrian Claverton," Lady Georgiana Claverton responded serenely as she emerged from the back of the shop, a white bundle in her arms.

*Oh well done.* Max smiled to himself as he stole a quick look to see how Grace was taking the exchange, but she remained buried in fashion plates apparently oblivious to the delicious scene taking place around her.

"A lady? In trade?" The Marchioness sniffed.

Lady Georgiana was not to be cowed. "Not only a lady, but, even better, a talented artist." At that moment the bundle began to squall. "Now look what you've done! You've upset Auguste. I certainly hope that a ride in the park will calm him down again or we shall all be in the basket. Come, Juliette," she turned to an exquisitely beautiful young woman who also emerged from the back tying the ribbons of a prodigiously elegant Gypsy hat of white satin. "Mama is waiting." And without a backward glance, Lady Georgiana, with Juliette in her wake, sailed out to the ducal carriage that had just that moment pulled up in front of the shop.

"Well, I never!" The Marchioness flicked her fringed shawl and turned on her heel.

"But Mother, are you not going to make an appointment? Even you must admit that the clientele is unexceptionable."

"Do be quiet, Max. Come along." And snatching his arm again, the Marchioness marched her son—if an able-bodied man well over six feet could be said to be marched—out of the door and onto the pavement where Max looked desperately for a hackney.

The gods were smiling on him, as one rounded the corner the minute they reached the curb, and Max was able to bundle his mother into it and send her off before she even knew what he was about.

Before the carriage had even turned the corner into Burlington Gardens, Max hurried back into the shop, but Grace was nowhere to be seen. Damn and blast! So *that* was the Juliette whose French lessons Grace had taken over because she was married—not only married, but into one of the first families of the realm—and she also appeared to be the proprietress of one of the exclusive temples of *a la modality* where fashionable women worshipped. How intriguing. Truly, Helen Gerrard had created something unique, if this is what came out of her establishment. Max had hardly been able to credit it when Grace told him about all the lessons and the investment plans, but now he was seeing it with his own eyes.

Grace was thinking much the same thing as she hurried down Piccadilly. She had no footman or maid; Rose had agreed to meet her at Maison Juliette after an errand, but Grace could not wait for the maid's return. She had to get away from Lord Maximilian and his mother, and besides, it was only the reputations of ladies that suffered if they wandered unaccompanied in London, and Grace was no longer a lady.

Grace had hurried over to Maison Juliette the minute she'd received Juliette's note saying that she was in town. Lord Adrian, though raising his own racing stock on his estate near Newmarket through careful breeding, still felt the need for regular trips to Tattersall's, and Juliette welcomed the opportunity to check on her shop. Even though Alice managed the shop's day-to-day operations overseeing the seamstresses who turned Juliette's creations into stunning reality, and Dora handled the accounts more competently than Juliette ever had, the new Lady Adrian had dreamt so long and fought so hard for Maison Juliette that she needed to be part of it, to immerse herself in rich and multi-hued fabrics, to ponder extravagant trimmings and try them against this satin or that crape. As much as she adored her husband and doted on her son, Juliette missed her friends, Helen's ladies, with whom she had shared so much.

After the baby had been given his lunch, Juliette had plied Grace for news. In fact, she learned more about her brothers-in-law from Grace than from her redoubtable mother-in-law. The Duke and Duchess of Roxburgh were fond enough of their offspring but they did not share Freddy's obsession with snuff boxes, waistcoats, or opera, nor did they understand John's passion for saving souls, other than the oblivious wealthy and well-fed ones that made up his parish of St. George's, Hanover Square. And neither the Duke nor the Duchess had the slightest inkling of John's infatuation with mathematics, much less shared it. Fortunately for the Claverton brothers, Helen Gerrard did understand them and had given Freddy free rein in his designing the new look in her drawing room, discussed opera knowledgeably with him, while her ladies provided a constant supply of conversation on the latest in bonnets or walking dresses, the merits of spencers over pelisses that dominated the drawing room in the early afternoon when its customers were engaged in other pursuits. As for Freddy's brother, and the establishment's spiritual advisor, she understood Lord John's need to save the lost, the damaged, and the hopeless. Did she not have the same drive herself? And no one had a better grasp of mathematical theory than the girl whose father had given her a better education than most men and indulged her with every mathematical treatise he had been able to lay his hands on.

"And Freddy," Juliette had asked, "How does he go on? He is the dearest man in nature, but no correspondent, as you might guess."

"He and Helen are deep in the project for re-doing the drawing room. He is closeted with her at least an hour a day." Grace refrained from mentioning that the absence of Juliette had drawn these two closer together, but she could not help adding, "He misses you, you know. No one can discuss materials and colors and draping as well as you."

"But he does have Maison Juliette and Alice, and Alice is very clever at sewing."

"Alice is all that is excellent, but you will admit she does not have your depth of knowledge or charm. Fortunately, Lady Georgiana brings him with her whenever she is thinking about a new gown. If the truth be told, I think she comes in a good deal more often than necessary simply to give Freddy an excuse to avoid Lady Lavinia."

"Georgie is no better a correspondent than her brother, but she does write that Lavinia is determined that *this* year they *will* be married. Poor Freddy. I am afraid he cannot continue avoiding his fate much longer; He has had time to re-build Wrothingham Abbey several times over in all the years he has been *getting it ready* for Her-Grace-to-be. I dearly love my father-in-law, but I shall love him more if he lives to be one hundred. Poor Freddy would not have to be duke for many years to come and Lavinia will be in her dotage by the time she becomes Duchess of Roxburgh."

"Why Juliette!" In spite of her words, Grace did not look the least bit shocked.

Her friend grinned and then, gazing down at her sleeping son, she shook her head, smiling. "I do hate to see poor Freddy under the cat's paw, especially the paw of such an ill-tempered cat, but we do need an heir, or two, so that dear little Auguste is free to enjoy life as his father has.

*As his father had, for the most part,* Grace thought. Barely surviving Waterloo and struggling to walk with a cane could not be said to be enjoying life, but given the alternativess of death or amputation, perhaps he could be said to be appreciating it.

The arrival of Lady Georgiana had broken up the *tete-a-tete,* and, if it had been too short a visit for Grace, she was glad to see how eager Georgie was to be with her sister-in-law and her nephew.

It was plain to see that Juliette was happy. She had always been quick enough to laugh and tease, to share her *joie de vivre* with her friends, but there had been an undercurrent of determination, and intensity that was now gone, replaced by a softer, quieter glow of true contentment. She loved and she was loved. True, she had also realized her dream of becoming a modiste, but even in the days before her marriage to Lord Adrian, when the success of Maison Juliette was assured and the incomparables were clamoring for appointments, there had been excitement and enthusiasm, but not the look of fulfillment Grace now saw in her friend's eyes, heard in her laugh, and felt in her movements which, graceful as always, were now relaxed and assured.

Was that what it took? Love? Being able to follow one's passion, to realize one's dream, and to support oneself at the same time should bring the same fulfillment as love, but it had not for Juliette, not until love, in the form of Adrian had claimed her. Surely it was not that way for everyone? Surely when she, Grace Owen, finally held the audience in a theater in breathless silence, captive to the power of her voice, that same fulfillment would come to her? The change in Juliette had shaken Grace. They had been so alike, sisters in their single-minded pursuits of their dreams and in their devotion to succeeding on their own without anyone's help. There was only one solution to such troubling thoughts.

Hardly acknowledging Fenwick as he opened Mrs. Gerrard's massive door, Grace hurried up the stairs and, not even bothering to remove her bonnet, she flung herself at the pianoforte. Her work, her music. That was all there was for her. Outside of that, what more could she want? Nothing! And it certainly wasn't a man, so why had the sight of Lord Maximilian Hawkesbury sent her running back to St. James' Square in such haste? *That* was even more unnerving to contemplate than the change in Juliette. Why should his presence affect her at all? But she had not been the only one who was unnerved. Grace had felt his eyes on her, seen how he edged as far away as possible from that harpy of a mother and as close as possible to Grace. She had even caught sight of him out of the corner of her eye practically pushing the woman out on the street and into a carriage as Grace had made her own escape. No, Lord Maximilian was nothing in her life and certainly not worth a second's reflection.

# CHAPTER 10

Grace Owen, however, was causing Lord Maximilian Hawkesbury to do some serious reflecting of his own. Never in his life had he had the least difficulty in dealing with women—mostly he avoided them and the variety of lures cast to attract his attention. No matter how they indicated their interest in him—a shoelace broken in front of his door, a sudden longing for fresh air if he mentioned his curricle, the shy fluttering of eyelashes on a demure young miss longing for a dance partner, the frank appreciation of a maid looking for something more rewarding than a tumble in the hay with a village lad—he easily ignored them because he knew that for all the different modes ways in which it was expressed, the interest was not in him, Max, the person, but in who he was and what he could do for them, which was to confer money or status, or both. His mother had taught him well. Max had learned early on that he was nothing to her but an accoutrement, the clever, self-possessed son, then, the handsome young man with a brilliant future whose sense of duty could be played upon for more pin money, or escort duty, or pity for a woman virtually impoverished by his sybaritic, self-indulgent father. But she had never once, by the slightest gesture, shown that she cared in the least for him or even knew anything about him. No other woman Max had encountered since had been any different.

Until now, until Grace Owen had summarily dismissed him, not once, but twice, even though the second time had been a little less brutal. The irony of it all was that, theoretically, it was easier to arrange another meeting with her than it would be with almost any other woman. All he had to do was pay. But he didn't want to pay. He wanted to be her friend. He wanted to help her achieve her dream.

Max swirled his glass of port as he stared into the fire. Having bundled his mother into the hackney, he had headed home to the impregnable serenity of his own chambers and the stimulating company of the dispatches just arrived from Paris. There was still much concern over Russia in general and the Tsar's motivations in particular, as well as rampant mistrust among all the parties involved in peace negotiations. Max, with his level head and pragmatic approach to one and all was sorely missed for his ability to cut through the quagmire of egos and motives to find a resolution for even the most intractable issues. Now he was faced with a complicated issue of his own. Surely if he thought enough about it, he could come up with a clever solution in which all parties could be satisfied while maintaining their pride and independence.

Pride and independence—the vision of Grace Owen, her chin raised and her blue eyes flashing, rose before him. She was pride and independence personified, and dammit, he admired her for it. And he wanted to help her gain more of it, which was really rather counterintuitive because, as he knew better than most, the way to pride and independence was to rely solely on oneself, to do everything on one's own. So how was he to help?

Max was still mulling this over in his mind the next morning as he made his way down Piccadilly towards Hyde Park in the hopes that the fresh air and peaceful green vistas would clear his mind.

But peaceful green vistas were not to be his. "Max?"

Surely someone had called his name, but he had been absent from London so many years there was no one in town who would be expecting to encounter him there. It couldn't be his mother; he could not be so unlucky as to fall into her clutches again so soon?

"Max!"

This time it was not a question. He turned to discover a petite dark-haired woman, flanked by two dark-haired girls in matching bonnets.

"Henrietta?"

While Max's brother had restored the family estate by marrying a fortune, and Max had wiped away his less than happy memories of home by escaping to Cambridge and then the diplomatic corps, Max's sister had defiantly chosen to find happiness in a family of her own, far away from both the chillingly formal environs of Swanton Hall and the frantic, glittering world of the *ton* which had robbed all three of them of their parents. In fact, Henrietta had never actually seen the Marquess and Marchioness of Swanton in the same room together, she being the product of her parents' last interaction together in a drunken coupling in which both parents had mistaken one another for their current lovers at a house party whose hostess had made the mistake of inviting both of them and their *cheres amis*. Since then, Henrietta, ten years younger than Max, had been pretty much left to her own devices, which had culminated in her refusing to have anything to do with a Season and choosing a husband of her own, brother of a school friend, a man who cherished her as deeply as she had been ignored by her family, and loathed the false gaiety of the *ton* as much as she did.

Max had thought she and Lord Edgefield were happily ensconced in their snug little estate in Wiltshire, but apparently not.

"What are you doing here? I thought you had wiped the boring English soil off your boots forever."

"I have, but duty calls. I am seeing to Uncle Richard's estate."

"Poor Max, caught up at last by family responsibility in spite of your best efforts."

He chuckled. There was no resisting the flash of dimples or the teasing glint in Henrietta's dark brown eyes. So much of his life had been spent abroad that he barely remembered his sister, but there was no forgetting her mischievous smile. With no one paying attention to her as she grew up, she had always run her life pretty much according to her own desires and had become something of a force of nature in the process—a charming force, but a force, nevertheless.

"And," he neatly turned the tables on her, "what are *you* doing here? I thought you and Edgefield avoided this den of iniquity and ruthless social competition like the plague."

"We do." Again the dimples flashed. "But Edgefield really *does* take his parliamentary duties seriously and he misses the girls so much when he is away that we have taken a house in Brook Street to be with him."

"Without informing any family members, interested or otherwise, I'll be bound."

Henrietta had the grace to look sheepish. "Well," she fiddled with her bonnet ribbon, "as we don't go out in the *ton* much, there really was not the least need for anyone to know."

"And also it is far more convenient for you to live just as you please, undisturbed by the demands of importunate relatives who might ask you to lend a helping hand introducing their son to the most selective circles in the Upper Ten Thousand."

"Oh!" She raised one gloved hand to her lips. "Oh dear. I take it that these, *importunate relatives* found someone else to, er, importune."

"Precisely." He did not bother to stifle the sardonic tone.

"I *am* sorry. I had no idea you were in town, or that Randall was either." And to her credit, Henrietta did look genuinely sorry. "But why did Hubert not ask our mother for assistance. If anyone knows the ways of the *ton* . . ."

"Would you *ask our mother for assistance*?"

"Well no, but . . ."

"Enough said."

"Again, I am sorry, but," she tilted her head, peeping up at him without an ounce of apology in her dark eyes, "but I am sure you are much better at that sort of thing than I would be, introducing a young man to the fashionable world, I mean."

"Not half so good as a married woman and her member-of-the-Parliament husband."

"Oh Edgefield," she shook her head dismissively, refusing to take the bait. "He has less interest in the *ton* than I do, which is to say none at all."

At that point, one of the girls holding onto his sister's hand became restive. "Mama, are we not going to the Egyptian Hall?"

"Hush, Beatrice, Mama is talking." Then, belatedly remembering her manners, "This is your Uncle Max. Max, my daughters Beatrice, she urged the hand-tugger forward, "and Laura."

The taller, and Max presumed, the elder of the two, regarded him seriously. "It is a pleasure to meet you, Uncle. Are you going to the Egyptian Hall too? Mama has promised to take us to see all the exhibits."

"I am going to see an elephant and a rhinoceros and a cameoleopard, and . . ." Laura was not about to let her sister monopolize the conversation.

"And *almost every known quadraped* that is on display there," Beatrice finished smoothly.

"As you can see, we must bid you good day," his sister shook her head in fond exasperation, "but I do hope you will visit us. I shall send you our direction. You are at Albany?"

He nodded, unable to suppress a grin as she was towed off down the street by her enthusiastic offspring. Clearly the girls had inherited their mother's headstrong nature. He very much doubted that Henrietta, after spending a morning with those two, would have the energy to deal with the all-consuming spectacle that was the world of the *ton*. Anyone who had spent several hours shepherding two eager girls through the crowds gawking at the exhibits would be more in need of a nap than a rout or an evening at the theater. Why did Henrietta not have a nursemaid or governess to spare her the exertion? Then he was struck with a thought so brilliant in the solution it offered to two problems that he was even surprised at his own cleverness.

Why not have Grace Owen teach music to his nieces, giving his sister some time to herself and Miss Owen a chance to apply her musical skill?

Why not indeed, other than the fact that he had not the least notion if the girls or their parents wanted them to learn music or if Miss Owen would agree to share her considerable talents with two active young ladies who undoubtedly possessed the attention spans of two gnats. Of course most people would question the wisdom of introducing a denizen of Mrs. Gerrard's into the respectable household of a member of Parliament, but somehow, though he was not about to let Randall stray into Grace Owen's orbit, Max had no qualms about thrusting Grace into Henrietta's. His sister was a law unto herself and thus had very little use for society's. She would not give a fig for what the rest of the world might call Grace Owen if she could make Henry's daughters happy. And for the oddest reason, which he could not explain to himself, Max felt certain that Grace Owen could.

Now all that he had to do was convince Grace to allow herself to be introduced into the household of a member of Parliament. That was going to be the more difficult part of the bargain, that, and convincing Grace to see him again, because even though he could simply call on her at Mrs. Gerrards, he knew that paying her a visit would not guarantee that she would allow herself to be visited.

# CHAPTER 11

Hᴇ ᴡᴀs ǫᴜɪᴛᴇ ʀɪɢʜᴛ. The next morning when Fenwick announced that a gentleman, a Lord Maximilian Hawkesbury was asking to see her, Grace set down the chocolate pot with a derisive snort. "Tell his lordship that I am not at home."

"Oh come now, Grace," Dora peered at her over her own cup of chocolate, "are you not even going to find out what his lordship wants?"

"I know what his lordship . . ."

"He said to tell you that it has to do with your music, Miss," Fenwick interrupted apologetically."

"My music?"

"I would see the man," Dora insisted. "He does not strike me as someone who does anything without a great deal of thought and purpose. Do you not agree, Fenwick?"

"A most accurate assessment, Miss Dora." The butler stood his ground politely, but firmly

"Oh, very well. Show him to the drawing room, Fenwick. I shall be down directly."

"There, what did I say?" The right moment and the right circumstances will come along."

"Dora! The man knows nothing about music."

"Perhaps he does, perhaps he does not, but his nephew does."

"The nephew he forbade me to see because I am one of Mrs. Gerrard's ladies."

"For which he apologized handsomely."

"Not for asking me never to sully Lord Farnsworth with my presence, but for misjudging my good sense in already sparing Lord Randall the contamination of my companionship."

"Oh come now, Grace, surely the man is not *that* censorious. He apologized, did he not? And now he has come to see you again and he makes certain that you know it is your musical talent and not your person that interests him. Are you not a little curious?"

In fact, Grace was a great deal curious, and just the tiniest bit flattered that he was interested enough in her, after hearing her story, to want to see her again. Yes, she was curious, and she was going to the drawing room, but she was *not* going to check her reflection in the looking glass first because she really did *not* care what he thought of her.

She did not look happy to see him. Max had not thought of himself as a vain sort of person, but perhaps he was after all, a lowering thought. Of course, not everyone he called on was ecstatic, but they rarely looked annoyed, as though he had interrupted something far more interesting than he was. "Miss Owen," he had already prepared himself to act as though his unexpected appearance was the most natural thing in the world. Now he struggled to remain unfazed by her tepid reception. "I am forced to admit that I am here to ask a favor." There. That had gotten her attention.

"A favor?"

"Yes. My sister is in town with her two daughters, and she mentioned their need for music lessons." He must remember to tell Henrietta this when he next saw her. "They are very spirited young ladies and I doubt that the average pianoforte instructor would be able to deal with them, much less teach them anything. You, on the other hand, look as though you could." He was making this up, but as soon as the words were out of his mouth, he realized they were true. Grace Owen struck him as being an amazingly competent woman, capable of handling anything, even a precocious and outspoken eight-year-old and her equally outspoken five-year-old sister.

"Why would you think that?" Grace was so taken aback by the entire proposition that she could only goggle stupidly. This man wouldn't let her near his nephew, but he wanted her to teach his young nieces. Was he mad? And was *she* mad for wanting to do so without knowing anything more?

"Well," Max smiled apologetically, "you *did* tell me that you give pianoforte lessons here. Of course I would have to ask you to come to Brook Street to give the lessons, but I also thought . . . well, actually, I thought you might be more inspiring than the average teacher."

It was the slightly sheepish way in which he gazed off in the distance as he tried to find the right words that caused Grace's heart, a previously non-existent organ, to warm with a sudden glow of . . . she was not quite sure what. He was feeling awkward, this seemingly invincible Lord Maximilian

Hawkesbury, but he trusted her enough to let her see it. He was treating her as an equal. Sudden tears pricked her eyes and she glanced quickly at her hands to hide them. An unwilling smile tugged at one corner of her mouth as, determined to treat him as an equal too, she forced herself to meet his gaze. "I expect I am."

The smile did it. For a moment, he thought he'd never seen a woman look so beautiful—vulnerable, humorous, proud, all at the same time. It was a heady combination, and he wanted more of it, more of her.

"And so I told him I would think about it," Grace confided to Dora when, after the feeblest of excuses, she had escaped from Lord Max and his proposition and hurried back to her own bed chamber to mull over this surprising turn of events. Never one to miss out on a good story, Dora had materialized in her doorway before Grace even had a chance to sit down.

"And what do you think? If ever there was someone who knew her own mind, you do," Dora teased.

"Ah, but do I? Why would a man who despises my company for his nephew seek it out for his nieces?"

*Why indeed?* Dora, eminently pragmatic though she was, could only think of one, or possible two reasons, neither of which had to do with practicality. Either Lord Maximilian wanted to see Grace again and not in *that sort of way*, or he wanted to help her achieve her goal of supporting herself with her music. Either, or both, meant that somehow, in a very short pace of time after meeting her, he had become genuinely interested in Grace Owen and her welfare. And Dora, who had seen far too much of the world for someone so young, viewed this as a most promising turn of events, most promising indeed.

Grace herself was not so sure. Could she go to a respectable house and become, in essence, a member of that household, even though she would be nothing more than a servant there, without feeling self-conscious or at least something of an imposter? Surely Lord Maximilian had not told his sister where Grace lived or what she did. And how could she, a woman of ill repute in most peoples' eyes, teach two innocent and well brought up young girls? What would their mother say if she knew?

Their mother, who for once in her headstrong, redoubtable existence was utterly nonplussed when her brother called on her in Brook Street the next day. "You are recommending a music teacher, Max? You, who never wishes to beholden to anyone or to have anyone be beholden to you? This must be an extremely superior person or an extremely unusual circumstance."

"It is just that I thought that if your girls were to have music lessons you might have more time to yourself."

"They *have* a nursemaid, and what would make you think I want more time to myself? Out with it. There is more to this than a desire to help a sister you do not see more than once or twice in a decade. Who is this person and why do you wish to help her?"

Really, he was losing his touch, and he was more affected than he liked to think by Grace Owen and her story if his sister had so little difficulty seeing through him. "This person, Miss Owen, is an excellent musician who has fallen on hard times and . . ."

"Since when did you ever care for such a thing? I am surprised at you, Max. I had thought our mother had cured you of every chivalrous impulse you might have possessed. Besides, what do you know of music?"

"Nothing," he admitted cautiously, "but Randall does, and Randall says . . ."

"Then why is not Randall here convincing me to hire this Miss Owen?"

Why indeed? "Because Randall is a very . . . Randall is young . . ." Max could not remember when his glibness had ever failed him. It had not, not until he had looked into Grace Owen's eyes and felt ashamed of himself, not until he'd looked into Grace Owen's eyes and wanted to help her. Not until he'd looked into Grace Owen's eyes, period. Ever since then he had not been himself.

"Because I told her to stay away from him," he admitted.

It was rare for Henrietta to be bereft of speech, but at this moment she appeared incapable of anything except raising a skeptical eyebrow.

"I told her to stay away because Randall is an innocent young man and she is a woman of . . . she is rather unusual . . . in fact she is a Cyprian."

The skeptical look gave way to pure amusement. "And yet this person, who is unfit for Randall's company, is perfectly fit to teach my daughters music?"

"Exactly! I always *knew* you were a clever girl, Henrietta."

Then she *did* burst out laughing. "Oh Max, you must be very far gone even to give the time of day to one of those *bloodsuckers* as I think I once heard you call Papa's *other interests.*"

"Not far gone," he protested, but his sister saw the flush cross his high cheekbones, even as he did his best to appear nonchalant, "just hoping to help a talented musician launch her career."

"By teaching my daughters music?"

"It's a start. If she teaches in a respectable household, she could be invited to sing at some society matron's musicale, and then, who knows . . ."

"You wretch! I am *not* a society matron. Well, technically I *am* a matron, I suppose, but *not* a society matron."

"As I said, it's a start. I shall call on you in a day or two for your answer." And with that, he bowed and hurried out of the room, leaving his sister, as he always did, utterly frustrated.

# Chapter 12

Henrietta was not the only one beset with questions. Just when Grace had convinced herself she did deserve a place in a respectable household in spite of what she was, she remembered the look in Max's eyes when she had promised to think about it—so understanding, so kind, even. And when had she started thinking of him as Max? No, she could not do this. It was way too big a risk. She had already shared too much with him. She could already feel the tough protective shell she had so carefully constructed against the world's hurts softening into . . . into what? Trust? Friendship? No. The only friends she could count on were the ones who shared the elegant mansion in St. James' Square with her. They were bound together by their sordid pasts and their hopes for the future. They could be counted on in a way she had never been able to count on anyone before. It would be folly to hope for something like that from anyone, especially a man who condemned her one minute, apologized the next, and offered her a job the next.

Before her resolution could fail, Grace sat down at her dressing table and wrote to Lord Maximilian declining his offer and thanking him for his interest in her musical career. It took several tries before she got the right mixture of graciousness and firmness. Helen, with her encyclopedic knowledge of the *ton* could be counted on to know his direction, even if Grace didn't. She was about to ring for Tom Sandys to deliver it when he knocked on her door. "A letter for you, Miss Grace."

"A letter?" Even the most besotted of her admirers never sent her letters, nor did she have any surviving relations or friends outside of Mrs. Gerrard's. But when Grace took the heavy cream-colored missive in her hands, saw the crest with which it was sealed and the distinctly feminine hand in which it was addressed, she was even more mystified. Why would a lady of rank be writing to Grace Owen? The message inside did little to dispel the mystery. *The Countess of Edgefield requests the honor of a visit from Miss Grace Owen at her residence in Brook St. at her earliest convenience.*

Once again, Helen, with her Debrett's and her ability to put two and two together, supplied the answer. "It's Hawkesbury's sister. You must have made quite an impression on the man if the Countess of Edgefield is inviting you to call on her." Helen gazed off into space, a tiny frown wrinkling her brow. "Most curious. It is rumored that she avoids the *ton* in general and never comes to town. I wonder why she is here, and even more," she quirked one delicate brow, a teasing smile tugging at the corner of her mouth, "how she happens to know about you." Then, fixing Grace with the penetrating eyes that never missed a trick at cards, or in life, she continued. "I should oblige her, if I were you, no matter what your opinion of her brother."

"Her brother wants me to give pianoforte lessons to her little girls."

"Does he now?"

Grace felt the heat of the flush that would rise to her cheeks no matter how much she wished to ignore it. "It is very kind of him."

"Though you can't, for the life of you, figure why he would suggest such a thing."

"No. I cannot."

"Well, I can." The catlike smile appeared again, more pronounced this time. "And if his sister knows your direction, then she must know who and what you are, which says a great deal for her character, and an even greater deal for her brother's interest in you. Yes, I should definitely oblige the Countess at the earliest possible moment." And with that pronouncement, the establishment's proprietress rose in one fluid motion and glided from the room.

There was nothing for it, Grace supposed, except to accede to the Countess' request. "If for no other reason," Dora responded upon hearing about it, "than to satisfy our rampant curiosity . . . or hers. What sort of society matron would allow a Fashionable Impure to darken her doorway unless she is insatiably curious herself? I must say, I quite like her already."

Grace was not so sure that curiosity lay behind the invitation, but whatever did, it was best to learn earlier rather than later. Having responded to the Countess' note, she consulted with Juliette on her toilette. The new Lady Adrian Claverton sat in her upstairs sitting room at Maison Juliette, gently rocking her son's cradle with one foot as she pondered the question. "If I remember correctly, you have a muslin walking dress that will do very well, but you need something to add *eclat* , but not too much. Ah, I have it." She gave the cradle a push strong enough to set it rocking on its own as she rummaged through the shelves of the large cupboard that took up an entire wall of the room. "Here it is." She shook out a blush colored spencer. "I had it made up as a sample to show Lady Allston, but kept the color nondescript so she could imagine the spencer in whatever shade she liked. It will go very well with your dark hair and, with a little work, should fit you to perfection." She held it up for Grace to slip in her arms. "Excellent. Understated, but stylish, and if you get slippers to match, it should produce just the right effect I think."

Whether it did or not, Grace could not tell because the Countess appeared so eager to learn more about her when Grace was ushered into the drawing room at Brook Street, she hardly spared her a glance before launching into her welcome, "I do thank you for coming. Max assured me that you are amazingly accomplished; of course, he never would have recommended you otherwise for he is extremely punctilious in everything he does, but you do understand that if I am to entrust my girls to your teaching, I want to know what sort of person you are."

Grace could only imagine what the Countess might be thinking, but she nodded reassuringly. "Of course, my lady, it is the natural concern of a mother."

"And a sister." Henrietta added slyly. "But where are my manners? Please do sit down and make yourself comfortable while I ring for tea."

Grace took a moment to glance around the room which was elegantly, but sparsely furnished in creams and golds, and the vivacious Countess, with her dark curly hair, large brown eyes, and vivid coloring dominated her understated surroundings.

Henrietta studied her for a moment, her curiosity so obviously at war with her duties both as a hostess and the Countess of Edgefield that Grace couldn't help smiling.

"Ah, I see you understand me, and I can also see that we can be comfortable with one another so I can admit that it is more for Max's sake than my daughters that I wanted to meet you."

"His lordship?"

"Precisely. I don't recall Max ever having mentioned a woman in his life to me, not that we see one another every often, but no matter. He has no particular use for women—take our mother for example—even though they pursue him like mad. He seems to have very little use for the sex in general and your sort in particular, if you will excuse me for saying so—quite the opposite. You are confused. I don't blame you. I am making a dreadful muddle of it. To speak plainly, our father ruined himself, and the family, with one expensive mistress after another, and our mother, who quite possibly drove him to it in the first place, was no better in her way than he was. Between the two of them, they gave Max quite a distaste for the fair sex. And then to have him not only speak of a woman, but recommend her as someone qualified to teach my children . . . well you can see why I had to meet you."

"I . . . I suppose so. But truly, my lady, I am quite qualified to teach your daughters. I learned to play the pianoforte almost before I could talk. My father was a music professor, you see, and my mother was also a brilliant musician. Now I am studying with Signor Lanza." Grace could not keep the pride out of her voice though she knew the renowned teacher's name would mean nothing to the Countess.

"Oh, I have no doubt you are extraordinarily talented. Max is too awake on every suit to recommend someone who is not the very best, but to have thought of it all himself . . ." Chin in hand, the Countess gazed off into space for some moments while Grace did her best to look respectfully interested. "Yes, the person came before the idea." Then seeing Grace's blank expression, she laughed. "Do forgive me. My husband tells me I am the most obscure person in the world. My thoughts get ahead of my tongue. What I mean is that I never mentioned the need for a music teacher to Max or anyone. I hadn't thought of such a thing even at home, much less in London. Don't you see? Max wanted to help you and *then* he decided my daughters needed music lessons, not the other way around. If I had not been in town, he would have found someone else who needed your musical talent. It's plain as pikestaff. He wants to help you, and Max never wants to help anyone. He cannot abide social entanglements. Couple that with his distaste for women of your . . . er . . . persuas . . . well anyway, you can see how intriguing it is. I've never known him to offer assistance to anyone, much less a . . ."

"Woman of questionable reputation," Grace finished drily. "But I do not need his assistance. I do not *want* his assistance."

"Part of the attraction, I am sure. Oh my, this is too delicious. I *do* beg your pardon. I sound like some scheming female or matchmaking mama, but I am fond of Max. He is brilliant, honest, principled, and works hard, but he is utterly alone. I am glad he has found someone interesting enough to want to help."

"But I don't need . . ." What didn't she need, for Lord Max to help her or for Lord Max to be interested in her or both? "I do not wish to be beholden to his lordship."

"Perfect."

Oddly enough, Grace had the feeling that her vehement protest gratified the Countess more than her easy acceptance would have. "I mean, do not distress yourself. In the end, you will actually be beholden to me and not Max." A conspiratorial smile flashed quickly as she leaned over the tea tray that had just been set in front of her and began to pour. She turned to the footman as he handed Grace her cup. "Walter, would you be so good as to bring the girls to meet Miss Owen?" Again the conspiratorial smile. "I believe that once you have met my girls, you will be completely convinced that this is the right thing to do."

Indeed it had been, Grace mused as the hackney drove her back to St. James's Square. The little girls had been charmingly interested. "Can you sing for us," the elder of the two had asked.

"I expect I could." Grace had risen and, with a questioning glance at their mother, sat down at the pianoforte in the far corner of the room. "After all, it does make sense to establish that one's music teacher can, in fact, produce music." Beatrice looked to be extremely gratified by her own cleverness, while Laura, less easily convinced, held back. But when Grace launched into *The Marriage of Frog and Mouse* the little girls laughed and clapped their hands.

"More!" Laura begged.

Grace couldn't help smiling at her enthusiasm. "Well here is one you must know. It is not so silly as *Frog and Mouse*, but it is pretty."

"Oh, *Cherry Ripe!*" Laura was not to be outdone by her sister. "We do know that, but you sing it ever so beautifully."

A lump rose in Grace's throat as she looked down into the serious young face whose eyes were warm with shy admiration. Who would have thought that Grace Owen, fallen woman—no she must not think like that—but who would have known how gratifying such innocent, untutored admiration could be? "Why thank you. I am so glad you think so. And now I will sing something for your mother, shall I? I hope she likes Mozart."

Absolute silence fell as she began *Gently Caressing Zephyrs*, the two girls standing so still and quiet thy might have been statues. The Countess' vivacious countenance smoothed into dreamy contemplation of nothing in particular, and the silence continued some minutes after the last note.

"That was . . ." the Countess drew a deep breath, "exquisite! You are wasted on my two little heathens, but if you would be so good as to teach them, until, that is, you become the next Catalani, we should be ever so grateful."

Grace cocked her head, smiling at Beatrice and Laura. "What do you think?"

"Oh yes!"

"Yes please," Beatrice added, remembering her manners.

"I shall write to my brother, shall I, thanking him for his suggestion and letting him know you will be commencing music lessons here next week?"

"Yes please," Grace answered immediately, relieved that any need for further contact with Max had been taken out of her hands by his very capable and extremely clever sister. Max was not the only one in the family blessed with diplomatic aplomb. The Countess' knowing dark eyes missed nothing, nor, apparently, did her kind heart.

# Chapter 13

GRACE MIGHT HAVE BEEN GRATEFUL to the Countess for sparing her writing a thank you to Max, but Max was not. "What do you mean you have already spoken with her?" he demanded, invading Henrietta's drawing room the day after Grace had reluctantly accepted her invitation.

"You were right, of course, Max," his sister responded tranquilly enough, but, if he had been less prey to his own disturbing emotions, he would have recognized the mischievous twinkle in her eyes. "Do sit down. You look like a caged lion."

He rather felt like a caged lion. His cravat was too tight and he wanted to wrap his hands around someone's neck. His sister's? Grace's? Most disturbing of all was why he wanted to do so. He should have been delighted that his sister had not only taken his suggestion, but followed up immediately. But he wasn't. He was infuriated. Now he had no excuse to see Miss Grace Owen ever again. His sister, blast her, had deprived him of it, or at least of receiving a note from Grace informing him of her engagement and thanking him so much for his generosity in conceiving of and arranging such a wonderful opportunity . . . or not. It had been in the realm of possibility that Grace, having shown herself to be both proud and independent, would have refused his suggestion, but even then she would have written him a note of some sort that he would then have responded to by calling on her to remonstrate with her. He shot a suspicious glance at Henrietta, his sister knew it, dammit, all of it. Clearly Grace did not *want* to see him ever again if she'd let his sister answer for her, and why that should matter to him so much, he could not say, but it did. "Well," he concluded sourly as he turned to go, "I am glad you arranged it all."

"Yes, she is coming from ten until noon every Monday and Friday. Beatrice and Laura are quite taken with her." Her words floated after him as he strode out of the room.

Henrietta smiled to herself. She wasn't sure he'd gotten the part about Beatrice and Laura, but she was quite sure he'd heard the Monday and Friday from ten until noon. Now all she had to do was sit back and await developments, for there would surely be developments. She would swear to that. Henrietta had seen the grateful look when she promised Grace to let Max know about the lessons, but she had also seen the uneasiness. Obviously Grace was drawn to Max, as he was to her; otherwise, why did she seem so relieved not to have to contact him again? Yes, Henrietta rested her chin in her hands, there had been a vehemence in Grace's wish not to be beholden to Max that betrayed how much he affected her. And he? He had looked positively bearish at the way his sister had eliminated the need for further interaction between the two of them. He could, of course, call on her at Mrs. Gerrard's, but Henrietta did not think her brother wanted Grace in that sort of way. Well, of course he did—what man did not—but his interest in Grace Owen went much deeper than that. Max's soul was involved in this one. Not that Henrietta knew her brother—ten years her senior and mostly absent—that well, but she did know of all the times he had avoided contact with her or the rest of the family, and that he seemed not to care much about anyone or anything except Uncle Richard and the diplomatic service, all of which made his interest in the very inconveniently female, and the even more inconveniently Cyprian, Grace, very telling indeed.

Henry was willing to wager a considerable sum that it would not be very long before her brother found some excuse to turn up in Brook Street on either a Monday or a Friday between the hours of ten and noon.

In the meantime, someone else had turned up in Brook Street and was causing no end of commotion. Beatrice and Laura had been the first to notice the scraggly little dog huddled miserably in the gutter. "Oh Mama, look! Poor thing." Beatrice immediately bent down to examine the mass of dirty fur that licked her hand feebly. "Oh Mama, may we keep him? Please?:

She started to pick the dog up, but her mother stopped her. "Be careful, he may have been kicked by a horse or have some injury."

The Countess had no sooner uttered the words when the poor thing heaved a tremendous sigh and struggled to its feet. "I'll help you carry it Bea. If we join hands to make a kind of basket . . ." Laura took her sister's hands, and together they carefully scooped up the wretched creature and tenderly bore it up the front steps.

"Disgusting." A haughty lady dressed in a plain muslin walking dress and severely cut lavender pelisse sniffed, giving the girls and their burden wide berth as she strode past. "Such behavior. Gracious, where is your mother?"

"Right here," Henrietta responded serenely, looking the haughty lady squarely in the eye. "And you are?"

"Well, I never!" Clearly the haughty lady had been too focused on the offending little girls to notice their mother standing close by. "Lady Lavinia Harcourt." And with an angry swish of her skirts, the haughty lady stalked on down the street.

"I don't like her," Laura whispered as they struggled up the steps. "She has mean eyes."

"And she is our neighbor." *Unfortunately*, Henrietta thought as she watched Lady Lavinia mount the steps of another house several doors down. "But come now, let's get this poor fellow cleaned up. What shall we call him?"

"Pippin." Laura didn't hesitate.

"But why? He isn't really . . ."

Halting on the top step, Laura gave her bossy elder sister *the look*, which everyone in the family knew brooked no argument, "Because I like the sound of it."

"Then Pippin it is," Henrietta winked at her eldest, "but now let's take him to the kitchen so we can feed him as well as clean him up."

Fortunately for Pippin, the girls were a great favorite with Mrs. Barnes the cook who otherwise might not have taken kindly to having a dirty pile of fur dumped on her clean kitchen floor.

"Ooh, he's ever so sweet." The scullery maid left off peeling potatoes to bend over the new arrival who licked her fingers hungrily.

Mrs. Barnes fixed her with a glacial stare. "Then you, Sally, may be responsible for seeing that he does not disrupt this kitchen in any way."

It turned out that Pippin was rarely ever in the kitchen, for he rewarded his young benefactresses with his constant and devoted attention, following them everywhere, and sitting quietly and patiently as they played with their dolls and did their lessons. His favorite, of course, was walking with them in the park, and that was how Grace first made his acquaintance one morning as they returned to Brook Street just as she was arriving for the girls' lesson.

Coincidentally enough, their haughty neighbor was also returning home at this unfashionably early hour. "Disgusting little mongrel," she hissed, swishing her skirts disdainfully away from any possible contact with the little dog.

"That's the lady with the mean . . ."

"Lady Lavinia Harcourt," the Countess of Edgefield quelled her youngest daughter with a look that tolerated no discussion.

So *that* was Freddy's fiancée, poor man. Grace had heard of the Claverton-Harcourt betrothal tradition, and now, having seen the flint-faced Lady Lavinia herself, she pitied Freddy even more. No wonder he spent so much of his time at Mrs. Gerrard's where the women were not only congenial, but supportive.

Lady Lavinia certainly did not look like the sort of person who enjoyed anything, and undoubtedly begrudged everyone else any small pleasure they might take in something as well.

Pippin, who clearly shared the general opinion of Lady Lavinia, whimpered and clung close to Laura as they mounted the steps. Still cringing, he followed them all into the music room.

"Poor thing. He still remembers the day we found him." Laura knelt down by the pianoforte, clasping the little dog to her chest.

"I know just the thing." Stripping off her gloves, but not bothering to remove her pelisse, Grace sat down. "Mozart." She smiled encouragingly at the girls. "My cat, when I was growing up, was very fond of Mozart. There was something he seemed to find soothing in a Mozart piano sonata." Swallowing the lump that rose in her throat remembering those happy days when she knew where she belonged, Grace laid her hands on the keys. "Sonata 16 or Sonata Facile. One day I shall teach you to play it."

As the notes rippled across the room, Pippin raised his head.

"Oh look, he likes it." Beatrice reached over to stroke his head as he slowly sank out of her sister's arms to lie on the floor. His nose dropped between his paws as lying, eyes fixed on the instrument, he swished his tail slowly back and forth in time to the music.

Now, if only she could do that with Max, Henrietta thought. There is a man who needs to relax and enjoy life more than he does.

# CHAPTER 14

MAX WAS DEFINITELY NOT RELAXED AS he pored over his uncle's account book the next day. Usually he was intrigued by the investments Richard seemed to think would turn a profit—some of them not so obvious—which made them even more interesting, and some of them which showed he had paid attention to the letters his nephew had sent from the continent which was rather gratifying since no one else in his family paid attention to anything he said. At least someone in his family was proud of him, or, if not proud, at least considered his opinion to be worth something.

Max paused over one particular reference to his letters, struck by the thought that he might not be giving his nephew Randall his due or taking his interests seriously enough in the same way others had ignored him. There was nothing wrong with music, or, actually, anything as a profession, if one did it with passion and one did it well. Did Randall do it well? Max had no idea, but he knew someone who would. Had Grace ever heard Randall play the organ? Randall had praised Grace's singing and spoken of her as an equal, someone who could appreciate and understand his talents just as he did hers. Perhaps Randall had shared his talents with Grace as well.

Why that thought should make his cravat seem too tight or inspire him to rise and pace the room was nothing Max wanted to think about. It would have been a great deal less upsetting if Grace had been what he at first thought her— a rapacious courtesan out to fleece an innocent young man with a respectable allowance—but no, she had just wanted to share her talents and interests with someone who could understand and appreciate them. How irritating.

It was not even a Monday or a Friday so he could not casually drop by his sister's and, just as casually, run into her. He certainly was not going to call in St.

James' Square like every other benighted fool who had fallen victim to a pretty face and charming conversation, though, come to think of it, most of their conversations had been more combative than charming. A rueful grin tugged at the corners of his mouth. Grace Owen was definitely no one's fool, and she gave as good as she got. That was one thing they had in common.

His chambers, like his cravat, were growing uncomfortably confining, so grabbing his curly brimmed beaver, Max headed out, away from introspection, in search of action, distraction, anything to restore his ordinarily well-ordered mind to its usual channels. A brisk walk in the park was just the action and distraction he needed.

Striding down Piccadilly at a most unfashionable pace, he soon felt better. There were enough equipages jostling for position in the busy thoroughfare to distract, and an abundance of fresh air and bright blue sky to clear his head . . . until he saw her.

No! How could it be that Grace Owen, graceful, and more self-possessed than any woman had a right to be, and the height of elegance in a deep flounced muslin walking dress was stepping out of Hatchett's Hotel. It was purest misfortune that he arrived at the moment she was pausing underneath the pillared portico before plunging into Piccadilly. In another second, she would have turned up or down the street and the deep brim of her bonnet would have completely obscured her features and her vision. As it was, the dark blue eyes fixed on him immediately, widening in what could, by no stretch of the imagination, be called a welcoming look.

"Miss Owen." Surely the man who could converse with potentates from all over the globe in all sorts of languages could have mustered up something more clever to say—even *good day* would have been better—but apparently not.

"My lord."

Fortunately for Max's ego, Miss Owen was proving no more glib than he. Now if he could just stop himself wondering what she had been doing in Hatchett's. Actually, he wasn't wondering. He knew. What else would a fashionable impure be doing at a London hotel? If he had thought about it—but Max, admiring the dark curls clustered around the heart-shaped face, long dark lashes fringing eyes that saw entirely too much, and lush red lips, was not thinking at all—he would have known that none of the ladies from Mrs. Gerrard's elegant establishment would have deigned to meet anyone anywhere, but in its select drawing room, and that they would have been dressed far more alluringly than a muslin walking dress and blush-colored spencer. The ensemble, along with matching blush gloves, shoes, and bonnet, was infinitely becoming, but decidedly demure for someone engaged in dalliance, of whatever kind.

A sudden gust of wind caught the reticule that dangled loosely in one hand, nearly ripping it from Grace's grasp, and a scrap of paper fell from the opening.

Max grabbed for it before the next gust could take it away. He did not want to look, but he could not help it. A slip of newspaper was the last thing he expected, a note of assignation, yes, but not an advertisement for *Oxford Canal . . . 13 shares . . . particulars at Hatchett's Hotel, Piccadilly.*

"Canal shares?"

"What of it?" Grace did not mean to sound defensive. There was no reason in the world why she should be. After all, everyone had a perfect right to buy canal shares, but the expression of astonishment on Lord Hawkesbury's face was decidedly infuriating. There was something about the incredulously raised eyebrow over eyes whose skeptical expression conveyed an air of irritating superiority she did not find at all attractive. It was, in fact, extremely, well, irritating.

"Actually it is the turnpike bond lists below," she continued, "that are more attractive at five percent, which is two percent more than I can get in the consols."

"But why turnpike shares?"

"And why not?" Really, the conversation was descending from the merely irritating to the truly annoying. But then he grinned.

"I beg your pardon. I must sound like the veriest coxcomb."

"You do," she admitted, her tone only slightly less frosty.

"But," he offered her his arm as determined passers-by bumped into the obstacle they made on the busy thoroughfare, "I am curious why a musician and a woman who . . . who . . ."

"Who already earns her own keep?" Grace tilted her head provocatively.

Once again she was enjoying his confusion, blast it. But she was right, his inarticulateness *was* amusing. ". . . *who already earns her own keep* is investing in turnpike shares."

"As I said, I already have money in the consols, and turnpike shares not only pay much more, but they and canal shares spread out the risk. I do not have enough savings to purchase land or an estate, but one day I shall."

He still looked confused.

"Helen teaches us all to invest, to build capital for our dreams. Now Juliette's dream of owning a shop brought her even more capital, and so will Dora's dream of owning an inn, but my dream of becoming a great opera singer is once again dependent on me to earn my money. I need something else to produce an income so I shall never ever have to need or depend on anyone!"

The fierceness of the last statement quite took his breath away. No one of his entire acquaintance had ever had to depend solely on themselves for support, nor would they want to, Max thought cynically. What an amazing woman. No, what an amazing person, Grace Owens was. How could he help?

"Have you thought of insurance?"

Now it was her turn to look blank. "I don't own any property and I have no family so . . ."

"I mean as an investment." Slowly he began walking with her back down Piccadilly, since that seemed to be where she was headed.

"But, isn't that terribly speculative?"

"Not if one applies the right predictive mathematical formulae, no. Insurance companies can make their shareholders a good deal of money."

"But, but . . . I thought you were a diplomat, not a financier."

Hah! Now *she* was the one who looked bewildered. "I am. But, like you, I have investments, and I am drawn to insurance because . . . because . . . I am fascinated by mathematics," he admitted sheepishly.

"Have you read Mr. Bonnycastle's *Treatise of Algebra,* then?"

Not the response he was expecting. "Nnno, well,er, not yet," he hastened to add, unwilling to be at a disadvantage in the face of what was obviously a challenge.

"Helen and Lord John have been discussing it this age. They seem to share a passion for such things, heaven knows why, and are forever giving one another new treatises. They like the predictability of it all, and they try to convince me that as a musician, I should share this interest, but I cannot see it. Perhaps you might like to join them in their discussions some evening. Or you might like to join them in a card game. They are fiendish players." Grace had no idea why she was inviting a man who detested Cyprians to a very den of them except that there had been just the tiniest wistful note in his admission about mathematics that hinted at a deep loneliness in the man, the loneliness of unshared interests.

Grace had been many things—despised, abused, scorned, and yes, lonely—but she'd always had people around her with whom she could share her music. What if she had not even had that to sustain her? How truly lost she would have been.

She was answered by a deafening silence. She had overstepped the bounds this time. Or perhaps he did not approve of gaming either. She could not remember if Helen had said his father was a gambler as well as a womanizer. The politic thing would be to thank him for his escort and continue towards her next errand at Chappell's, but for some reason, she did not want to give up. He had wanted to help her by getting her hired as music teacher to his nieces. She wanted to help him in return, and something inside her told her that Lord Maximilian Hawkesbury, diplomat and man of the world though he might be, needed this chance at friendship, strange though the circumstances might be. "Well, then, tea, maybe," she amended.

"Tea?"

"Yes. Lord John always stays for tea on Sunday afternoon." There. Nothing could be more unexceptionable than that.

She looked like a mulish two-year-old, determined to have her way, and she was enchanting. Max's lip quivered. "Tea then. By the way, where am I escorting you?"

"Chappell's. It is . . ."

"Randall's favorite haunt. Yes I know."

"Of course."

Her slightly conscious expression made Max feel guilty all over again. He *had* been rather brutal with her, allowing his own past to color his first encounter with her, a mistake he would never have made in any other situation, even the most inconsequential of diplomatic negotiations. It was a neophyte's blunder and he could see she still felt it. "If you spend as much on music as my nephew does, no wonder you are looking for better terms on your investment. My brother made a mistake in asking me to keep an eye on Randall in the *ton*; he should instead have asked me to make sure he did not spend his entire fortune on music. What are you looking for?"

"Howell's *Practical Instructions for Piano-Forte*, Jousse's *The Piano Forte, Made Easy*, and anything else that might help me learn the best way to teach your nieces."

"But I thought you already gave lessons."

"To the ladies at Mrs. Gerrard's who know me well enough to complain if something is not clear. When one has lived with music all one's life, it is all too easy to make assumptions at the expense of explanations. I don't want to do that with your nieces. I want to make music fun for them and easy and natural, as it should be."

The difficult moment had passed and her equilibrium re-established as he held the door of the shop open for her.

"Ah, Miss Owen! How delightful to see you. We have just gotten in the music for Signor Rossini's new opera *Il Barbiere di Seviglia*. The lead is a contralto, but with some transposition up it would be perfect for you, especially *Una Voce Poco Fa*. And for your *lesser audiences*, we have Mr. Moore's *Oft in the Stilly Night*. And did I hear this gentleman speak of Lord Farnsworth? Like you, he is another extremely knowledgeable customer who it is always a pleasure to serve."

Max didn't think he could remember feeling quite so insignificant. The clerk's adoring expression, and the ceremony with which he welcomed Grace, proclaimed Miss Owen to be not only a valued patron, but a highly respected one. Actually, Max quite enjoyed it, and when he thought about it, he realized this was the first time he had witnessed admiration for a woman's skill and intelligence, not the obsequiousness of one inferior in rank to one who was superior, but genuine recognition of expertise. He was glad, for from all that he had learned about this woman, she deserved it. She also deserved *his* respect, and the best way to prove that was to trust her judgment and follow through on her invitation to tea on Sunday at Mrs. Gerrard's.

# CHAPTER 15

A SKING HIS YOUNGER SELF, who had sworn vengeance on predatory women, if he were completely mad, Max climbed the steps to Mrs. Gerrard's Sunday afternoon. Before he reached the last one, the door swung open, held by its venerable butler—Fenwick, if he recalled correctly, and he usually did.

"Good afternoon, my lord."

"Good afternoon, Fenwick." Max thought he saw the butler's glacial visage thaw just the tiniest bit. "Is Miss Owen in?"

"I shall take you to the drawing room." Fenwick deftly avoided the last question. "They will be finished directly."

"Ah." Max didn't want to know. *Finished with what?*

"With holy services, sir," Fenwick added as though such goings on were the most natural occurrence in London's most select seraglio.

Apparently Max's expression was not as blasé as he had hoped for the butler went on to explain. "His lordship, sir, the Reverend Lord John Claverton that is, performs them here every Sunday—after he is finished up at St. George's, and then he stays for tea."

Claverton. Max knew the name of course, which meant that St. George's could only be of Hanover Square, spiritual home of the religiously inclined of the *haut ton.* Vicar of an exclusive parish, mathematical enthusiast, and spiritual advisor to a bevy of fashionable impures? Max could not help being intrigued, and he suspected that, that was precisely how Grace Owen meant him to feel.

He had no further time for speculation as he heard a door open down the hall, and a number of female voices floated in his direction. A tall, red-haired woman wearing a lemon-colored morning dress whose superb cut and dashing color emphasized the elegance of her figure and the brilliance of her auburn curls, led them. "My lord," she smiled warmly enough as she greeted him, but the green eyes were watchful, assessing him in a critical, but not unfriendly, way. "Grace told us to expect you. I gather that, like us," she glanced over her shoulder at the tall, soberly clad blond gentleman behind her, "you are a mathematical devotee."

"An interested amateur at best," Max demurred. There was something about her self-possession that told him this woman was not someone who wasted her time with idle enthusiasts.

"Come, come, sir. From what Grace tells me, you are not the sort to do anything in a dilettantish sort of way."

She had said that about him? It was rather lowering to realize how much it pleased him that Grace not only took him seriously, but talked about him.

"*Not* an amateur, I think," the tall man stepped from behind the woman who was obviously Grace's *Helen*, to offer his hand. "I believe I saw you at Mr. Mitchell's lecture to the Mathematical Society, did I not? John Claverton, by the way."

Now that he was directly in front of him, the man did look familiar. Max had also noticed him at the lecture and had been struck by his intensity which stood out in that audience where no one could have been called uninterested. "Yes, I thought his discussion of probabilities fascinating, both from a mathematical, and from a practical point of view in applying them to insurance and benefit clubs. But Grace, er Miss Owen, tells me you are reading Mr. Bonnycastle's work."

Max liked the way the man's eyes lit up and the infectious smile that instantly transformed his angular features.

"Yes. Mrs. Gerrard and I argue over some of the smaller details," he tossed Helen the teasing, collegial glance of a close friend, "but, in the main, we agree it is excellently done."

Mrs. Gerrard disposed herself gracefully on a sofa facing the fire and motioned the two gentlemen to chairs on either side. "His lordship is inclined to be a little less rigorous."

"Well, more charitable, shall we say." The smile widened to a grin.

Helen's emerald pendant earrings twinkled as she shook her head in mock dismay. "An occupational hazard, I suppose. But tell me, my lord, have you not read it?"

Max shook his head.

"Tom, be so good as to bring the book on my desk for his lordship when you are through here." She nodded to the footman who had just entered bearing a massive tea tray.

The footman returned from his errand in no time.

"Here. Take it home, read it, and tell us what you think. I am sure," her eyes flashed challengingly at Lord John, "you will agree with me."

And so it went with the banter; the tone was light and the mathematics thought-provoking. In the background was the gentle hum of female voices as the other occupants of the house slowly sauntered in and took their tea. And under it all, the gentle, barely heard tones of the pianoforte moved the conversation along like some placidly flowing river, smoothly, but effectively.

Max hadn't even noticed Grace come in, but now she sat at the pianoforte, her hands moving swiftly and surely over the keys, her expression dreamy. Obviously she was in another world. Did she even know he was here? It was a lowering thought. Max was not a coxcomb, but he was accustomed to being noticed. On the other hand, the idea of a woman who was so wrapped up in something—anything—that she didn't even see a man was something he'd never experienced. Despite its reflection on him, Max found it oddly attractive.

His reverie, and hers, were broken by the entrance of a large fair man, exquisitely clad in a blue coat of Bath superfine, biscuit-colored pantaloons, delicately embroidered waistcoat, and intricately tied cravat. His somewhat chubby features seemed almost boyish, and his curls, so fair they were almost white, were swept into a Coup au Vent. "Hallo, everyone." His breezy greeting might have included everyone, but he headed right for Grace, waving what looked like papers. "I have got it! *Together Let Us Range the Fields,* the duet Miss Frith and Mr. Bradbury sang in the Argyll Rooms the other evening. All we have to do is find a gentleman to accompany you. It really is an enchanting piece."

Grace noticed *this* man, and it irritated Max that this bothered him, even though there was not an ounce of flirtatiousness in her welcoming smile—just friendliness. When he thought about it, a friendly smile between a woman and a man who were not related was a rare and precious thing. Max could barely count on one hand the men who gave him friendly smiles, much less women, and he envied it.

"My brother, Freddy," Lord John explained as though he somehow needed to do so. "It was his interest in Mademoiselle Juliette's, er, Lady Adrian Claverton's gown that introduced my brothers and me to Helen and company. Freddy is a connoisseur," he hastened to explain, "and it was his admiration of my sister-in-law's silk gown that brought him here to learn more about it, both because it was French silk and we were at war with France, and because it was so exquisitely fashioned. What he discovered was a kindred spirit, and he and Juliette have been collaborating on designs ever since. They have even gotten my sister Georgie interested, which is saying a great deal. Now that Lady Adrian has established Maison Juliette, he is helping Mrs. Gerrard re-decorate here. Forgive me, you had no earthly need to know this," he grinned at Max's stupefied expression. "I apologize."

"Hello, Freddy," John rose as his brother headed back toward Helen, a swatch of blue damask in his outstretched hand. "I see you have come to turn Helen's attention away from mere mathematics to aesthetics. I had best take my leave. Do you care to accompany me?" He turned to Max. "I have some questions on the lecture we attended and would be most interested in hearing your thoughts."

Max should have felt grateful at being extricated so easily from this den of iniquity without being subject to uncomfortable solicitations, but he was not. He glanced around the room. Dora happened to look up from a conversation with a slim, blond woman who looked more like the daughter of a vicar or a country solicitor—which in fact she was—than a Cyprian, and she gave him a friendly smile, a friendly smile of his own, before going back to her discussion. Trying not to be obvious, he rose, turning toward the pianoforte as he did so, but Grace was too busy leafing through the music to see him.

But Max had reckoned without Lord John Claverton. His lordship might complain that there was very little work for him among his extremely comfortable parishioners, but he was a sensitive man, and took up the Lord's work wherever he found it. Striving always to sympathize with the needs of his fellow me, he led Max over to the pianoforte. "You were quite right to introduce us to Lord Maximilian, Miss Owen. He is indeed a worthy addition to our mathematical discussions."

Max was rewarded with a blush as Grace looked up, or was she looking at Lord John?

"I am so glad, my lord." She turned toward Max and he was struck all over again by how very beautiful she was. "I do hope you enjoyed it as well." And that was all she said before setting the music on the stand and placing her hands on the keys.

He should have been glad she was not interested in him. He should have been relieved that she was not after him like the blood-sucking, well, gold-sucking, harpies who had ruined his father, but at this particular moment, all he felt was disappointment that she let him go so easily, without even hinting at a possible meeting in the near future. What was it about her that made him wish she would? Was it the dark blue eyes so alive to the world, the long white neck caressed by a few dark silky curls, or the passion that radiated from her when she was at the pianoforte? Whatever it was, it was becoming disturbingly irresistible.

# Chapter 16

"I TRULY DID WISH TO DISCUSS MR. MITCHELL'S LECTURE WITH YOU," John said as they walked towards Piccadilly, again with a disarming smile that was also extremely knowing. Max wondered just how deliberate the entire thing was. Had the Vicar of St. George's, Hanover Square engineered their exit to protect him from Grace, Grace from him, or because Lord John Claverton genuinely wanted to discuss Mr. Mitchell's thesis? No one at Mrs. Gerrard's had acted the way he had expected them to. On the one hand, they had been as natural and unconcerned as if they were taking tea in any elegant London drawing room, without the least hint of ulterior motives, such as luring him upstairs to steal his soul or his fortune. On the other hand, the discussions were more lively and intelligent—both his and the snatches of others he overheard— than he had encountered in all the other elegant London drawing rooms he had ever visited, drawing rooms where there actually *were* ulterior motives, such as marrying his title and his fortune.

"You see, Mrs. Gerrard and I have been thinking about setting up a Female Friendly Society, something along the lines of the York Female Friendly Society, which can provide for her ladies in case of illness or worse. She pays them well and encourages them to save a goodly portion of their earnings so they can start new lives, but . . . well . . . accidents happen, and life can turn upside down in an instant, as these women well know. Grace mentioned that you are interested in insurance, and the thing is, we want to be precise in our calculations so that it is successful. If it is successful, we would like to establish others so that women in service or shops, or whatever trade, have something between themselves and utter destitution should they become ill or unable to fend for themselves."

Max liked the enthusiasm brightening the other man's eyes. Here was passion as well, and he could not help being drawn to it, besides which, it was the sort of interesting intellectual problem that tickled his brain. Perhaps he was mistaken, perhaps Lord John, enthusiast that he was, had not intended to draw him from Grace, but had simply wanted to discuss risk and probabilities in greater detail

By now they had reached Albany and Max said goodbye to his new friend, but not before he had promised to call on him in the rectory.

"It is rather large for one occupant so I would welcome the company, though I must warn you that its proximity to Grosvenor Square makes it far too easy for my mother and sister to drop in unannounced." He grinned. "They are both good sorts so I don't usually mind the interruption. I am also eager," he pointed to the book in Max's hand, "to hear your opinion of Bonnycastle. He writes very clearly, I think, no matter what you think of his thesis." A quick bow, and he was off down Piccadilly, his tall, loping figure easily distinguishable in the crowd.

Max turned into his own quarters, eager for solitude and a chance to sort through a myriad of thoughts and impressions precipitated by his visit to Mrs. Gerrard's. Pouring himself a glass of port, he sank into a chair, opened Bonnycastle's *Treatise of Algebra* and stared at the page in front of him without reading a word. When had anyone given him anything without any expectation of something in return? The Max of even a few weeks ago would have been sure that Helen Gerrard had designs on him, or, to be more precise, his pocketbook, but there was something in that lady's self-possessed air that made him know she was completely trustworthy. It had been enthusiasm for the subject and their discussion that had prompted the gift, and nothing more. When he considered it, everything about that afternoon had been nothing more or less than it had appeared—women having genuine conversations with one another—no glancing around to see if others were noticing or admiring them, a pianist lost in her playing, a friend bringing her a new piece of music simply because they shared an appreciation for it. How relaxed, how natural, and how pleasant it had all been.

He had Grace Owen to thank for it, the Grace Owen who had merely nodded at him as though she had invited him all for his benefit, not hers. And that bothered Max. It bothered him that she hadn't invited him there for herself, and it bothered him that it bothered him. Perhaps, after all, she didn't find him as intriguing . . . and attractive as he found her. Perhaps she didn't feel that spark of connection he did every time he looked into her eyes, saw the understanding, the humor, and the challenge in them. Perhaps she didn't enjoy sparring with him the way he did with her, as though what they said to one another really mattered, as though each one of them had at last found the worthy opponent they'd been seeking their entire lives.

How was he to know for sure? He couldn't just call on her at Mrs. Gerrard's like some besotted suitor or, worse yet, patron. That was not the sort of relationship he thought they had . . . until she had dismissed him so easily.

He took a sip of port, swirling it around on his tongue as he pondered the problem, trying not to think of those eyes and that long white neck. Aha! He had it. Max set his glass down with a snap. He would call on his sister . . . on a Monday or a Friday between 10 and 12.

So it was that the very next day Max presented himself in Brook Street at a little after 10—hardly the hour to be making a call, even on one's sister. No doubt Henrietta would pepper him with all sorts of leading questions, or, at the very least, smile knowingly, but he didn't care. And he really didn't care when he heard the sounds of halting piano music coming from the drawing room.

"I'll announce myself," he informed the astonished butler from half way up the stairway. Max halted his precipitate entry at the landing just outside the drawing room and crept forward noiselessly. He did not know what he expected, but it hadn't been to have his heart punched by the scene in front of him.

She was sitting with a little girl on either side of her, her arm around the delicate shoulders of each one, head bent forward, smiling at the smallest one. In between her and the recipient of the smile, a furry thing waved rhythmically back and forth. A duster? No. It belonged to a small dog wedged cozily in between Grace and his niece. But it was the expression on Grace's face that made him catch his breath. It glowed with joy and tenderness; and the gentle loveliness suffused her entire being. If the Grace Owen who played and sang like an angel was riveting, this Grace was radiant in a way that moved something deep inside him, something so foreign as to be unidentifiable, indescribable, but real and powerful, nevertheless.

Equally moving was the look on both the girls' faces as they smiled adoringly up at their teacher, and Max was bowled over by the unexpected, almost irrelevant, but obvious thought that Grace Owen was not only a beautiful talented woman, she was a good one.

The smallest niece—Laura, he now remembered—planted her tiny hands in a final chord and the dog between her and Grace reached up to lick her cheek in approval. "Uncle Max!" She caught sight of him out of the corner of her eye as she turned to pat the dog. "Come meet Pippin."

"How do you do, Pippin." Max took the little dog's paw in his hand and shook it gently, much to the delight of both his nieces. He was not so sure about Grace though; her expression was as unreadable as any skilled diplomat in the most intense of negotiations.

"I do beg your pardon for interrupting, Miss Owen."

"Not at all, my lord," she responded serenely, much to his frustration. After all, it was not every member of his Majesty's diplomatic corps, or gentleman bachelor who would allow himself to be found in the customary province of governesses or fond mamas. Didn't she see she could trust him to be her friend?

"Uncle Max, I can play *Baa Baa Black Sheep*. Do you want to hear me?"

"Very much." Max took a seat in a nearby chair as Grace and Beatrice moved over to give Laura pride of place in front of the keys. It was a very creditable rendition and, as he applauded, Max was surprised to discover how pleased he was by her success. Then he remembered his manners. "Excellent performance. Obviously you have a very good teacher." He winked at Grace. "I am sure Beatrice has learned something as well?" That won him an appraising look from Grace, not to mention a shyly grateful smile from her other pupil.

It was Beatrice's turn to move to the center of the pianoforte where she began *Oranges and Lemons* which, if less rousingly performed than *Baa Baa Black Sheep* was rather more accurate.

"Excellent, excellent. It is clear that you two have been most diligent, so it must be fair to say that Miss Owen is as fortunate to have you as pupils as you are to have her as your teacher."

"Laura, Beatrice . . ." Henrietta whisked into the room and came to a dead stop inside the doorway. "Oh hello, Max. Did I know you were coming?" She grinned impishly as she came over to give him an unexpected peck on the cheek.

"No, actually not, but I was just on my way to . . ." Where *was* he on his way to? "To Tattersall's and, since I was passing by, I thought I would inquire as to how you all were doing."

Even Henrietta was not buying this since Brook Street could barely be said to be on the way to the famous horse auctioneers.

"Well, I was taking a long walk around Hyde Park, you see . . ." Max searched quickly for a change of subject before he got himself in any deeper, "and I was delighted to hear music when I entered, so, naturally I begged to be allowed to join the lesson."

All this was too much for Grace, who was barely keeping herself from laughing. Grace laughing—a sight he would have walked far more than the circumference of Hyde Park to see. Warmth and something else—could it be happiness—seeped through Max's veins. So this is what it was like to have a family, simply to *be*, with nothing expected, nothing demanded, just acceptance of him, as a person. He hadn't realized that he wanted it until now. How delightful it was. Now he saw clearly how Grace, cast off by society in general, or at least *respectable* society at any rate, must have longed for the very same thing, and how she must have found it among her companions at Mrs. Gerrard's. Or, judging from the longing in her eyes as she smiled at her pupils and absently stroked the little dog's head, she had found most, but not all of it at the elegant establishment in St. James' Square.

Grace's expression was not the only thing transformed. The wink as Max had complimented Laura and praised her teacher had done it. Grace, who had remained unmoved by multitudes of exquisitely wrought compliments and extravagant presents, even fairly creditable poetry, was undone by the simple conspiratorial gesture, at once so intimate, and yet so utterly un-lover-like. What was it about one man, well, actually, this particular intense, sometimes arrogant, sometimes toplofty man sharing a secret smile with her that turned her bones to water while making her pulses race. And then he had actually given in to a self-deprecatory, sheepish grin at being caught in such an obviously concocted excuse for appearing in Brook Street. It was . . . endearing. What right did a dark-browed, chiseled-faced man have to look endearing, not to mention devastatingly attractive?

Pippin struggled slightly and looked up at Grace curiously as her hand stopped stroking his fur and clutched it instead. And then, with a dog's intuition, he turned toward Max, and, tongue hanging out, grinned his own toothy grin.

"Look! He likes him. Pippin likes Uncle Max." Laura slid off the bench with the dog and danced over to her uncle with him and the moment was broken, but not before Max's sister had caught the exchange and smiled her own secret smile. Henrietta had already tumbled to the fact that Grace Owen was someone special to her brother, and it appeared that he was special to Grace as well. Now she had proof, what was she going to do about it? The Countess of Edgefield was not quite sure how she was going to bring them closer together, but she knew that ultimately she would find a way. They were both too unique to be wasted on people who were simply ordinary, or worse, like the fiercely determined Lady Caroline Daventry who, on the slimmest pretexts—her father's diplomatic service with Max—had called with her mother on Max's sister a few days ago. Henrietta had not been fooled. She had seen the acquisitive glint in Lady Caroline's eyes and had not liked it one little bit.

# CHAPTER 17

"COME GIRLS, WE MUST NOT TAKE UP ALL OF MISS OWEN'S TIME, you know. She has other things to do besides teaching piano to you two," the Countess smiled ruefully at Grace.

"Arf."

"Or you, Pippin. Come along. It is high time for your other lessons. Don't look so glum; learning your letters and geography may not be so entertaining as music, and it is only your mother teaching them to you, but they are equally as useful. If you'll excuse us?" Henrietta turned to Max and Grace, then, taking a daughter's hand in each of hers, she sailed from the room, Pippin at her heels. *And that,* she thought triumphantly, *is that.*

For a moment Grace and Max just stared at one another, and then he chuckled. Somehow it was so infectious Grace couldn't help chuckling herself, and soon the two of them were laughing so hard tears stung their eyes. "She really is incorrigible."

"Who? Laura? She is at that."

"No, Henrietta, my sister. I wish I had known her when I was growing up, but by the time she came along, I was away at school and did not come home if I could help it. She must have run the household ragged with no one to control her."

"But surely your mother . . ."

"My mother is not interested in anything but herself, money, and men, and never was. She only bothers with Hubert because he is head of the family, not that there is much to be head of since, thanks to my father, the estates are mortgaged to the hilt. My inheritance, such as it is, is irreparably tainted by trade, my Uncle Richard having decided to do something more interesting with his life than ride to the hounds." The laughter had fled from his eyes, leaving them dark as slate, and the amused twist of his lips had thinned into a mocking sneer.

"I am sorry." Grace laid a hand on his arm and felt the tension in the rigid muscles underneath his coat. Here was someone who felt things as strongly as she did, and worked just as hard as she did to keep them bottled up under a controlled exterior.

The sneer quirked into the ghost of a smile and the eyes warmed. "I do believe you are."

"Is that so surprising? Who could understand better?"

The more he considered it, the more he realized there was some truth to what she said. Even though he was wealthy, titled, and a man, he had never truly belonged anywhere, except possibly in the heady moments when he had convinced wrangling diplomats to agree. But how much worse it was for a woman with no money and less power. From that vantage point, the decisions she had made about her life not only made sense, they were the only ones she could have made.

"Of course I could have saved my *respectability* by becoming a servant, but with no references, such positions, no matter how lowly, are nigh impossible to come by. And who would marry a woman such as I with no money and no connections except someone who wanted a docile slave?"

The sound of rapid footsteps interrupted and Grace turned towards them. "And here is Rose, come to walk me home, for we denizens of Mrs. Gerrard's establishment must always maintain our outward signs of respectability. You are surprised, my lord. Did you not see her trailing behind us down Piccadilly the other day?"

In fact, he, usually so acutely aware of his surroundings, had been oblivious to everything else but Grace Owen—her beauty, her cleverness, her surprising depths—that he had, had no thought for anything else.

Grace chuckled again. "No need to admit to it. It is written all over your face."

He grinned. "It is a very complicated life you lead, Miss Grace Owen, a very complicated life indeed."

"Yes. We ape the trappings of the most rigidly respectable in order to escape their notice so that we may live our utterly un-respectable lives in peace."

"Not so different from the rest of the *ton*."

There was no missing the sardonic tone, and Grace looked up to discover again a surprising wealth of sympathy in his eyes. "You will find no slavish admirer of the *ton* in me, Miss Owen. After all, my parents were considered *respectable*. In spite of his licentious and spendthrift ways, my father was always welcomed in the *best* of houses, as was, of course his wife, though rarely together, the *best* of houses usually being too tactful for that."

Grace studied her hands, absorbing all these things before replying. "How odd. You actually make me appreciate that my life, irregular as it is in so many ways, is refreshingly honest."

She looked so much like a serious student considering a complex problem that Max couldn't help smiling. "I do believe you are in the right of that," he agreed. And who would have thought that Lord Maximilian Hawkesbury would ever have reached such an astounding conclusion?

But now the butler was handing Grace her bonnet and spencer, and Rose was tying the strings of her own bonnet as they moved towards the door.

"I would be delighted to escort you wherever you are going." Max was loath to end the conversation, despite the bitter memories it brought back.

"That is kind of you, but there is no need . . ."

"Except that I enjoy talking to you."

"Do you now?" She cocked her head.

He could not remember when he'd been examined quite so critically, except, perhaps when he had lied to his nurse about washing his hands before dinner.

Then she smiled and took his arm. "I do believe you do. How very flattering." And it was. There was far more interest than admiration in his expression. Grace could think of no man, except Freddy, well, and his brothers, who had looked at her as a person instead of a woman. To someone who was privately bored to death with admiration, this interest was more flattering than all the poetic compliments in the world.

"And where are you going?"

"Home, to St. James's Square." Odd how easily the word *home* came to her when speaking of Mrs. Gerrards, but not so odd, really, when its inhabitants paid more attention to her and knew her far better than her parents ever had. To be sure, she had been their darling daughter, living proof of their love, but if the truth were told, they had eyes more for one another than they ever did for her. Certainly when her mother had died, her father had found absolutely no solace in their daughter.

"Excellent."

She looked up at him, not a little disappointed, even though she hated to admit it. So he was more interested in visiting Mrs. Gerrard's than he was in her.

The look in her eyes was not lost on Max. Somehow he was forever making a fool of himself in front of Grace Owen. "I beg your pardon. That came out all wrong. What I meant was that I wish to escort you, wish to go for the pleasure of your company, but I am glad the destination is St. James's Square rather than, say, Chappell's, because I wish to speak to Mrs. Gerrard about a scheme to set up a female friendly society . . . to provide for all of you in case of misfortune," he hastened to explain.

Grace didn't know what to think. Here was a man who despised her kind, and now he wanted to help them? And he actually looked intrigued at the prospect.

"It was Mrs. Gerrard's idea," he hastened to explain, "but I thought it would be much more useful if, while we are setting it up, we teach everyone something about how it works. I thought perhaps I might just stop in and volunteer my services to Mrs. Gerrard, and I also wanted to suggest setting up an annuity that would pay you all a regular allowance in your old age."

She still didn't reply, and it made Max uneasy. Did it seem like a deceitful ploy to her? Truly he had been so taken with the notion that it hadn't crossed his mind that she might mistrust his motives. "I quite like the idea and I think I might actually be good at teaching. I am often called upon to do the explaining in our negotiations so I expect that I might be a dab hand at teaching.

He looked so eager she could not help be touched by this man who helped decide the fate of nations, yet seemed unsure that he would be allowed to teach a group of fallen women about insurance and annuities. "I think it an excellent scheme, and I shall be the first to sign up for lessons. Now tell me more so that I may sound intelligent when Helen interrogates me, for interrogate me, she will."

# CHAPTER 18

Grace was entirely correct in her prediction; Helen did interrogate her—mercilessly—but not about female friendly societies. "When a man, whose family fortune was entirely lost to rapacious courtesans, offers to teach finance to a seraglio full of them, one does have to ask the question." Helen fixed Grace with a *look* as she nibbled on the pencil that had been vigorously calculating accounts, "Why? And the *why* is disturbing, considering he does not seem to wish to avail himself of our, er *services* in the usual way."

"But Freddy does not avail himself of our *services* in the usual way either," Grace objected, completely sidestepping the issue.

"The Marquess of Wrothingham has very clear aesthetic interests, not to mention a very clear distaste for his fiancee's withering company; that makes it only natural for him to seek us out. I see nothing similar in Lord Maximilian's case, which leads me to believe it is a very strong interest in one of us that accounts for his offer." Raising an accusatory brow, Helen stopped nibbling on the pencil and set it down with a snap. "You *know* how dangerous it is if a gentleman pursues one of us without any apparent . . . carnal persuasions. It can lead to foolish romantic tendencies."

Grace nodded. "I know, but the gentleman in question has mostly demonstrated combative tendencies where I am concerned."

"Most combative, at the outset, yes, but immediately softened by procuring you a position in his sister's household." Seeing the look in her employee's eyes, Helen relented. "Make no mistake, my dear, I honor the man for being an honest, decent, and even generous human being. He has shown that rare capacity to learn and change his perspective—unusual to nonexistent in anyone, but particularly in the male of the species. I do think you should . . ."

"I know, and I thank you for wanting to protect my feelings, but I have none—except for music, of course. It is just that I think the idea you and Lord John propose of a mutual friendly society to protect us in case of misfortune is an excellent one, and Lord John apparently felt confident enough of Lord Maximilian's usefulness that he enlisted his aid. Lord Maximilian explained most clearly to me how it all works. In fact, he had already suggested insurance to me as a way of distributing risk in my investments."

*A romantic conversation if there ever was one,* Helen could not help thinking ironically, but still, there was a glow about Grace that gave her pause.

"And he even suggested that we consider setting up a *Mrs. Gerrard's Establishment Annuity,* separate from the insurance, that would pay us in our old age. Apparently he is fascinated by the actuarial mathematics involved in the setting up of assurance and annuity tables. If you could see how much he enjoyed explaining it all to me . . . I mean, I don't think he has many opportunities to speak about that sort of thing. I could see how much his discussion with you and Lord John meant to him; he looked like a different person afterwards."

"And here I thought you were playing the pianoforte," Helen murmured as she watched the delicate flush creep into Grace's cheeks. *No, no feelings involved at all. We'll see about that, my dear.*

"I was, but I am always aware of my audience, whether they are listening or not."

"I know, dear girl. I see how your music sets the tone of the evening—soothing us when discussions become too heated, enlivening us when they drift into dullness. Of course you are aware of all of us, but some perhaps more than others?"

Grace laughed ruefully. "You are brutally honest, but truly, Lord Maximilian is nothing to me. I just find it rather fascinating that such a worldly, cynical man should be so transformed by a simple conversation. It makes me think that maybe he is lonely. How odd."

"But you and I see scores of lonely men every day. As we both know, it is offering our congenial company to lonely people that is our greatest charm."

"Yes, but all those others are so very . . . social, and lead such social lives. Lord Maximilian is so very self-sufficient."

"I expect he had to be . . . as we all have had to be."

Grace nodded, recalling the bleak look on Max's face and the bitter twist of his lips as he had described his distant, self-indulgent parents, and then she took herself to task for wanting to make up for his lonely childhood. Lord Maximilian Hawkesbury was a wealthy, powerful man who could quite obviously, given who he had become, take care of himself. He did not need any help from anyone, least of all a fashionable impure. Why on earth should she care about his happiness? But she did.

Watching her quietly, Helen had a fair idea of the thoughts roiling around in her protégé's mind, for she too had observed how Lord Maximilian's severe features had softened as he had warmed to the topic he had been discussing with her and Lord John, betraying a passionate mind behind a forbidding exterior. In a way, he reminded her of Freddy and Lord John and Lord Adrian, though all of them were more easy-going than her establishment's most recent visitor. Like Lord Maximilian, the Clavertons were also men whose entire beings became animated when speaking of their particular interests, and it made all of them, Lord Maximilian included, dangerously attractive to people like her and Juliette and Grace who had their own special obsessions. But that did not mean one had to fall victim to that attraction.

"I do think his suggestion of an annuity has a good deal of merit," she mused. "I find other areas of mathematics more diverting than statistics and probability, but I can see how others would find them fascinating." Helen rose, putting an end to all further discussion. "But now I must consult with Fenwick about our supply of claret. I was not best pleased by the last bottle that was served."

The motivation behind Lord Maximilian's offer of instruction and investment assistance, as well as any concerns for his happiness were all forgotten several days later as he stood before them all in the *schoolroom,* an impressive figure carrying a pointer and a roll of papers.

"Now I know Mrs. Gerrard has encouraged all of you to save your earnings so that you may do as your friend Lady Adrian has done and invest them in dreams of your own." As Max looked at their expectant faces, more riveted on the speaker than any he had seen in all the lectures he attended at Cambridge, he asked himself if he were crazed to think he could help them invest what they made—what he had previously considered *stolen* from the birthrights of families like his, until he had met an unapologetic, determined young woman who had done the only thing she could do to save herself in the face of misfortune. Had he, like his father, fallen victim to a beautiful face and charming manner? Was he, possibly also like his father, seeking out the comfort he had not found at home among the denizens of Mrs. Gerrard's? It was a lowering thought. No! He was not like his father. He was not doing this out of weakness. And he had not been charmed. Challenged? Yes. Charmed? No. *Frosty* was the word that came to mind when he thought of their first meeting, and then came *clever* and *interesting,* but there had not been an ounce of flirtation in any of their encounters and that was what made her so intriguing. Blast!

The silence was deafening. Max took a breath and continued as smoothly as he could. "As you all know, disaster can strike at any time," Max felt, rather than saw, Grace's eyes fixed upon him encouragingly, but he received the message loud and clear, "but you do not need to fall victim to it if you plan. And I am going to help you plan."

This time he did look up, and the expression in her eyes lighted his soul. No one, that he could remember in all his life, except, possibly Castlereagh, or Uncle Richard, had given him their approval. Yes, Castlereagh and Uncle Richard congratulated him on jobs well done, but this was more, so much more, and he could not help smiling back at her . . . and the others. They were nodding and smiling too, warming him with their appreciation. Yes, he *did* want to do his utmost to keep his promise to the ladies of Mrs. Gerrard's and help them find security in an uncertain world as best he could.

# CHAPTER 19

Grace had watched as he unrolled his charts of life expectancies and explained the mathematics for calculating interest but she had not really listened. She was far more interested in the way he smiled when Dora pinned him down with a difficult question. Instead of dismissing her, as most men would have, he clearly relished the question. "Yes, it is an issue that others have struggled with, though it is not obvious to most. Let me explain how they addressed it," which he proceeded to do in a way that made clear he respected her knowledge and her curiosity. Dora was a confident, forthright creature, but she positively glowed with pride as he went back and forth with her. Who would have thought that a man so brutally dismissive in their first meeting would be so complimentary now?

But it was not complimentary in the ordinary way. Lord Maximilian Hawkesbury was not speaking facile words that left him uninvolved; he was bestowing dignity by taking the ladies of Mrs. Gerrard's seriously, by engaging them in discussion instead of lecturing, by showing that he enjoyed learning and exploring with them. No wonder he was a successful diplomat, for he had the gift of honest appreciation that made others trust him. She could see it in her friends' eyes and hear it in their voices, these women who rarely trusted anyone outside of their own little world, and almost never a man.

Grace gave herself a mental shake. Helen was right to have warned her. She could actually end up liking the man. How foolish was that?

But Grace was not the only fool. "He is rather a tough character," Dora confided later. "In our first encounter, he made it clear that he had no use for me, but he appears to have changed his mind." She grinned, "And he seemed to like it that I gave as good as I got. If he can do all he says he can, then we owe him a great deal of thanks."

Clarissa agreed. "He explained it so even I could understand. It's the sign of a clever man if he understands complicated things so well he can make them comprehensible to others . . . and to look so dashing when he does it," she added with a sly smile.

"We are fortunate he is willing to share his time with us when he must have so many other important affairs to attend to," Jane spoke up.

"And why shouldn't he share his time?" Dora demanded. "Not only are we all clever and charming, but we are going to make money for him as well as for ourselves. Don't forget that, no matter how grateful we are."

The gratitude, however, was not one-sided.

Wishing to distract herself from feelings that were far too admiring towards Lord Maximilian Hawkesbury, Grace had hurried out of the room while others were clustered around him, in search of her one true companion—her pianoforte. As her fingers touched the keys, these absurd thoughts subsided as the music washed away the dangerous attraction that always seemed to wrap her in its grip whenever she was around him. And then she felt that unnerving sensation that told her he was standing right behind her.

Amid the hubbub of questions and comments, Max, his senses, always alert where *she* was involved, had seen Grace slip out the door, and immediately knew where she was going. She was avoiding him again. But why? He thought she had been pleased with his presentation.

She whisked around on the pianoforte bench, her eyes wide with an emotion he could not quite read. It was not surprise. The rest of her did not seem startled. It almost appeared to be apprehension, or, could it be, defiance? What had he done? Exactly what she had wanted him to do—or so he thought. Then he noticed her hands, usually so strong and capable, wringing themselves one over the other. It tore at his heart to see her so agitated.

Without thinking, he gathered them in his own. "Thank you."

"Whaaaat?"

"Thank you. I enjoyed myself. I liked it, feeling useful—helpful, I hope. And I enjoyed discussing some of my favorite topics with your friends." He spoke without thinking, not knowing what he was thinking until he uttered the words."

"And they enjoyed you." Grace could not help chuckling as she pictured them all clustered around him like a throng of admiring schoolgirls instead of London's most sophisticated courtesans—anything to ignore the warmth and strength of his hands. When had anyone's touch been so . . . so overwhelming, but at the same time so reassuring?

"I do think they found it interesting; at least they seemed to." His hopeful tone was both endearing and irresistible.

"Oh they did." She smiled. How could you not like a man who was just a bit unsure of himself? Grace wished he would revert to the browbeating, dismissive intruder she had first met. *That* man she could keep at arm's length with no difficulty at all. This man? She could not even retrieve her own hands from this man.

"Oh, there you are, my lord," Rose hovered on the threshold, "I do beg your pardon, Miss Grace, but Mrs. Gerrard said to tell you that Lord John is come, my lord, and you might wish to discuss *next steps* with them. They are in her office, and I am to send Mr. Sandys in with tea."

"Duty calls," Max smiled ruefully. "And now I will get a true reading on my performance, and my usefulness. I leave you to your music, which I apologize for interrupting."

Much to her disgust, Grace could not come up with a suitable reply but nodded in the weakest sort of way. Really, she was deteriorating into the most impressionable, missish . . . Well, it was time to sort herself out. She had a career to pursue.

# Chapter 20

Henrietta happened to be looking out the drawing room window a few days later, before gathering her girls for their pianoforte lesson, when she saw a suspicious looking man sidle up to Grace and Rose as they approached the Edgefield's townhouse. Actually, he didn't look suspicious—he was well enough, though carelessly, dressed—but his manner alerted her. She could see the sly smile that made his rat-like features even less attractive, but mostly it was the way he hovered over Grace, insinuating yet threatening at the same time that gave her pause. And Grace, drawing herself taller as she flicked her skirts disdainfully away from the stranger, did not look pleased by the encounter.

Before Henrietta could think, the girls came racing into the drawing room and she heard Walter opening the front door and welcoming the two women.

Distracted by her daughters' enthusiastic recital of all that Miss Grace had taught them during the last lesson and the new song she had promised to teach them today, Henrietta forgot about the unnerving scene until some days later when she was accosted by their haughty neighbor.

Henrietta and the girls had been out for a walk, and Beatrice and Laura had run on ahead for their tea while their mother came along more slowly, urging a reluctant Pippin who was tugging on the least to investigate some very interesting smells.

"What you see in that mongrel, I have not the least notion," Lady Lavinia Harcourt sniffed as she edged away from all possible canine contact, "but I must take this opportunity to warn you, my dear Countess, that your music teacher is not all she should be."

"I was not aware that you knew I had a music teacher, but your concern is misplaced, I assure you. Miss Owen comes highly recommended as a pupil of Signor Lanza, in addition to being an excellent teacher." Henrietta, hoping she was successfully imitating her brother at his haughtiest, tried to sound both distant and dismissive while ruthlessly squelching the desire to inquire of this interfering busybody if the two of them had even been introduced, which Henrietta was quite sure they had not.

Lady Lavinia sniffed again as Pippin, distracted by a situation more interesting than any random smells, plunked himself down on the pavement, fixing their neighbor with a minatory look. "Musician she may be, but she is also an . . . er, other less respectable things."

Henrietta raised an incredulous eyebrow.

"My brother, Basil, Viscount Wormleigh, tells me she is a . . . well, she has a most unsavory reputation."

"And I suppose your brother would know because . . . ?"

The flush rising in Lady Lavinia's gaunt cheeks only emphasized the hatchet-like features. "Don't say I did not do my Christian duty in warning you," she snapped. "Good day, Madam." Gathering her skirts even more closely to her, Lavinia sailed off with as much dignity as she could muster.

"If she calls *that* Christian," Henrietta muttered to Pippin, "I'd like to see who she considers an Infidel."

Later on that evening, her husband confirmed what his wife already suspected. "Viscount Wormleigh?" Edgefield looked up from his dinner in some surprise. "Shocking loose screw. However did you come across the man?"

"I didn't come across him," Henrietta hastened to reassure him, "his sister happened to mention him."

"Well I would stay as far away as possible from him as I could. The Harcourts may be an ancient family, but that does not mean that all of them are the sort of people you should know."

And that was saying a lot, for no one stood on less ceremony than Edgefield. In fact, it was her husband's total lack of interest in such things that had first attracted Henrietta to him, that and the fact that he had been madly in love with her ever since they had met when he was visiting a friend at a neighboring estate to Swanton Hall.

Now that she had identified the *gentleman* of Grace's uncomfortable encounter, Henrietta, being Henrietta, demanded the entire story the next time Grace was in Brook Street.

"Yes, he is a nasty piece of work." Grace confirmed her suspicions. "He forced his way into Mrs. Gerrard's on his future brother-in-law's coattails, and then proceeded to assault Dora. Needless to say, Mrs. Gerrard, well Lord Adrian, really, got rid of him in very short order, and he hasn't been seen in the vicinity since. It is a great deal too bad that Freddy, er, the Marquess of Wrothingham, has been engaged to Lady Lavinia since birth, for her brother, according to Lord Adrian, is thoroughly despicable."

"Not unlike the sister, in my opinion," Henrietta responded drily. "You seem surprised. She may not actually be disreputable like her brother, but she is a thoroughly *nasty piece of work* herself. Yet she had the effrontery to warn me against you. Don't look so worried." A sly smile stole across the Countess' face. "I think it is time to introduce you to society. Mind you, I am not normally one to court the *ton*, but neither can I abide self-righteous tabbies . . ." her voice trailed off as the smile deepened, "yes, I think a musicale would be just the thing to make your talents known. And the Marquess of Wrothingham's name will be first on the list of guests. The girls mentioned a song he brought you the other day. I take it *he* is impressed by your musical ability."

"He is most kind."

"Nonsense. If he has a brain in his head, he knows how talented you are, and my guess is that he is a fervent admirer. Aha! You cannot hide it, he is enraptured by your talent. Oh, this is delicious. I can hardly wait to tell Max; he will be so delighted."

Grace looked skeptical

"I know he will. Oh, very well, have it your way, not delighted, but intrigued."

"Certainly that." Grace laughed. There was no resisting the Countess of Edgefield's mischievousness nor her forthright manner of speaking.

His sister was right, Max was intrigued. He only wished it had been his idea. "Very clever, dear Sister. I find it highly irritating that you thought of it before I did."

"You can't be the only intelligent one in the family, and you are full enough of yourself as it is."

"I?" He clutched his breast in mock horror. "The man who listens with the utmost respect to pompous diplomats without so much as the flutter of an eyelash?"

"Yes, but that's your profession. I am talking about ordinary daily life."

She was joking. Of course she was. Max could tell by the teasing smile and the twinkle in her eye, but there was just enough of an edge to her voice to give him pause. Was he insufferably pompous, or, at the very least, just pompous? Was that what Mrs. Gerrard's ladies thought of him? Was that why Grace had been in such a hurry to quit the schoolroom after his talk? Surely not.

Watching him closely, Henrietta sensed that her remarks had hit home. Good. He needed to be taken down a peg or two once in a while. On the other hand, her brother was a good man. If it hadn't been for him, she wouldn't be able to offer Grace the opportunity to distinguish herself in a musicale though

Henrietta had the grace to admit to herself, the idea of a musicale, had been more to put Lady Lavinia's nose out of joint than to advance Grace Owen's musical career.

"Come," taking pity on Max, his sister beckoned him to the drawing room sofa, "help me plan the guest list. Of course Edgefield can invite his colleagues in Parliament, and we must make certain it is an evening when Mama has been invited somewhere else much more important. Then, I thought the Marquess of Wrothingham and his fiancée . . ."

"Wrothingham's fiancée?" Max raised a skeptical eyebrow

"Well, Lady Lavinia lives just a few doors down and . . ."

"Henrietta!"

Blast! She knew her brother to be awake on all suits, but she had not known he was that awake. "Well, she does and . . . and," and then she found herself confessing All to her brother.

He laughed until he had to wipe tears from his eyes. "Too rich by half. Henrietta, you are a minx, but do let me warn you never to play poker. Your face gave it away the moment you mentioned Wrothingham's fiancée. No, don't look so defensive. I like your idea even better now I know the entire story. What a little troublemaker you are—in your own quiet way."

"I am, aren't I?" Henrietta grinned, loving the feeling of sharing something with her distant, clever, older brother. "I must get started. The Countess of Edgefield rarely entertains, but when she does, by God the *ton* will know. You will ask Wrothingham who else in the musical world should be invited?"

"Yes, and I will consult with Randall as well. He may not have much use for, or many acquaintances among the Upper Ten Thousand, but his musical connections are impeccable, if a trifle pedantic."

"Poor Randall," his aunt sighed. "I fear those disapproving parents of his are doing their best to kill his interest in music—prating on and on about the duties of the heir to Swanton."

"It is more than an interest," Max felt bound to defend his nephew, "Miss Owen and the clerks at Chappell's assure me he is extremely knowledgeable."

"I stand corrected," Henrietta fixed him with an unreadable look as she marveled at how wide-ranging Grace Owen's influence had become.

# CHAPTER 21

So it was, a few weeks later, that Grace took her place next to the pianoforte in the Countess of Edgefield's drawing room. She had arrived early, at the special request of Beatrice and Laura who wanted to see her in the dress she would wear for her concert.

"You look like a fairy princess," Beatrice breathed as she took in the white lace gown with the blush colored slip festooned at the hem with roses.

"And look, she has a crown!" Never to be outdone, Laura pointed at the wreath of roses Rose had so cunningly threaded through the glossy dark curls.

"Very elegant indeed," their Mama agreed. "A Maison Juliette creation, of course?"

"Of course." Grace grinned. "And Lady Adrian will be looking at it so critically, seeking out any possible flaws in design that she won't hear a note I sing."

"Well, let's hope she is the only one, for you're here to be heard, not seen, in spite of how lovely you look. And now, speaking of *seen* and *heard*, you two," she fixed her daughters with a look, "are neither to be seen nor heard. Now off to bed."

"But Mama . . ."

"I will tell you all about it at our lesson tomorrow," Grace promised.

"All of it?" Beatrice retreated backwards out of the room in the direction of her mother's pointing finger.

"All of it."

"You promise?" Laura slowly followed her sister.

"I promise."

And now Grace stood by the pianoforte, surveying the glittering throng in front of her. Of course she was accustomed to accompanying herself, but the Countess, who wanted her guests' attention focused solely on Grace's singing, had hired a pianist, an earnest young man recommended by her equally earnest young nephew who had arrived early that evening with his Uncle Max. They sat in the back, broad-shouldered and encouraging, chatting companionably with an ease and intimacy Hentrietta had not expected. A little in front of them were the Clavertons, Lady Georgiana, her mother, Lord Adrian, Juliette, and the Marquess of Wrothingham, who had brought with him Thomas Greatorex, Conductor of the Concert of Ancient Music, and William Dance, Director of the Royal Philharmonic.

"Of course I am the veriest amateur and you two are so kindly humoring me," Freddy confided in his endearing way to both guests, knowing full well that no one refused the invitation of a duke's son, "but I assure you I am not asking you to waste your time on a whim. I feel certain that someday, not immediately perhaps, but some day, both of you will be asking Miss Owen to sing with your musicians."

Henrietta had, of course, encouraged Freddy to bring his fiancée, excusing herself with the most limpid expression of innocence in her brown eyes, "I invite her through you because we have not been formally introduced, and one hates to put oneself forward."

Henry was glad her brother was not around to hear this absolute plumper, for she had no intention of Lady Lavinia Harcourt ever crossing her threshold, but his lordship did not suspect a thing, making apologies for his fiancée as his hostess greeted him that evening. "Lady Lavinia had a prior engagement which is indeed unfortunate because she is very fond of music. I expect she would have received quite an impression of Miss Owen's performance, had she been able to attend."

"I am sure she would," Henrietta responded sweetly, *and it wouldn't have been a positive one, nor would it have had anything to do with Miss Owen's formidable talent.* The dear Marquess, poor man, was utterly oblivious to the ironic glint in her eyes. Henrietta had known that the Marquess' fiancée would never appear at a musicale featuring Miss Owen, but she would never have dreamed that Wrothingham would bring such illustrious guests, though she did her best not to sound too eager as she welcomed them. "I am honored, gentlemen, and I do hope the evening is to your liking."

It was a gratifyingly large crowd that eyed Grace expectantly as her accompanist struck the first chord, which had more to do with the hostess of the event than the performer, but Grace was flattered. Dear Henrietta, and dear, dear Freddy for dragooning Mr. Greatorex and Mr. Dance, not that they would necessarily be impressed, but Freddy's kindness melted her heart. And so, she drew a deep breath, and plunged in.

The more Grace sang, the quieter the audience became, until one could not so much as hear the rustle of a fan or even a cough. She had begun with a few familiar songs, then moved to some of the new ones Freddy had brought her, finishing up with a soprano version of *Una Voce Poco Fa*, and finally, *Der Holle Rache Kocht in Meinem Herzen*.

This was greeted with such stunned silence that Grace's heart fell, but, being the professional she was, she bowed regally and prepared to retire when the thunderous applause burst forth. She let out a long sigh of relief. She knew she was good, but still, this, her first public concert, had been a test to see if she were really as good as she thought she was, or as her friends told her she was. And she had proven herself. Even more gratifying were the animated expressions on Mr. Greatorex' and Mr. Dance's faces as they discussed her performance with Freddy who looked just as gratified, if not more so, than Grace felt.

At the back of the room, Max watched her eyes seek out Freddy and his guests and cynically chided himself for being disappointed that she didn't look to him first. Of course she hadn't. What did he know about music? She might have at least looked to Randall who did though. And, in a roundabout way, Max was partly responsible for this obviously resounding triumph.

"My lord, you have turned out to be a surprising musical devotee. One had no idea."

Blast! Lady Caroline Daventry. Henrietta had warned Max. "I am so sorry," she had apologized, shamefaced, "but Lady Caroline *would* foist herself on us when the girls and I were walking Pippin in the park. Naturally she had to quiz the girls about their stay in London, all in the most delightful fun, of course," Henrietta gritted her teeth "and naturally Beatrice had to mention the piano lessons, and naturally, Laura, not to be outdone, had to mention the musicale, so there was nothing to do but invite her. Even *I* did not have the temerity to tell her that I do not welcome predatory females into my home, especially when they are after my brother."

Max would have forgiven his sister anyway, but she had looked so genuinely distressed he couldn't help smiling. "Forewarned is forearmed, eh?" Except his thoughts had been so taken up with Grace Owen he had forgotten to be on his guard, which was not like Lord Maximilian Hawkesbury. He must be slipping. He *knew* he was slipping. He rarely, if ever, spared a second thought on a woman, and here he was sparing seconds and thirds on Grace Owen until he was beginning to wonder about himself. Unable to escape, he turned to acknowledge his pursuer.

"Max, may I introduce you to the Duchess of Roxburgh and her daughter Lady Georgiana. I was telling them how thrilling it is for Miss Owen that Wrothingham brought Mr. Greatorex and Mr. Dance," Henry's voice broke into his fit of self-recrimination. Max hadn't a clue who the two gentlemen in question were, other than that they were the ones accompanying Freddy who had caught Grace's eye, but at the moment he did not care. Smiling gratefully at his clever sister with her naughty, knowing smile, he turned with relief to the Duchess and her daughter, leaving Lady Caroline to her own devices.

It was not the cut direct—he was too polished for that—but the young lady knew when she had been upstaged. "I see Mama waving at me. So delightful to see you, my lord. I look forward to seeing you again very soon." She flashed and intimate smile as she patted his arm and then flitted across the room.

"I do hope we are not interrupting . . ." Georgie began.

"Not in the least," Max reassured her, "merely the daughter of a colleague in Paris. But, tell me how do you think the concert went?" Lady Georgiana's frank smile, her direct way of speaking offered such a blessed contrast to the coquettish Lady Caroline that Max could see why Grace had spoken of Freddy's sister in such a friendly fashion.

Across the room, Grace was brought up short by the sight of an elegant blond woman smiling up at Max and patting his arm as though they had been on the best of terms for years. Why should she care who spoke to Lord Maximilian Hawkesbury? She never cared who flirted with whom at Mrs. Gerrard's, if she even noticed it at all.

But years of having her illusions shattered had turned Grace into a realist who was brutally frank, even where her own illusions were concerned. Lord Maximilian was just a man who had intruded upon her life in a high-handed way, had the grace to admit his fault, and then offer his interest and his friendship. It was friendship, nothing more, but then, she admitted to herself, she was not the slightest bit curious about the woman laughing with Freddy or the one talking earnestly with Lord John. The fact was, Grace *was* curious about the unfortunately pretty young woman demanding Max's attention, and she *did* care about who she was and what she was to Max. How very upsetting. How very unnerving. Then all thoughts of Max were driven from her mind by the portly figure in front of her.

"Well, well, the lovely Miss Owen. Who would ever have thought to see *you* here?"

Grace drew a steadying breath. Lord Wayland was a regular at Mrs. Gerrard's whose enormous girth and florid face had always seemed jovial in Helen's drawing room; now, however, they appeared menacing. But what could he do? Destroy her reputation? She had none, and the reputation she was trying to establish as a singer was not likely to suffer, as singers' reputations were always suspect anyway. Grace took another breath, smiling at him calmly as though she had never encountered him before, but her knees were shaking.

His eyes flickered to a stylishly dressed woman across the room. "Have no fear, I am as eager to keep our acquaintance secret from Lady Wayland as you are to keep it from the rest of the world. Brilliant performance, by the way."

"And you would know?" She raised an incredulous eyebrow, for Lord Wayland was noted for three things only: wine, food, and women, and in that order.

"No, but I can hear, and the comments being bandied about are most favorable. Congratulations."

He moved on and Grace let out a sigh of relief. Only then did she take a real look at the woman he had indicated across the room.

# CHAPTER 22

LADY WAYLAND WAS PRETTY ENOUGH, in a blond spiritless fashion, but it was the way her eyes followed her husband, and the expression on her face as he moved away, bowing to Grace, that knocked the wind out of her as though she had fallen off a horse. The woman was jealous. Grace herself had just received an inkling of what that might feel like, and it wasn't pleasant. But Lady Wayland also looked hurt and unhappy. All of a sudden, the drawing room with its brilliant chandeliers and crowd of silks and satins, perfumes and twinkling jewels, not to mention the heat, was overwhelming, suffocating.

Grace had to get away. With no other thought but escape, she hurried blindly from the room, not caring who saw her or what they thought. She clambered down the marble staircase, searching for darkness and solitude, and, spying a door at the back of the house, fled into the garden.

Grace collapsed on a small bench in the back, partially hidden by shrubbery, and buried her head in her hands. It had all seemed so simple and straightforward, honest even, when she had come to work at Mrs. Gerrard's. Men wanted certain things, and they gave money for them. How could she not have thought about their wives, except to envy their lives of ease and respectability? A great sob rose inside her and she rubbed ineffectively as the stinging tears began to flow.

"Here, take my handkerchief."

She gasped and looked up to find Max, his brows knotted in concern, offering her a large white handkerchief.

"Tha . . . thank you," she managed to gasp as she mopped up her tears.

"My poor girl," he sank down beside her, taking the handkerchief and gently wiping away the remaining tears, "whatever is amiss? When last I saw you, you were at the apex of your triumph."

"It was . . . it was Lady Wayland."

"Lady Wayland! My dear girl, whatever did she do? Whatever did she say to you?"

"She . . . she didn't say anything, but she saw me with her husband and she looked so miserable. I have only met him in passing at Helen's, but . . . but how many other women have I made miserable? How could I?"

"As I recall, my poor Grace," he responded drily, "you had no choice in the matter." Max gathered her hands in his, holding them tight against his chest. "Listen to me. If the men who frequent Helen's drawing room were happy with their wives, they would not be there. They would be at home instead, which is infinitely cheaper, isn't it? Sheer logic proves that." His conspiratorial grin was rewarded with a watery chuckle. "Besides, I happen to know Lucinda—only slightly, fortunately. She came out the first Season I was in London and it was well known she was on the catch for a rich husband. She might have caught a much bigger fish than Wayland if she'd had an ounce of spirit. She was pretty enough, but a prosy, sanctimonious bore. Believe me, I was once unavoidably her partner, and she could talk of nothing but herself. She cares nothing for Wayland except for his title and his income, and I doubt she's changed since I knew her, which means she still cares for nothing but herself. The one to be pitied here is Wayland, not his wife."

Max saw she still wasn't convinced. "Tell me, do you think men plump down so much money, at Mrs. Gerrard's for a simple *roll in the hay*, if I may be so blunt? No, they come for company, companionship, to talk to people who are interested in them, which means that their nearest and dearest are not. Take my own father, for example. I barely remember my mother's ever speaking to him, except to criticize." And as Max thought about the Dowager Marchioness of Swanton and how he had always done his level best to avoid her himself, he suffered a momentary twinge of sympathy for his father for the very first time—old reprobate that he had been.

This time Grace really looked at him, and he could see his words sinking in as she nodded slowly, thoughtfully. Then the agonized look of self-reproach reappeared. "But . . . but I should have asked . . . or something." She pulled away her hands to cover her face.

"My darling girl," he dragged her into his arms, "*they* sought *you* out, not the other way 'round. You don't entrap anyone, lure anyone. You, and every-one else at Mrs. Gerrard's are simply there, charging an agreed-upon price for agreed-upon services—to state it in the crudest, most businesslike terms—and in the end it *is* a business. Very few, if any marriages are based on such honesty. Think of the men who have been lured, perfectly *respectably*, I might add, by a pretty face, to confer their names, their titles, and their wealth on designing women determined to *marry well*.

Grace nodded slowly and looked up at him, all the spirit and sparkle washed from her eyes. "I know. You are right. It was just the sudden shock of seeing things in a different way."

"And," he looked deep into those troubled eyes, "you are blaming yourself for all sorts of things that are not your fault."

How had he come to be so wise? How had he come to be so understanding, this man who hadn't even wanted his nephew to know her? And how had his arms come to feel so strong and comforting around her? Grace hadn't known that comforting feeling since she'd been a young girl in her mother's embrace.

He smiled down at her. "Not only should you not be blaming yourself, you should be congratulating yourself on your triumphant performance."

Grace gave a shaky laugh.

"That's my girl." He meant only to give her a reassuring kiss on the forehead, but somehow she looked up at him and he was pressing his lips against hers. And then he could not stop. Her lips were so warm, so soft, so yielding, as though they were that way just for him. He was lost. Max tightened his hold on her, sliding one hand up her spine to bury it in the silky dark curls, tilting her head back so he could cover her lips, her eyes, her nose, her delicious neck with kisses as he inhaled the rosewater with a tantalizing hint of something else that made the scent all hers. He was enveloped in the silky softness of her, her skin, her hair, her breath against his cheek, her everything, and he could not stop kissing her or longing for her, or craving a closeness, a connection he had never wanted before.

Then his brilliant, rational, logical, annoying mind reasserted itself, What was he doing? She was his friend, and he was giving in to his own desires, desires he had not known existed until now. What must she, she who was used to men losing their heads over her on a regular basis, think of him?

It was that thought that stopped him cold. Grace Owen's friendship was infinitely precious to him, and he wanted desperately for his friendship to be infinitely precious to her. He was ruining it! Max lifted his head, drawing a ragged breath as he released her. "I do beg your pardon. I have no ide . . . I mean, I . . ."

"What?" Grace looked groggily up at him.

"I apologize. I shouldn't have taken advantage of you . . . of . . . of your distress like that. Please forgive me. Please say we can remain friends."

If her brain . . . no if her *body* hadn't been in such a turmoil, Grace would have found his confusion amusing in the extreme. Why should any man apologize to any fashionable impure for doing anything to her? But this was Max, and he *had* done something to her, but it was not what he was apologizing for since he had no idea what he'd done. He had no idea that for the first time in her life, Grace *wanted* a man to kiss her, *wanted* to feel his arms around her, holding her so close she could feel his heart beat. And it was not just her body that wanted it, her heart wanted it too.

Her body, always so tightly under control, was suddenly warm and languorous, throbbing with longing, for what she was not sure. What she was sure of was that Max could give it to her. Why she was so certain of this, Grace had no idea. That was the incredible mystery of it, she who had never believed in anything her mind could not explain.

Her mind and body were in turmoil, so all she could do was gaze dumbly at him, noting irrelevantly, how intense his eyes were in the angular face, how dark the lock of hair falling over his forehead, how totally breathtaking he was—her breath. At last the years of self-control reasserted themselves. "Please, think nothing of it. You were doing your best to be kind, and I thank you for it." The intensity vanished from his eyes, the tautness from his face, and his breathing slowed as he relaxed, and, God help her, Grace was sorry for it.

"I . . . well I thank you for your gracious understanding . . . well . . . never mind." A smile tugged at the corner of his mouth. "What I should be doing is congratulating you on your resounding success. No," he held up a hand, "no need to point out that I wouldn't have the slightest idea of the difference between a good performance and a mediocre one, but Randall does, and he tells me you were superb. He also tells me he recognized some very important men with Freddy who were also much struck, and he assures me that they are far more difficult to impress than all the patronesses of Almack's combined. I am so pleased that you are finally taking your rightful place in the world."

He did look pleased. Tears stung Grace's eyes. How dear of him to be so happy for her.

"But now," he took her hand, raising it to his lips, "you must get back to your admirers and, much as I would like to, I must not escort you back. We don't want any talk about London's latest sensation. I shall sit here and contemplate the garden for an appropriate period of time. Now off with you, accept the congratulations that are your due." He gave her a gentle shove towards the door which, fortunately, was shrouded in shadows.

# Chapter 23

GRACE FOUND HER WAY BACK TO THE DRAWING ROOM, smiled, made conversation, *Yes this was her first appearance. No she had not studied on the Continent. Yes, she had an excellent teacher, Signor Lanza,* but her mind was elsewhere. It took every ounce of concentration she possessed to respond to the questions. She was beginning to think it would never end when Henrietta, seeing Grace's smiles growing mechanical, and hearing her voice lose energy and timbre, appeared at her side. "My guests have monopolized you enough, Miss Owen. It was an exquisite performance, and we are so grateful, but we want you to save yourself and your voice for another day."

"You do look rather done up, you know," she whispered *sotto voce* to Grace as she led her away. "Is anything amiss? I mean it when I say we are very grateful, and you were a resounding success. Even I could see that, heathen that I am."

"I am quite well, thank you. It is just that I am not yet accustomed to a crowd, but I shall be, thanks to you. Lady Georgiana is already badgering her mother to have me sing at Claverton House. It is I who am grateful."

But the Countess was not fooled. It was not the heat or the crowd. After her concert had finished, Grace had been happy and sparkling among her admirers, and then Henrietta had lost sight of her as she attended to the rest of her guests. When she had eventually caught a glimpse of Grace again, the sparkle had been replaced by a faint air of abstraction, not noticeable to the average person, but Henrietta was not the average person, especially where people she cared about were concerned. And, speaking of people she cared about, where was Max?

At last she saw him hovering by the entrance to the drawing room looking somewhat distracted himself. Hmmm. Her busy mind sorted through the possible explanations. It didn't have anything to do with Lady Caroline Daventry, whom he abhorred, or the Duchess of Roxburgh and Lady Georgiana, with whom he'd conversed most amicably . . . so . . . it could be. A curious smile tugged at the corners of her mouth as she unsuccessfully tried to remember if she had seen Grace and Max together, but they had both disappeared from her view for some time and she didn't think that they had been there all along and she'd just failed to notice them. Preoccupied with her guests she might have been, but not *that* preoccupied.

"Exquisitely done, Miss Owen. My wife is so fortunate you agreed to honor us with your talent."

Dear Edward—Henrietta came to with a start—always there when she needed him, helping her in the few social duties she took on. She mentally shook herself as she continued with the task that had sent her to Grace's side in the first place. "As I said, you do look a bit done up, and you must be longing to get home to put your feet up. Edward will order the carriage and you can slip away while I make your excuses."

It was cowardly of her, Grace knew it, and Helen would definitely not approve of such craven behavior, but she gratefully acquiesced to the Countess' suggestion, and, in what seemed like no time at all, was leaning back against the velvet squabs of the Edgefield carriage as it made its way sedately back through the streets of Mayfair to St. James' Square and home.

It had never felt so much like home as when she reached her damask-hung chamber where Rose lit more candles, helped her into her dressing gown, and brought her a soothing cup of tea. Bless Helen for giving her such a haven as this—odd though it might seem to the rest of the world—where she could sit in peace, comfort, and quiet, alone with her thoughts.

Fortunately the establishment was relatively peaceful and quiet tonight—Grace had slipped in quickly and unobtrusively, avoiding any possible encounter—because her thoughts were not. It was not just her thoughts that were in a turmoil, her body seemed to have taken on a mind of its own and was just as turbulent and confused as her brain. Except for hunger, cold, and exhaustion, Grace's body did not speak to her. It hadn't since the day at the Sans Pareil Theater when the loathsome Smedley had pushed her back over his desk and plunged his fat sweaty hands down her bodice and up her skirt as he whispered roughly in her ear, "If you want your father to remain in his position, you will do everything I say and keep quiet about it." She did, and she had. And her body had not belonged to her since then

Now it was speaking up, telling her how it felt to have Max's lips caressing her neck, how exquisite were the sensations that prickled her skin as he threaded his fingers through her hair, how her lips throbbed as they opened under his, and how her heart thudded as she awoke to feelings that swept her body from head to toes, feelings that inundated the mind which she had kept as separate from her body as her heart, more than separate, because, until this moment, she had not even known she had a heart.

And now she could feel the tug of it inside her as she remembered the concern in those eyes that missed nothing, felt the sympathy in the strong arms that held her so close, and heard the angry resolve in a voice that insisted nothing was her fault. Her mother had loved her and caressed her; Helen had championed and defended her, but no one had done both . . . until Max.

What was she to do? There was only one thing *to* do, what she had done ever since her mother had died—pretend it hadn't happened and carry on.

Which was just what Grace did, arising from her bed the next day after her morning chocolate and dressing and going for a drive in the park as she and her companions did every day that it was fine enough to so.

But she wasn't fooling herself, nor was she fooling any other sharp observers who were legion in a place that had seen as much of the world as the denizens of Mrs. Gerrard's had seen. As Mrs. Gerrard's elegantly appointed barouche rolled sedately through the park, Dora gave Grace a sharp look from under her Gypsy hat whose elaborate bow emphasized the delightful oval of her face, her brown eyes empty of their usual sparkle. "I expected you to be in high gig over your success last night. Freddy said it was a splendid performance."

It is kind of Freddy to say so, though it is hard for me to know. I think it went well enough. People were very kind."

"Very kind!" Dora snorted. I know you. You are too afraid to admit that you astounded them all because then you will have to do something about it.

When Grace chuckled, but did not respond, Dora knew it was something entirely different from music that absorbed her friend's thoughts. But what else was there to bring on such a fit of abstraction in such an ordinarily determined woman? It could be only one thing . . . and there was only one way to find out—the direct way. "Hmmm. I think it is more than music on your mind." A betraying blush crept up Grace's usually pale neck. Having found out all she needed to know, Dora took pity on her. "But I won't press you."

Her friend's grateful smile said it all, and Dora chattered on inconsequentially about Auguste's teething and how fussy Juliette said he was, the effrontery of the new wine merchant whom Helen had decided not to patronize, and what a clever scheme it was to set up their own friendly society.

At the mention of the friendly society, Grace's color, which had returned to normal, suddenly deepened, and Dora saw it all, then chastised herself for not having recognized the signs sooner. After all, she had seen the same signs in Juliette when Lord Adrian's was mentioned. Of course, she had not recognized those signs at the time either, but now, with the sharpened senses of hindsight,

Dora saw it all very clearly. Grace had developed a tendre for Lord Maximilian Hawkesbury.

Now the question was, did Grace recognize it herself, and, if she did, what was she going to do about it? Dora was willing to give any help she could. They all would—sisters in horror, loneliness and social condemnation as they were—but they also knew that all they could give one another was support; the solution to any problems lay within themselves. And Grace's solution was usually music.

Music! Dora resolved to contact Freddy the moment they returned to St James' Square. He had reported to Helen's ladies, eagerly waiting to hear about Grace's recital, that two very knowledgeable scions of London's musical establishment had been much struck by her performance. "It was not just her range and her brilliance, but her expression," he explained to the little group gathered around him in the drawing room, "and every note so clear and true. She is on her way, mark my words."

If anyone could give a little push to the gentlemen who might ensure that Grace was *on her way*, it was the Marquess of Wrothingham, connoisseur and guiding light for those in the Upper Ten Thousand who aspired to be known in exclusive circles for their artistic taste.

But Dora had reckoned without the competing efforts of another equally determined supporter. The Countess of Edgefield, having brought Grace's musical prowess to the attention of the attention of the *ton*, and having witnessed the hint of consciousness in both Max's and Grace's behavior, now focused her energies on bringing them together in ways that would prove to both of them what Henrietta already knew—they were perfect for one another.

# Chapter 24

Dora was right. Music was the cure for whatever ailed Grace, and, fortunately, lesson day was two days after the concert. Nothing spoke distraction like two adoring little girls, a welcoming dog, and a pianoforte.

"Mama said you did brilliantly at the musicale," Beatrice offered shyly.

"And there were ever so many important people there. I saw," Laura added triumphantly.

"You did not!"

"Yes I did." Laura stuck her chin out in a way that brooked no argument. "*You* were asleep, but *I* crept down the stairs ever so quietly and I saw. But no one saw me," she added hastily.

Her older sister rolled her eyes in such a perfect imitation of their mother that Grace was hard put not to laugh.

But she was not laughing at the end of the lesson when the Countess asked to speak to her privately. "Run along girls and get ready for our drive in the park. I must speak to Miss Owen first, and then I shall be up."

What was amiss? Grace tried to keep her heart from hammering as she reviewed possible disasters in her mind. Had Lord Wayland betrayed her after all? But then, Max's sister was fully aware of Grace's story. Had Lady Wayland? Had . . .

"There." Henrietta took a seat on one end of the sofa and patted a place at the other. "Now we may be comfortable. Do not look so alarmed, I merely have a favor to ask of you, which you are perfectly welcome to refuse. It is just that Parliament will be ending soon and we shall be returning to Edgefield Park," she paused for a moment and then added in a rush, "and the girls are very much looking forward to riding their ponies and all their country pursuits, but the thing of it is, they have become very fond of you and will miss you and their music lessons and . . . and . . . it would be the most wonderful thing if you could come down with us. I know you have obligations, but surely they won't be so demanding as London will be very thin of company at this time of year. Do you think Mrs. Gerrard could see her way to letting you come with us? Max says you teach French, and if you are going to be an opera singer, you probably know Italian as well. The girls would be enchanted to learn those as well as music. I know it will not be nearly so busy and interesting as London with all its shops and diversions, but mightn't it be a nice change after city life?"

She looked so hopeful and eager, more like her daughters than a countess and wife of a member of Parliament that Grace had to laugh. "I confess, such an unusual idea would never have entered my head, and I have not been in the country this age . . ."

"But you will consider it? Promise me you will at least consider it."

"Yes, I will con . . ."

"Mama," Laura appeared in the doorway, "you are not ready yet, and Uncle Max is here. I just saw his carriage from the drawing room window." And giving her mother another reproving look, Laura raced out to greet her uncle.

"Oh dear," the Countess pulled a rueful grimace, "once again I have fallen short. You have no idea how rigorous a critic a five-year-old can be. I do hope you will excuse me while I fetch my bonnet."

Grace was left with nothing, but to pull her chaotic thoughts together and retrieve her own bonnet and gloves from Rose who was hovering outside the door. With her mind already in a whirl, the last thing Grace needed was to cross paths with the man she had been desperately trying to banish from her thoughts, if not her life. She knew that he would be visiting Mrs. Gerrard's to continue the project for insuring the futures of its residents, but she had hoped, without having the least idea how it was to be accomplished, and without being obvious, that she would be able to avoid the man who had been dominating her thoughts and causing her heart to beat faster and her breath to come quicker than it should. Grace smoothed on her lemon kid gloves and focused all her attention on trying the ribbons of her French bonnet, trying for unruffled composure as she descended the staircase.

"Uncle Max, here is Miss Owen. Mama said you were at the concert the other night, Uncle. Wasn't she beautiful as a princess?" Laura tugged at her uncle's sleeve with a look that brooked no disagreement.

"Most certainly she looked like a princess." He smiled down at his niece, but not before giving a conspiratorial wink to her piano teacher.

"See, Miss Owen? I said you looked like a princess because I have seen pictures of princesses in books, but Uncle Max *knows* princesses, lots of them, because there were lots when he was in . . . ah . . . Vie ah . . ."

"The Congress of Vienna," her elder sister corrected her.

"Well, yes, there were rather a lot of princesses in Vienna," Max admitted ruefully, "but not all of them could have been called pretty by any stretch of the imagination. Actually, Miss Owen is more like a fairy princess. Regular princesses are either born that way or they marry a prince, but Miss Owen is a princess because she possesses magical gifts like a fairy princess."

"Magic?" Laura's eyes were as round as saucers

"Why yes, her music is magic. It makes people happy. It makes people feel beautiful inside. It makes them feel peaceful, or it inspires them, and *that* is magic, a magic that she works very hard to make the best she can. So you see, that is why she is like a fairy princess."

"But she is very beautiful." Laura, not entirely convinced by his argument, was determined to win her point.

"Oh undoubtedly, but to my way of thinking, the magic is better."

The lump in Graces throat was so achingly big that she could not have articulated a reply even if she had wanted to, but all she could do was stand there dumbly, overwhelmed by the surprising sweetness of a worldly man.

Fortunately, she was spared further awkwardness by the arrival of the Countess, briskly smoothing on her own gloves and calling to her girls, "Come, Bea, Laura, we must not delay, for if there is anything men particularly dislike, it is to have their horses kept waiting. You will excuse us, Miss Owen?" She cast a quick, far too observant look at Grace before allowing Max to offer her his arm and lead her down the steps, trailed by her daughters.

"Come, Rose, we must be off." Grace headed briskly down the stairs behind them and turned in the opposite direction the waiting carriage was facing. Fortunately, this led to the distraction of the shops on Bond Street, but even if it had not, she would have hurried away from the disturbing presence of Lord Maximilian Hawkesbury as fast as she could.

What was wrong with her? Grace Owen did not run away from a challenge. Taking life head-on had been the only way she had survived. She had even fought off the lecherous Smedley until her father's livelihood had been threatened. Now, a man whose touch made her weak with longing, whose conspiratorial wink warmed her soul, and whose surprising understanding tugged at her heart, sent her fleeing as far and as fast as she could—not just toward Bond Street, but to the wilds of Wiltshire, because the more she thought about it, the more the Countess' offer seemed heaven-sent. To be away from Max, his eagerly awaited lectures on insurance in Helen's *schoolroom* or the possibility of running into him—remote though it might be—as he went about settling his uncle's affairs, felt like the only thing she could do to save herself from this madness which seemed to have taken her so tightly in its grasp.

Now, all she had to do was convince Helen to let her go, but surely she could. The Countess had been correct in thinking London would be woefully thin of company in the next few months. Lord Huntley went to Brighton. Freddy would undoubtedly be down at Wrothingham Abbey overseeing the never-ending renovations that kept forestalling his wedding day, and the rest would flit off to various estates and welcoming country houses.

Helen agreed. "It will be rather slow here. Dora, who is a better business-woman than I ever could be, keeps suggesting that our taking a house in Brighton for the season would be extraordinarily lucrative, except," she drew a breath, "one does enjoy the peace and quiet here—at least at the start. I am glad the Countess thinks so highly of you, and I certainly appreciate her consideration of your *duties* here. It demonstrates a level of understanding rarely encountered in the *ton*. Bye the bye, what has she offered you in return, if I may be so bold as to ask?"

"Fifty guineas."

"Fifty guineas!" Helen's delicate brows rose in astonishment. "That is generous indeed. It is a rare governess who can command that much a year, even in the best of households."

"She is very kind."

"I should say so." Her eyes darkened speculatively, but too briefly for Grace to notice. "Kind, but ingenuous, when the best among us here can earn that in an evening, and certainly in a week. But go, I expect the country air and youthful companionship will do you good."

"Thank you. You are very kind." Grace rose and headed toward the door.

"Only when it is in my best interests." It was Helen's usual tart rejoinder, but in this case, she meant it. Grace Owen had been unsettled lately, and Helen did not have far to look for the cause. Lord Maximilian Hawkesbury was an unsettling person where anyone was concerned. Too quick by half, he never missed a trick, at cards or—the more she thought about him, she realized—apparently at anything else. And he was dangerously charming, oh, not in the way that made young ladies or *tonnish* matrons swoon, though they probably did, the matrons anyway, but in an interested, curious way that showed genuine respect and a desire to learn about a person. That mixture of respect and interest was more headily seductive to the unimpressionable, worldly women in Helen's employ than all the admiring glances, winning smiles, or flattering phrases so effective among the gently bred young ladies in the Upper Ten Thousand.

It was in Helen's and Grace's best interests that Grace not fall victim to this intoxicating mixture of energy, intelligence, and interest that could only end in misery. To be sure, Juliette had found love and happiness with Lord Adrian Claverton, but everyone knew such things only happened in fairy stores, and if they occurred once in real life, they were never repeated.

Fortunately, the Countess of Edgefield had come up with a solution to this burgeoning problem: distance. Distance and distraction and time for Grace to forget about dangerously attractive men who were drawn to her more than they should be.

Dora, however, was not quite so sanguine about the Countess' motives. "From what Juliette tells me, the Countess looked very pleased whenever she saw her brother glancing in Grace's direction," she confided to Helen when she was told of Grace's plans, "and she did her best to separate him from a Lady Caroline Daventry who is shamelessly pursuing him. Juliette thinks the Countess is a deep one. We shall just have to wait and see what her game is—if she has one."

Helen frowned thoughtfully, but did not reply.

# CHAPTER 25

H ELEN WAS NOT THE ONLY ONE CONSIDERING the salutary effect of distance. "You have asked Gr . . . er Miss Owen to Edgefield Park?" Max remarked later that day, surprise, not unmixed with suspicion,

"Why not? The girls adore her and I quite enjoy her company. She is far more learned and intelligent than most females I know. Besides, I should imagine country living might provide a welcome respite from London's hectic pace," Henrietta responded serenely. Max did not look enamored of the idea. Good! Let him fret and discover how necessary Grace Owen was to his happiness. He was entirely too self-sufficient by half. It would do him no harm to realize that it was good for people to enjoy one another's company, to need one another, and to be there for one another.

"When do you leave?"

"Oh sometime next week I should think," was the airy reply, as though Henry had not planned their departure down to the last minute and arranged everything for Grace as well.

"Well," Max recovered himself at last, "that is exceedingly kind of you, and I am sure Miss Owen must be very grateful." He remained chatting with his sister for a few minutes just to prove that her announcement had not affected him in the least before suddenly remembering that he had promised to lend Dora Mr. Bailey's *Doctrine of Life Annuities*. And if he happened to run into Grace in the course of delivering it, so much the better.

"You remembered! Thank you, my lord." Dora's wide smile and her surprise and delight that someone like him had not only noticed her special interest in what he was teaching, but had respected it enough to offer her a book from his library, wiped all thoughts of Grace Owen from his mind—for a moment or two.

"You did express a wish to read the actual text of what I was discussing, so here you are."

"Thank you." She clutched the book to her chest as though it were her most precious possession, looking for the moment more like a little girl surprised with a longed-for present than a sophisticated courtesan. And Max was astounded how happy that made him.

"I do hope you can put it to good use. It strikes me that you have a head for business."

She flushed with pleasure at the compliment, but there was confidence in her voice as she replied, "That I do, sir."

"Then we shall see that it is given every advantage." He truly meant it. The thought of helping this other young woman realize her dream, whatever that dream was, was important to him—not so important as Grace Owen and her dream, but important, nevertheless. What was happening to him? He was becoming as enthusiastic as Helen and John in their zeal to help Helen's ladies reclaim their lives.

"And I say again, that is most kind of you, my lord. Oh, here is Grace. I am sure that she too, since it was her invitation to tea that started the entire thing in the first place, would be happy to learn how well things are going." Dora, very aware of the undercurrent of attraction between Max and Grace, and sensing that she, herself was only Max's ostensible reason for being there, had been watching for Grace during the entire encounter and had just caught a glimpse of her friend's hastily retreating form as she overheard their conversation.

Grace had just emerged from her talk with Helen when she caught sight of Dora and Max in the drawing room, and now she was caught. There was nothing for it, but to come forward and greet Max as nonchalantly as though her breathing had not become ridiculously erratic and her heartbeat increasingly irregular.

Dora noted the elevated rise and fall of the lace on Grace's corsage as well as the faintest tinge of pink on her cheeks. Good. She had made the right decision. The previous day when Grace had mentioned the invitation from the Countess, there had been something in her hasty but determined response that made Dora think Grace meant to escape town without any further contact with Lord Maximilian Hawkesbury. Now Dora was sure of it as she witnessed her friend's reaction to Max, and she, Dora, was not about to let Grace dismiss him so swiftly and completely, not when Dora could plainly see how Grace, unwilling though she might be to admit it, was drawn to the man. One only had to observe how her eyes followed him when he was in the room and the way she looked at him to know that. Running away was never the answer. Grace's feelings were involved, and it was in her own best interest to face these feelings and decide what to do with them.

"If you've finished speaking to Helen, then I must report on the accounts she gave me to look over." And with that, Dora beat a strategic retreat, leaving Max and Grace to face one another, neither one quite sure how to begin.

Grace, determined never to show weakness or awkwardness with this man who affected her so strongly, plunged in. "This a fortunate meeting, my lord." It was not in the least fortunate, and Grace, who suspected that Dora had, had a hand in it, was ready to wring her neck, but she would deal with her later. Now was the moment to show that Lord Maximilian Hawkesbury meant nothing to her. Nothing to her at all. "It gives me the opportunity to thank you again for introducing me to your sister, who has been so kind to me, and who continues her kindness by asking me to carry on tutoring her girls down at Edgefield Park." There, she had been a miracle of cool, detached graciousness.

"I am delighted to hear it." Though he wasn't in the least because, all at once, the thought of London without the possibility of seeing Grace seemed very dull indeed. "I do hope you are able to do so." How stiff and ill-at-ease he sounded spouting meaningless platitudes, but caution told Max it was best not to let on to her even the tiniest bit that she had been the topic of his and his sister's discussion. "I imagine that not only Beatrice, Laura, and Pippin will be glad of your stimulating company, but my sister will be too. She is an original, Henrietta is, and more forthright than makes most country matrons comfortable.

That obviously pleased her and Max heaved an inner sigh of relief. "Come," he smiled, pointing to two chairs on either side of the fireplace, "tell me all that you plan to teach them and how you mean to go about it, for those two are a rare handful, having inherited every ounce of their mother's independent spirit, and neither one about to be outdone by the other."

The awkward moment had passed and they both forgot their reservations as they talked about the challenges involved in teaching two headstrong young girls.

Grace's eagerness to avoid Max dissolved in the pleasure of seeing how much real interest he took in his sister and her family, pleasure that betrayed how much he actually cared about their happiness and wellbeing. In fact, the disdainful, the critical Lord Maximilian seemed to care about the happiness of a number of people if Dora's glowing face and the book she clutched to her chest were anything to go by. What other man would . . . but here Grace's thoughts were again straying into dangerous territory and she brought herself up short. "It will be a challenge, but I think I shall quite like it, and I am looking forward to the change. There. Now he knew that she was not going to miss London at all—or any of the people inhabiting the city.

She looked so beautiful as she spoke, so alive with eagerness for her subject and the chance to make others as passionate about it as she was herself. Max had never met a woman so unselfconscious. She employed no arts to attract, no fluttering eyelashes or coy smiles, no subtle references to herself, to him, or to them, no attempt to charm. She was all energy and devotion to her craft and her students, and in that energy she was charm itself . . . at least for Max. He was helplessly drawn to that charm which had nearly caused him to forget himself the night of her concert. Even now he could feel the smooth warmth of her skin under his lips and . . . No, he would not think about that. It was a very good thing, after all, that she was going away. Now he would be able to forget her and concentrate on the business that had brought him to London in the first place, forget the way she made him feel and return to his comfortable and supremely rational life where senses and feelings were non-existent—and it was better that way.

Grace tilted her head, eyeing him speculatively. "And while I am gone, you can perhaps learn more about your nephew's musical aspirations. I have not yet heard him play, but if Sir George Smart has accepted him as a pupil, then I know he is very good, and very lonely, I think," she added speculatively. "Pursuing excellence in music is always a solitary task, but I would imagine that for him it is more so than for most, given that his family, naturally enough, expect great things from him as the heir. I fear there is little encouragement and less appreciation, if any, than he might like."

Encouragement and appreciation, two things notably lacking in Max's life, and he knew exactly how isolating that could be. Fortunately he had, had Uncle Richard and Castlereagh. It was time for him to be more of an uncle to Randall. Learning about the lad's passion would be a great deal more interesting and a great deal less onerous than shepherding him successfully among the *ton's* matchmaking mamas.

# Chapter 26

It was a great relief to both Max and Grace when early one morning the Edgefield traveling carriage left Brook Street with the Countess, her daughters, and Grace ensconced in as much comfort as any traveler could wish. "It is a good thing Edgefield is to come later so we have ample room for ourselves," Henrietta remarked as she settled the girls into opposite corners of the carriage, "and no, you have not done him out of a seat, for he never was planning to travel with us in the first place. Some last details of Parliamentary business to finish up."

The girls, thrilled at the prospect of seeing their ponies again, and of introducing them to the newest member of the household, chattered incessantly as they made their way through the streets of the metropolis while Pippin, having sniffed every nook and cranny of the vehicle, turned around twice on the seat next to Grace and settled down, his nose on her lap.

By the time they had reached Marlborough, the entire carriage had adopted poses similar to Pippin's. Laura had curled up with her head in her mother's lap and Beatrice, having discovered that snuggling in the corner of the carriage led to more jostling, slumped against Grace who, wrapping an arm around the little girl to steady her, began to feel drowsiness creeping over her as well as the sun sank low in the sky. It was a rare feeling to have two small creatures so relaxed and nestled so trustingly against her. How long had it been since she'd felt that closeness cuddled with her own mother? A lifetime ago. A different lifetime altogether.

A lump rose in Grace's throat. How peaceful it was, just being there together—no conversation, no observing or interpreting of looks or movements, no hidden implications, no striving, no social maneuvering, just being. A great sigh rose within her as she leaned her cheek against the head pressed to her shoulder, and she knew no more until the rhythm and the clop of hooves stopped and the sound of approaching footsteps and voices told her they had arrived at Edgefield Park.

The house was ablaze with light from tall windows in the two-storied bays on either side of the stone portico, up two flights of shallow stairs where servants lined up waiting to welcome them and help them inside, and a capable-looking woman, handsome in her black dress with a ring of keys at her waist, descended to greet them.

"Mrs. Hensham, Mrs. Hensham," Laura, her exhaustion forgotten, raced up the steps with Pippin in her arms, "We have been on the road ever so long, you can't imagine, and look what we have!" She set the little dog down, and Pippin, recognizing authority when he saw it, sank onto his haunches, his tail swishing back and forth ever so cautiously as he fixed the housekeeper with his most winning smile."

"Well," the housekeeper examined him critically, "he looks quite clean, and I expect he's an excellent ratter."

The tail wagged more confidently.

"He's ever so well behaved," Beatrice volunteered in her most grown-up voice. "We call him Pippin."

Hearing his name, the dog inched forward and placed a paw next to the housekeeper's foot. She nodded and then smiled at the girls. "He's a clever one too." Her eyes met the Countess' and she smiled. "It will be nice to have a dog in the house."

Grace heard Henrietta's sigh of relief and was suddenly struck with the thought that even a countess worried about what other people thought, and that quite possibly the opinion of an excellent housekeeper was more to be prized than that of a *tonnish* hostess.

"You will have to introduce him to the ponies tomorrow," Mrs. Hensham continued, smiling and leading the girls into an impressive black and white tiled hallway, and Grace could see why Laura and Beatrice had greeted her so eagerly. Here was someone who understood what was important in life. But Grace and the Countess were not forgotten. "Your bedchambers are ready, my lady, and I will send George up with trays to your rooms." She turned to Grace. "Welcome, Miss Owen," and then beckoned to a fresh-faced girl hovering in the background. "This is Daisy who will look after you while you are here. I trust you will find her satisfactory."

A maid? For a governess? Grace could hardly wait to write to Helen and Dora. Truly, she felt more like an honored guest than a governess. Her time in the country was becoming a very good thing indeed.

It was an even better thing when, after having eaten the excellent supper on a tray in her bedchamber and being helped out of her travelling clothes by Daisy, she walked over to the window and opened it. The air was soft and mild, sweet-scented and fresh, and the silence was exquisitely soothing after the myriad and ever-present sounds of London—late night revelers singing and shouting at the tops of their voices, the watch calling out the time. Peace, tinged with melancholy washed over her. It was so like home when she'd sat at her window in their cottage in Oxfordshire, dreaming of becoming as beautiful and talented as her mother, and as sought-after for her music as her father.

Her eyes began to feel heavy, her body limp after struggling to hold it erect and steady for hours on end in the carriage. She stumbled over to the bed and fell into lavender-scented sheets, dropping off to sleep as soon as her head hit the pillow.

Grace awoke to bird song and children's voices, and, for a moment, was surprised not to find herself in her tiny bed under the eaves, until she woke fully to the realization that the bird song was in Wiltshire, and the voices were those of Laura and Beatrice laughing as they threw a ball to Pippin and raced after him when he caught it. She stretched luxuriously and inhaled the country air. London had its shops, its theaters, and its museums, all of which she enjoyed to the fullest, but at the moment it was delicious to be in the countryside on a beautiful morning.

There was a rap on her door and Daisy appeared with morning chocolate. "Her ladyship thought you might like this before breakfast. I shall be back when you are ready to dress."

"Thank you, you may set it there, if you would," Grace pointed to a small table near the window, "but I am ready to begin the day."

"And a lovely one it is too, ma'am." Daisy smiled shyly as she awaited instructions for the items of clothing to be selected. Daisy was a country girl, simple and hardworking, utterly devoid of worldly experience, but even she knew that the dresses from which Miss Owen was choosing her morning's attire were far too fashionable and far too richly ornamented to belong to a governess. She would have to keep her ears open to find out what the other servants had to say about this new arrival.

But there was nothing said. Mrs. Hensham ran a tight ship and no such speculation, by even so much as a look, was allowed concerning the newest member of the household, no matter how unusual, or beautiful, or talented she was.

That she was talented soon became apparent.,,,and appreciated. The musical efforts of Beatrice and Laura were noticed and applauded as being the right sort of thing for properly raised girls of good family, but Miss Owen's music was something else altogether. Every afternoon, after music lessons, followed by French lessons, with some Italian thrown in, Grace was given three blissful hours entirely to herself while the Countess made certain that no one, not even her devoted pupils, interrupted her. That did not stop the footmen from arranging for their errands to make them pass by the music room, or the maids from surreptitiously dusting the tables and pictures in the hall outside as slowly as possible in order to savor the liquid notes pouring forth.

"It do make a person feel all calm and beautiful-like, ma'am, to hear that singing of hers," a housemaid offered in her defense when it was pointed out to her by the eagle-eyed Mrs. Hensham that she had been dusting that precise spot on a console table for quite some time.

But there were other blissful moments besides those at the pianoforte. Grace was given a well-mannered chestnut mare to ride, though at first she was hesitant to do so. "In addition to the fact that I am a governess, it has been years since I have been on a horse."

"Nonsense," came the Countess bracing reply, "one never forgets how to ride, and besides, you can ride with the girls. Is that *governess* enough for you?"

"Oh please!" The sisters, rarely in agreement about anything, spoke as one.

Grace had already been introduced to the ponies when Pippin had been taken to meet Prince and Caesar. "Mine is the most special so I named him Prince," Laura announced, tossing a challenging look at Beatrice. "Hers is only Caesar."

"Who was an *emperor* who ruled over all of the entire Roman Empire of which England was only a tiny part.

There was nothing to do in the face of such superior knowledge except scowl. "But Pippin likes Prince the best." And, after touching noses with the pony, Pippin clearly did.

Now rides around the park were a regular feature of their days, and Grace gloried being in the out-of-doors after the years in town—and oh the joy of the sun on one's face, the sound of birds, the gentle whuff of a horse's loving breath on one's cheek. She had forgotten all those simple pleasures that had brought such delight when she was young, not to mention the heady sense of freedom, galloping across the green expanses of pasture and stopping to take in beautiful vistas of church spires and fine old trees until the girls caught up with her.

So Grace left her London life and all attendant thoughts of it far behind as she enjoyed the lazy end of summer days at Edgefield Park.

# CHAPTER 27

Max, on the other hand, was immersed in challenging thoughts, made all the more unnerving by the hole created in his life by Grace's absence. It was not that he was not busy; things were progressing well enough with his uncle's estate that he had time to keep up with the letters from Lord Daventry and dispatches from the Foreign Office on the state of affairs in Paris as well as preliminary discussions of the issues to be dealt with at the future conference in Aix-la-Chapelle. And he had actually attended some concerts of the Philharmonic Society with Randall who became a surprisingly lively and entertaining companion when music was involved.

He also continued his regular sessions with the ladies at Mrs. Gerrard's as well as the card games and mathematical wrangles with John and Helen, all of which he enjoyed immensely, and all of which reminded him every time Fenwick greeted him at the door how much he missed Grace. He missed her saucy smile, her readiness to question his authority or his knowledge, her eagerness to learn—when she did recognize his authority and knowledge—and her devotion to her music, no matter how busy or tired she might be.

Talking to Dora, who possessed some of that same lively spirit only reminded him more strongly of her lovely friend who was absent, but it proved intriguing, nevertheless.

"I want to ask you something, my lord," Dora cornered Max one evening in the drawing room as he was making his way over where Helen and John were facing off against one another in a true battle of titans.

"I can see I shall not be a free man until I have answered to your satisfaction." Max gestured to a chair in front of the fire and took his own seat opposite her. "Ask away."

"Well," she began cautiously, fiddling with the fringe of a rose crape scarf draped over her arm, then, drawing a breath, and recalling her customary ebullient self, she plunged ahead, "I was reading the other day about building societies."

One mobile eyebrow shot up.

"The Kelley's Building Society, to be exact, and it sounded as though it might be a rather good idea. I know we have our savings in the consols, and some of us," she gave him a saucy smile, "in canal shares. And I know we are saving for our futures with insurance and annuities, but when we get too old, we will still need a place to live, and there is land available in Marylebone. If we don't need a place to live immediately, we could build something and rent it out until we did," she finished in a rush.

The mobile black brow sank back down to join its fellow in a thoughtful frown while Dora gave up twiddling with her fringe and began braiding it instead. "You might have an idea there, Miss Dora."

"I might?"

Once again that same look of gratification that transformed her when Max had given her his book slammed him in the chest and he could not help grinning back at her. "An excellent idea—an investment that would balance out annuities and consols and, er canal shares—an investment that could be lived in should one need to. I shall ask around and see what else I can learn, shall I?"

"Oh yes." Her eyes were shining, but she was not too gratified that she had missed his reaction each time canal shares were mentioned. Curious as to whether or not he felt Grace's absence at all, Dora had introduced her friend's particular favorite investment into the conversation and had been delighted to see just the hint of a conscious flush on those high cheekbones. So he did miss her despite his nonchalant air of indifference to the empty bench at the pianoforte. But now what was Dora to do? Did Grace miss him? There was no way to tell. Her letters had been so filled with descriptions of the gardens at Edgefield Park, their riding lessons, and the girl's progress at the pianoforte and their interlarding of French phrases into their conversations that it seemed there was no time to spare a thought for a clever dark-haired man who had, along with the Claverton brothers, become another regular contributor to the lives of the inhabitants of Mrs. Gerrard's.

As it was, Dora need not have worried. A series of encounters saved her the necessity to give either Grace or Max a push towards their deepening attraction.

Aside from sharing his dinners and a desultory rubber or two of whist with the members of Brooks's and his evenings at Mrs. Gerrard's where interesting conversation could be had without the slightest risk of running into his mother or Lady Caroline Daventry, Max lived a monk-like existence as far as the social opportunities London offered. It was safer that way, but it did give him far too much time to wonder about Grace. Was she enjoying herself down in the country? Were Laura and Beatrice behaving? Likely they weren't. Was she enjoying his sister's company or did she miss her friends at Mrs. Gerrard's? Did she miss him? Or, lowering thought, did she even notice he wasn't there?

After a particularly fruitless evening of posing these questions to himself and receiving no answer whatsoever, Max was just resolving to remedy the situation when he received an invitation to dinner from Castlereagh. Mixing again with foreign diplomats would be a welcome distraction . . . going to the Foreign Secretary's mansion in St. James' Square, not so much.

Resolutely ignoring a certain elegant façade in the square, and the mental image of one of its dangerously attractive inhabitants, Max welcomed the buzz of conversation and the sight of the brilliant company gathered in Castlereagh's drawing room.

"My lord, I have not cast eyes upon you this age. One was beginning to fear rumors of your demise."

At the light touch on his arm, Max turned to find himself surveyed by a pair of sparkling dark eyes set in a vivid, knowing face. One corner of the full red lips curved in a suggestively mysterious smile.

"You have been making yourself remarkably scarce, my lord, nor have you deigned to favor us with your presence at Almack's. What sort of churlish behavior is that?" Princess Lieven tilted her head provocatively. "Small wonder I have been bored to tears."

"Unconscionable behavior, I would gather, from the disapproval writ large upon your countenance." Max lifted her hand to his lips. He was accustomed to fencing with this clever woman, who took as much, if not more, pleasure from political conversations than she did from flirting, though, where Max was concerned, it was difficult to say. He'd first encountered her in Vienna, and then in ballrooms from Paris to London, finding her presence as stimulating and intriguing as she apparently found his.

Perhaps this was the heaven-sent answer to his worrisome preoccupation with a certain glorious dark-haired woman who made her home further around the square. Surely a flirtation with this fascinating lady would restore him to his senses and help him regain his customarily ironic perspective on life.

Thus, he was delighted to acquiesce when, seeing her husband and his host deep in conversation when they rejoined the ladies after dinner, she requested Max's escort home, "for my husband will be here until the early hours of the morning, and I prefer not to be. Too many late nights are not good for the complexion, you know." An arch smile told him she did not believe this any more than he did, nor did she expect him to.

As Max handed her into the carriage, she allowed her hand to clasp his for an extra moment before settling herself luxuriously against the rich upholstery. During the short ride, she kept up a vivacious litany of the latest *on-dits* until they reached Ashburnham House. The Russian ambassador's residence was ablaze with light, despite the absence of its master and mistress, and she turned to him at the door, acknowledging the welcoming glow from the drawing room windows.

"Though I did not relish staying up until the wee hours, it does seem a shame to retire quite so soon. Will you not join me in some refreshment before you go?"

The hunger in her eyes and the slight flick of her tongue across her parted lips told Max as clearly as if she had spoken that he was to be the refreshment.

His body recoiled, and then his mind reeled. What was wrong with him? For years he'd felt the tug of attraction in the presence of this patently seductive woman, and now he felt nothing? No, not nothing, but something almost akin to revulsion at the thought of kissing the lips she held up to him as the vision of another pair of lips, and blue eyes swimming in tears took possession of him. All of a sudden, the cloying scent of patchouli was overwhelming, and he fought the urge to tug at his cravat as the thought of his own empty masculine quarters became infinitely appealing.

"I thank you, Princess, but I have some dispatches from Lord Daventry to attend to, so I must decline your most flattering invitation." Max fervently hoped he did not sound as desperate as he felt, but he could see her face rearranging itself into its customarily aristocratic lines. "I do thank you, however." Once again, he raised her gloved hand to his lips and planted what he hoped was a suitably fervent kiss on it. With that, he nodded to the footman holding the door, bowed, and hurried on his way without a backward glance."

# CHAPTER 28

IF HE WAS HOPING TO FIND SOLACE in the privacy of his own chambers, Max soon discovered how wrong he was. As he sat in the flickering candlelight nursing a glass of port trying to banish all thoughts of Grace, he was inundated with visions of her facing off with him, her chin raised as she refused to be intimidated, the challenging gleam in her eye and the teasing curve of her lips as she argued the merits of her investments with him, or the way she tilted her head as she listened intently to his. And there was the tug at his heart as he pictured her on the pianoforte bench, sandwiched between her nieces and their dog, or the pain in her voice as she had asked despairingly, *How many women have I made miserable?*

He missed her. That was the long and short of it. He missed her dreadfully. Max had always considered his life to be rather interesting compared to most men's, but now it seemed sadly flat, and the time until he might expect to see Grace back in London an eternity. There was no help for it, it was time to repair to the country himself. To Wiltshire, to be more exact. To Edgefield Park, to be even more exact. Now all he had to do was come up with a pretext.

Max was not fool enough to believe that any pretext, no matter how plausible, would deceive his sister, but he knew he could rely on her to back up his story, whatever it was, just so long as it was not indefensibly lame.

"My brother appears to be paying us a visit in the very near future," the Countess entered the music room waving a letter as Grace was finishing her afternoon practice. "He says it is on a matter of business pertaining to me and the girls. One wonders what can be so urgent that he must journey all the way down here when he has never paid the least mind to us . . . until now."

If Henrietta had hoped to provoke a revealing reaction—or any reaction at all—which she had, she was destined to disappointment. As soon as Grace had heard the words *my brother* as the Countess sailed through the door of the music room, the rigid control she had spent so much time and effort cultivating, asserted itself. The one thing she could not master was the heat rising to her face, but fortunately, the afternoon sun pouring through the windows behind her obscured the faint flush that tinged her cheeks.

Henrietta noticed nothing, but Grace did, and cursed herself for it. What difference did Lord Maximilian Hawkesbury's presence make to her, whether he was in London or in Wiltshire? A very great difference, she ruefully admitted to herself, as she found herself fighting not to inquire of her hostess when he might be expected.

"He hopes to arrive in two days' time, but begs me to write him directly if that is not convenient. I do say, it *is* rather good of him to wonder if it is not, but then he is in the diplomatic service after all. I must tell the girls; they will be over the moon, for he has become quite a favorite with them." And she quit the room as precipitately as she had entered it, leaving Grace to wonder why her employer had bothered to inform her of the letter at all.

The more she considered it, the more Grace began to suspect that the Countess of Edgefield was a very deep one indeed. There had been a certain smug look in her eye that suggested she was not only quite pleased by the sudden turn of events, but not at all surprised. Grace shoved aside such useless speculation, too preoccupied with the prospect of living in the same house with Max to ponder his sister's reaction to his letter or its implications.

As their mother had predicted, Beatrice and Laura were delighted by their uncle's impending arrival, and from the moment they rose, two days after the receipt of the letter, they kept thinking up excuses to run to the windows overlooking the drive, in case a carriage should be appearing.

Needless to say, it was difficult to keep their minds on their lessons as they wondered if he would go riding with them, and if he would be impressed by the new tricks Pippin had learned. Such was their excitement when the post chaise finally drew up in front of the house, just as the sun was getting low in the sky, that, ignoring their mother's helpless remonstrances, they rushed to greet him, and Grace was able to absent herself without being missed.

She was not, however, able to avoid him completely, as the Countess had made it very clear that she was to join them for dinner when they were *en famille*. Admonishing herself for even bothering to think about how she would approach a man who had been occupying her thoughts far too much, Grace composed her face into a blandly indifferent smile as they gathered in the drawing room before dinner. But it was all for naught. She was lost from the moment she saw his eyes light up as she entered the room, and his lips curve in that rare, but special smile she could not help but feel was only for her—lips that had, not too long ago, made hers melt in response to their kiss, lips that had traced the outline of her jaw and slid enticingly down the length of her neck, trailing fire in their wake And now he was pressing them against the back of her hand which he clasped so warmly in his.

Contrary to all her hopes, and a concerted effort to ignore Lord Maximilian Hawkesbury's existence, Grace had forgotten nothing about this man, nor had her body; her heart hammered against her ribs, and each breath became something she consciously had to think about. She fought for a calming one. "I do hope you had a pleasant journey, my lord." There! It was spoken tranquilly, in a well-modulated tone. Helen's rigorous training had not been completely wasted on her.

"Thank you, I did." He cocked one disarmingly quizzical brow and Grace was lost. Worse yet, he seemed to know it. Then he took pity on her and, glancing in his sister's direction, continued smoothly, "But I had no idea I would receive such a welcome. Clearly Beatrice and Laura have been enjoying themselves immensely."

"Not that you would know it from their behavior." Their mother shook her head in mock dismay. "They act as though you were their savior, come on purpose to offer some diversion from us and enliven their dreadfully boring lives. It is too provoking, when their days have been a constant round of pony rides and playing with the dog and more games of shuttlecock than one cares to count. In fact, we have all been engaged in a riot of dissipation." The Countess sighed plaintively, but her eyes were dancing.

"What? No lessons? I thought there was to be music and French and Italian . . ."

"Oh there has been, but the other activities always seem to take priority, do they not, Grace?"

"Well, I suppose one occasionally has the sense they would prefer to be out exploring rather than sitting on the pianoforte bench."

"Hmmm. I think I have a remedy for that," Max offered, "I could teach them arithmetic. That would make music and French, and Italian seem positively frivolous in comparison.

"Arithmetic!" His sister looked at him as though he'd grown another head.

"I *am* rather good at it, you know. Miss Owen will tell you of the mathematical evenings I spend with Mrs. Gerrard and Lord John Claverton. Even her friend, Miss Barlow is beginning to have an appreciation for the finer points of numerical calculation."

Max's sister continued to stare, but Grace who knew him better than she cared to admit, heard the eagerness in his voice, and her heart was touched yet again by this man-of-affairs who was so ready to share his talents, and himself, with those who could use them.

"I would say that is an excellent idea!" Grace turned to Henrietta. "I have seen him hold a group of worldly women in thrall as he explained the intricacies of calculating risk and insurance. I have no doubt that he will be able to do the same with your daughters."

Max looked at her in surprise. She really meant it. His heart had risen and fallen more times in the last quarter of an hour than he could ever remember. Until he had met Grace Owen, it had been such a reliable organ, he had never thought of it at all. Now, it had thundered at the very first sight of her regal form and devastating dark blue gaze. And then, immediately plummeted at the cool smile and indifferent greeting. Now it was thudding again as she smiled conspiratorially at him as though they shared a special secret unknown to the rest of the world. Happiness made him almost garrulously indiscreet. "Yes, I have been instructing them in insurance and annuities, hoping to help Miss Owen's friends become women of independent means, reliant on no one, but themselves for their security. Which is why I have come down to Edgefield Park."

His sister's blank stare continued as he hastened to explain. "Well, talking with Hel . . . er Mrs. Gerrard, and Miss Owen," he glanced meaningfully at Grace, "I have come to see how important it is that women not be subject to the whims of fate, or, er . . . men, so I am trying to help them escape that. And then it struck me I should do the same for Laura and Beatrice, and . . . even you."

The blank stare grew incredulous, and Max hurried on rather apologetically. "I *know* Edgefield is all that one could wish in a husband and father, but, well, accidents do happen, crops can fail, weather can . . . well, er, life can be uncertain, and I have more resources than I know what to do with, which I did even before Uncle Richard left his entire estate to me so . . . er, so I came to discuss settling some of it on you and on Beatrice and Laura. I realize it is rather sudden, and all, and not quite the sort of thing one brings up this way, but, there it is. What do you think?"

"I think," completely at sea, the Countess struggled to reply, "I think . . . I think it is time for dinner." Henrietta smiled gratefully at the butler hovering in the doorway, and then gave her arm to her brother to lead her into the dining room as Grace, pray to a thousand conflicting emotions, followed. In fact, it was not her feelings that were conflicted so much as she herself was. She did not want to like this man, yet her first response was, *how very dear of him!* And her second, much to her chagrin was, *how very handsome he is* as he helped his sister to her chair and then, smiling that knee-weakening smile, turned to help her to hers.

# Chapter 29

Fortunately for Grace, Henrietta, in an effort to predict when her husband might be joining them, had plied her brother during dinner with questions about Parliamentary affairs. Between appearing to listen politely to them and concentrating on the food put before her, Grace made it through dinner without having to think or do much more than nod in an interested manner. Afterwards, as always when her mind was in a turmoil, she fled to the pianoforte where she could lose herself in her music under the guise of playing for them, and, an hour or so later, it was perfectly acceptable to plead fatigue and a wish to prepare for the girls' lessons in the morning and flee. But escaping to her bedchamber did not offer any particular refuge, as her thoughts and feelings plagued her with the recognition that she was very glad that Lord Maximilian Hawkesbury had taken the unprecedented step of visiting a family member voluntarily.

It was even more disconcerting to wake the next morning with a heightened sense of anticipation that the day held something special in store for her, only to realize that, of course it did, because Max had joined them. How utterly irritating it was to be looking forward to seeing him.

Others were there before her, however. As she descended the stairway, she caught sight of Max through the windows overlooking the side lawn. He had a girl on either side of him, each tugging on a hand as they led him in the direction of the stables. Grace chuckled to herself. Those two! She should have known they would waste no time in introducing their uncle to Prince and Caesar.

Grace watched as he bent over to catch something Laura was saying, then turned to Beatrice for what was clearly a big-sisterly tart rejoinder. Then he smiled at each of them in turn. It was a smile that did strange things to her heart, and strange, and far more threatening things to her well-being than his smile which did strange and surprising things to her body. A physical attraction like that could be erased by distance . . . eventually . . . Grace thought, but she had the uncomfortable suspicion that the heart thing would haunt her forever.

So, after morning chocolate, Grace retreated to the pianoforte where, in spite of her longing to practice the most tender songs she knew, she summoned up a picture of Signor Lanza at his most demanding and forced herself to do scales and vocal exercises instead until she was exhausted.

"Miss Owen, Miss Owen," Laura and Beatrice, closely followed by Pippin, raced into the room. "Uncle Max likes Prince," Laura, always determined to be the first, if not the most authoritative burst out.

"And Caesar." Beatrice settled herself regally on the bench next to Grace. *And* he has been teaching us to solve problems."

"Like going to the village. If one of us walked and one of us rode, who would get there faster."

"We *know* who would get there faster," Beatrice retorted loftily. "He taught us out how long the person on the horse would have to wait until the person walking could catch up."

"It's called math . . . math . . ."

"Mathematics. And Uncle Max calls it just another language for figuring things out." Beatrice wrinkled her brow thoughtfully.

Grace nodded. That sounded like Max, clever man that he was.

"He says it will teach us to be resourceful." Laura plopped down on the other side and smiled up at Grace. "Like you, Miss Owen."

"Like me?"

"That is what he said. Didn't you, Uncle Max?"

"You are entirely correct, Laura, I did say that." Max, having followed the girls at a more leisurely pace, confirmed, as he entered the music room. "And I meant it. Not only does Miss Owen sing beautifully, and speak both French and Italian, she knows how to think for herself."

He might be talking to his nieces, but the warmth and admiration in his voice were all for her—genuine admiration, not the flattery Grace was used to. How precious it was, and how rare, to look into another person's eyes and see respect. It was his gift to her, and Grace had no idea how to repay it.

But apparently she already had, unbeknownst to her. Later in the morning, the girls were visiting tenants with the Countess, who took her country responsibilities seriously, and was determined that her daughters would too, no matter what sort of estate they married into. The best way to insure this was to inculcate these duties to the less fortunate and those who depended on them into them early.

That left the morning free for Grace to practice to her heart's content, but somehow, her heart and mind were not in it. The green fields beckoned, and her thoughts were distracted. Why? She did not want to know, but a brisk solitary walk in the park seemed like the most effective antidote.

She had hardly stepped onto the garden path leading to the park beyond, when Max rounded the corner, clearly on his way to the stables. "Miss Owen."

Grace knew a moment of panic before she could summon her mantle of dignified calm, and, much to her chagrin, he seemed to have sensed it. "I beg your pardon. I do not mean to intrude on what must be a rare and welcome solitude, but . . . but . . ."

Now, he looked distinctly uneasy himself. How delightful. Grace raised a questioning eyebrow.

"It is just that I wanted to . . . ah . . . to thank you."

"To thank me?"

"Well yes, but it is rather difficult, and, frankly, rather humbling, to explain.

She stared at him. The always cool and composed Lord Maximilian Hawkesbury, star of many a delicate diplomatic negotiation, at a loss for words? How intriguing.

"It's just that I find myself enjoying the company of my nieces and their mother, who I actually never knew much at all. It is rather," he broke into a rueful grin, "actually, it is rather fun, seeing things through their eyes, enjoying things in a way I never . . . well, in the way things *should* be enjoyed. And if it hadn't been for you, I would never have found that out." Again, that utterly disarmingly rueful smile, and Grace was bowled over by the thought that perhaps her childhood in the simple Oxfordshire cottage had been a great deal more fortunate than his at the ancestral family seat.

His next words confirmed it. "You see, Hubert was ten years older than I so I was always utterly loathsome to him . . . and then, he was a very dull dog—still is," he paused reflectively, "But I think Randall, with his love of music might somehow have escaped that particular trait—dullness, I mean. I took your advice," he admitted, a self-conscious flush staining his cheekbones, "and we've taken in several concerts together. I have discovered that he is more intelligent and interesting than I had at first thought. At any rate," he continued, "Hubert went off to school before I was out of leading strings so other than my nurse, and a tyrannical tutor or two, I had no one my age to play with until I went off to school, by which time I had learnt to rely on myself for my own amusement. Not a bad thing really, but now I see, it can be a trifle lonely."

Grace's heart ached for the proud independent man next to her as they strolled along the path. What it must have cost him to reflect on his life in such a way, and then to acknowledge it—not just to himself, but to her, of all people. How he must trust her. She was overwhelmed by the thought, but before she could even think of how to respond, there was a sound of carriage wheels on the gravel and voices. "Uncle Max Uncle Max!"

The girls raced around the corner and came to a full stop in front of them. "Are you going riding?" Beatrice took in the shining top boots and buckskin breeches.

"Oh, may we come too? And Miss Owen?" Laura glanced at Grace, and, seeing she too was not dressed for equestrian activities, added "If we change our clothes quickly?"

No proof against such flattering enthusiasm, Max laughed, "I can wait, if you are quick about it. And you too, Miss Owen," he added with a teasing smile that brought the irritating flush to her cheeks.

# CHAPTER 30

THE GIRLS WERE AS GOOD AS THEIR WORD, and soon the little crowd was assembled at the stables. Max's Brutus, a magnificent gray, was already saddled and being walked back and forth.

The girls argued over the ride—through the pasture to the meadow, into the park, or along the stream? The pasture, with its opportunity to race against one another won out.

"Is the pasture to your liking Miss Owen?" Max asked, surveying her chestnut mare critically.

"Oh yes, Miss Owen loves to gallop. Don't you, Miss Owen?" Laura beamed up at Grace, evidently considering her a rider after her own heart.

"The pasture would be lovely." Grace glanced around for a spare groom or a mounting block, none of which was in sight as the grooms were busy with the little girls leaving, as she had feared, Max to assist her.

And it was worse than she had feared. Warm firm hands at her waist proved to her that her body had forgotten nothing since the evening of her concert. Heat flooded down from her waist, turning her knees, and other parts of her, to jelly, and up to her cheeks, which were flaming, but she managed to slide smoothly into the saddle, taking the reins easily as though attractive men tossed her effortlessly into the saddle every day.

Who knew that someone who spent his life sitting around tables debating with diplomats, studying risk and probability in his leisure hours, would mount his own enormous horse with the ease and skill of a natural-born athlete? Now that she was looking—and she was looking, God help her—she could see the strength in the muscles flexing under a jacket that was molded to his body, the square shoulders and broad chest, not to mention powerful thighs encased in buckskin breeches. Grace stifled a sigh, then, glancing up to discover him looking at her, she quickly turned toward her charges to see how they were faring before beckoning to them and heading off at a determined trot that became a canter and then a gallop as pent-up frustration with her own weakness burst forth.

"Huzza! Huzza!" Laura shouted as she gave chase, followed by Beatrice and Pippin bouncing through the grass behind her.

Max, however, followed at a leisurely pace, enjoying the scene in front of him. The high spirits of the girls and the dog were infectious, and he was half-tempted to race alongside them, but then his gaze fell on the leader of the procession, and he decided that the picture of Grace flying across the pasture was something not to be missed. It took his breath away, and not in the usual manner. This time it was not her beauty or her music, or her clever mind, but her strength and agility, the skill that made her become one with her mount, as powerful and dashing as the horse itself. And once again, he had to admit, as he had, had to before that she was as good at something as he was—well, perhaps not quite so good because she had been out of practice, but good enough to make him look to his laurels.

Grace had reined in at the end of the pasture and was trotting back, so the girls had circled back to their uncle. "Miss Owen rides very well, doesn't she?" Beatrice might have been asking her uncle, but her shy smile was for Grace.

"Indeed she does. I have not seen many to equal her, and that is not a compliment I give often."

"So it is all the more appreciated. I thank you." Grace appeared beside him, her cheeks flushed and her eyes sparkling with the pure joy of her ride, a pure joy that filled Max's soul as well.

A slight cough made him look down to see Pippin collapsed at Brutus' feet, panting heavily. "Poor fellow. He has kept up with us all this way and his legs are ten times shorter even than Prince's." Max dismounted, picked up the little dog, and placed him gently on the front of his saddle before remounting. "Now, be a good dog, and Brutus will be happy to give you a ride home," he instructed his passenger, who regarded him with great seriousness.

They headed back at a much more sedate pace with Pippin clinging close to Max, looking doubtfully around at first, then gradually relaxing as he became accustomed to the motion. By the time they reached the drive, he was sitting up, a dog in seventh heaven, as he surveyed the world from his lofty perch.

The girls too were in high spirits. "Look. He likes it, he likes it!" Laura cried, while Beatrice turned to her uncle with adoring eyes. "You are very clever, aren't you, Uncle Max? Just as Miss Owen told us you were," she added softly.

When had anyone actually told him he was clever? His Uncle Richard had said he had a good enough head on his shoulders. Oh Castlereagh might give

Max an acknowledging nod once in a very great while, but no one had ever made him feel as though he were in any way special or out-of-the-ordinary, or that his presence in any way contributed to anything. Max had always had to convince himself of that on his own. And now someone, and not just anyone, but a member of his own family was actually telling him he was clever, proving that, in spite of all his worldly experience, he hadn't experienced everything.

It was a heady moment, but all too brief, as Max caught sight of the traveling carriage in front of the door, where his sister and the servants had gathered, and recognized the woman being handed down from the vehicle. The Dowager Marchioness of Swanton. "Mother."

Muttered under his breath it sounded more like a curse than anything to the woman on the horse next to him as she turned to see him gazing in horror at Henrietta who, equally horrified, gazed back at him, shaking her head ever so slightly. Ever so quietly, Grace edged her horse away from the others as all eyes fixed themselves on the Dowager Marchioness of Swanton and her companion.

"London being so thin of company and all, it seemed only natural to visit you , and then Sir Digby happened to mention he was visiting friends in Bristol and, having no conveyance of my own," she looked daggers at her son, "it was fortunate that he offered to conduct me here." And with this airy excuse, the Dowager Marchioness snatched the arm of her unprepossessing companion and marched up the steps as though she, rather than her daughter, were mistress of the entire establishment.

"Of all the nerve!" Henrietta sputtered to her brother some half an hour later as he encountered her on his way to change out of his riding clothes.

"You mean you did not invite our dear mother?"

"Of course I did not, you wretched man! How could you think…" Henrietta looked at him more carefully. "Of course you are funning. She tells me she went to your lodgings after you didn't respond to her request for a carriage, only to be told you were in the country. Don't worry, no one in your employ admitted to knowing your destination. It was Randall who unwittingly divulged your whereabouts, poor naïve lad that he is. Now we *are* in the basket. However are we to rid ourselves of her?"

"Find someone with more *eclat* than we possess and bribe them to take her off our hands?" he offered, raising a satirical eyebrow as he resolved in the future to set Randall on his guard where the Dowager Duchess of Swanton was concerned.

"I am serious."

"And so am I, but short of murder, or Lady Jersey inviting her for a long overdue visit, I can think of nothing at the moment. What our mother wants, our mother gets, even if she has to cast her lot in with such a dubious ally as Sir Digby Staines."

"You know Sir Digby?"

"I know of him and it is nothing good." Max marched up the stairs, his previously bright outlook on the day completely clouded over.

It grew even gloomier when Grace brought the girls to show their grandmother all they had learned on the pianoforte."

"I know that my mother knows little and cares less what the girls are doing, but I cannot bear another minute of her wondering what we do for society and amusement around here. You must bring us some distraction," Henrietta had begged her.

So it was that Grace stood back and smiled encouragingly as first Laura and then Beatrice sat down at the pianoforte.

If she had hoped of an acknowledging smile, or even a friendly look of her own from Max, who, much to her relief, and her surprise, given his less than welcoming reaction to the new arrivals, was also part of the audience, she was destined for disappointment.

Not once meeting her gaze, he spent the entire performance eyeing Sir Digby who had insinuated himself into the little group with an inscrutable, but distinctly unnerving expression.

If she had thought about it at all, Grace would have realized that the predatory smirk that spread across Sir Digby's fleshy lips the moment she had entered the room was causing Max as much, if not more, uneasiness than it was causing her. It was the same look that had spread across Smedley's repulsive features whenever he saw her, the same look that had caused her so much misery.

# CHAPTER 31

Fortunately for Grace, the presence of guests meant that she no longer took her meals with the family, but in the schoolroom with the girls where the atmosphere was far more congenial than it was in the dining room, dominated by the Dowager's recitation of her social triumphs, relieved only occasionally by fawningly inane interjections from her opportunistic swain who clearly counted on her introducing him into the fashionable circles to which he aspired.

Grace kept a careful lookout for the uninvited guest the next day, only emerging from the environs of the schoolroom when she heard the carriage head off down the drive with Henrietta and the Dowager who insisted on social calls—not to her daughter's usual tenants and those in need, but the *best people* in the neighborhood.

Grace had spent a frustrating morning with the two little girls who would have infinitely preferred another ride like the previous day to the Italian lessons facing them. After much kicking the chairs with their feet and gazes constantly turning toward the window, they were induced to endure half an hour of verb drill until Nurse rescued all of them with the news that luncheon was on its way.

Seeing the girls in good hands, Grace hurried to the garden to enjoy the beautiful day and walk off the exasperations of the previous hour. Beatrice and Laura were dear girls and generally well behaved, but they were also high-spirited, which could be wearing to even the most patient of instructresses.

As Grace stepped outside, inhaling the rose-scented breeze, the tension drained from her shoulders. She took another deep breath and set off down the gravel path toward the folly by the lake. There was nothing like sunlight shimmering on the water and the coots darting here and there to clear the mind, inspire the senses, and reinvigorate the soul.

But as she neared the exquisite little Palladian shelter, the hair on the back of her neck rose. It was the footsteps behind her that did it. Not forthright strides, but the insidious and skulking crunch of gravel that told her, even before she turned around, that she had been mistaken in feeling secure. Sir Digby had not accompanied the ladies on their social rounds. He was right here, stalking her with a falsely innocent smile that told her she was in trouble.

"Miss Owen," he caught up to her and held out his arm. "How delightful to discover a fellow admirer of nature as I step out to explore these most exquisite grounds. Do let me escort you, for the path, well-kept as it is, is a little rough."

Ignoring the arm held out to her, Grace turned back towards the house. "In truth, I am only taking a quick breath of fresh air before returning to the young ladies who are expecting me momentarily."

"Oh come now," he grabbed her elbow as she made to pass him with what she erroneously thought was more than an arm's length between them.

"Truly, I must return." She twisted her arm out of his grasp, only to have him leap forward and grab her by both arms. Then, pulling her into a none-too-gentle embrace, he thrust his face toward her.

Too many years of practice came to Grace's aid as she twisted away and brought her half boot down hard on his insole.

"Ungrateful hussy! You will be sorry for this." He tightened his arms and planted his lips on her neck.

"I think not!" Rage boiled within her as, throwing caution to the winds, Grace dropped like a stone towards the ground.

Too far away to help, Max who, having resisted his mother's demands for his escort on their visits and retreated to the library, had risen from his paper-work the moment he saw Grace through the window and observed Sir Digby's sudden appearance, heaped self-recrimination on his own head for not having anticipated and forestalled the encounter, raced towards them. He watched in horror as Grace sank to her knees, evading his embrace. The horror that turned to astonishment as she rose to her feet and planted one of the finest left hooks Max had ever seen, in or out of Gentleman Jackson's. Sir Digby went down like a sack of potatoes, giving Max time to close the gap between him and Grace.

"Are you all right?" He pulled her into his arms, examining her anxiously for any signs of injury.

"No!" Her eyes were blazing. I cannot *think* of how I was so stupid as to allow myself to be accosted by that . . . that . . .," she directed a scornful glance at the prostrate figure now struggling to his knees.

Reassuring himself that she was indeed more angry than hurt—not even her knuckles appeared to have been bruised by her deftly delivered blow—Max marched over and, grabbing the vanquished abuser's collar, hauled him to his feet.

"I think you are quite finished here, sirrah, and if you know what is good for you, you will depart before my sister and mother return. Furthermore, you will forget Miss Owen and this entire incident as completely as if it had never happened."

"Now see here," Sir Digby managed to bluster, despite the hand gripping his collar, "you cannot . . ."

"I can and I will—if you so much breathe a word of this—bring about your utter ruin, not only in the *ton*, but in the City where not everyone is so aware of your connections with the slave trade that not only supplied your plantations in the Caribbean, but made you a great deal of money as well. I also venture to guess that you and your friend, the captain you are visiting in Bristol, have managed to smuggle them these past ten years despite the Royal Navy's best efforts to curtail that loathsome and illegal traffic. And," he tightened his hold as the unfortunate Digby struggled to speak, "as if that were not enough, I am also well aware of the income you derive from lending money at fifteen percent to moneylenders who then charge eighty percent to save young bucks from defaulting on their gambling debts. If you care nothing about the illegality of trading in human souls, I feel certain that you do not wish to be known by the *ton* as a damn cent-per-center, so be off with you, for I, unlike you and the reputation you have in the City, I am a man of my word."

Letting go of the collar, Max turned to offer his arm to Grace, allowing her thoroughly demolished assailant to crash to his knees again before gathering himself together and scuttling back towards the house. "Come, let us put as much distance between ourselves and that scum as we can." Pulling her hand through his elbow, Max held it in a warm, reassuring clasp as he led her gently toward the folly.

Grace followed numbly, the rage having subsided to leave her absolutely drained of all thought or feeling.

# Chapter 32

"There," Max opened the door, dusted off a bench with his handkerchief, and sat them both down as he scanned her face, eyes dark with concern. "I do apologize for not saving you from that nasty scene. I should have been more vigilant. But," a reluctant smile tugged one corner of his mouth, "you were magnificent. I've never seen a more effectively planted facer in my life, and I am not at all sure I could have done so well myself." Indeed, Max was having some difficulty reconciling his sudden desperate urge to protect and defend Miss Owen from all danger and discomfort with the lowering recognition that in point of fact, she did not in the least need him to do so.

"Ah, that was nothing, but you made sure he will never trouble me again. That I could not do."

Odd, how much better her words made him feel. "But where did you come by such pugilistic skills? That was no amateurish lucky hit."

"No it was not," she admitted with a hint of a grin. "It was Lord Adrian and Lord John. They taught us after Basil, er, Viscount Wormleigh attacked Dora. Juliette asked them to teach us to defend ourselves. She said . . ." Grace gulped back a sob that seemed to have come from nowhere, "she said that she wanted *to make bad men afraid*, and I do too, but I wish . . . I wish," tears stung her eyes, "I wish I were a man so I didn't even have to think about such things.

And to Grace's utter horror, she burst into tears.

"Oh my poor love." Max drew her into his arms, holding her close, gently stroking her hair, while she sobbed as though her heart would break—very nearly breaking his in the process. How could someone, anyone, not treat this magnificent woman with anything but the utmost admiration and respect? How could anyone want to do anything but cherish her and her dreams?

A black rage rose inside him as he contemplated going after Sir Digby and thrashing him within an inch of his life, possibly far less than an inch, but that was the easy part. Grace's misery was the hard part, the part that needed to be taken care of now.

Slowly the sobs subsided, and she raised her head from his shoulder to look at him with tear-drenched eyes. "I'm sorry. I don't know what came over me. I was angry, and I defended myself. I should be proud of that, but I've become a complete watering pot." She smiled slightly, but her eyes were haunted.

"It was not today that upset you, but before."

"How did you know?"

Max wiped away a tear with his finger. "I didn't for sure, but I guessed. Now, you must believe that defeating him today wipes out all those yesterdays so they will never haunt you again. Say that, *I will never think of it again.*"

"I will never think of it again," she echoed dutifully, like a child repeating its lessons.

"Very good. And with that, you have banished it from your life."

"I know, I know, and I *am* proud, that I defended myself, but that one person should have such power over another is . . ." she drew an angry breath, "utterly despicable."

"It is. And people exert that despicable power over others whether they are women or men. The only defense against such tyrants is to be strong and steadfast in your belief in yourself. And you are strong and steadfast." He smiled down at her. "Believe me, you are."

Grace's eyes lit up at his words, and without thinking, he bent to seal them with a kiss. It was only meant to reinforce what he had said, but her lips parted under his as she drew in a deep breath and he was lost.

Max drew her close in his arms, overwhelmed by her scent, the beating of her heart against his and the silky warmth of her lips under his. "Oh my love."

He didn't realize that he had spoken his thought until she pulled away from him, regarding him so curiously he could not help chuckling. "You *are* my love, you know. My fierce, challenging, independent, and utterly overwhelming love. You bested me the first time I met you, and I confess, without the least shame, I have been captivated by you ever since, even though you continue to best me."

She shook her head wonderingly as though such a thing were simply not possible.

"Here, let me convince you that I adore you from the top of your head," he laced his fingers in her hair, tilting her head so he could kiss the glossy black curls, "to . . ." his lips moved to her forehead, her temple, trailing kisses along her cheek to the tantalizingly sensitive spot below her ear, then slowly down her neck, until Grace could hardly breathe for the sweetness of it—and something else, something she had never felt before. She had known the tender caresses of her parents, but this was new. This was overwhelming, sweeping her with a longing that was at once languorous and exhilarating. Blood sparked through her veins. Every cell of her skin was alive to his touch. She could hardly breathe for wanting more—more of him, more of his hands and mouth caressing her inch by inch, everywhere.

So this was what it was like! This was why Juliette got that special secret smile on her face whenever she spoke of Adrian. Yes, one could easily see the warmth of love in her eyes, but Grace had never quite been able to understand that smile—until now. Now she understood completely as she reached up and pulled Max's mouth down hard on hers as she molded her body to his, the hardness of his chest pressing against nipples that were all at once tinglingly alive. His hands slid down her shoulders to her waist, pulling her against him and, God help her, she wanted them to slide lower still to parts of her body she had never considered anything but dead, now melting with desire. "Aaah," she murmured against those wonderful warm demanding lips.

Max pulled away to look into her eyes, his own filled with questions. "You know how much I adore you. It is not just physi . . . .I am not like those men . . ."

Grace raised one eyebrow.

"Yes, yes, I want you. I admit to what you so obviously know." He reached up to trace her jaw, then drew his fingers slowly gently down her neck, and around her breast before returning them to cup her cheek. "But that is nothing compared to how I feel about you . . . about us, about having someone to share things with when I have never had anyone to share anything with ever before in my life."

And then, in the midst of her passion, Grace saw the lonely little boy he must have been, ignored by his parents, too young to be anything, but a nuisance to his older brother, too intelligent to be totally absorbed, and therefore accepted, in the foolish games of his schoolmates. Her eyes stung as she reached up to smooth away the lock of dark hair that fell across his forehead. "I do know." She smiled.

"Oh Grace, my darling girl." Max pulled her back into his arms and they remained silent, stunned by the wondrous sweetness, the miracle of it all.

"Uncle Max, Uncle Max!" Laura came flying down the path toward the folly as they disentangled themselves and rose to meet her. "Mama says a messenger has arrived for you and . . . and . . ." breathless with self-importance, she struggled for an appropriately serious expression, "and he needs a reply so you are to come directly."

Max cast a rueful look at Grace before turning to his niece. "Very well, lead on oh fearless messenger."

Grace watched them go, a tender smile on her face and confusion in her heart. What was she to do? She had broken the cardinal rule at Mrs. Gerrard's.

She had unbelievably, incredibly, against all possible odds, fallen in love. Worse yet, it was not just the cardinal rule at Mrs. Gerrard's, it had been Grace's cardinal rule and guiding principle since her mother had died and her father had been destroyed by the loss. Love was the enemy. Love took away your soul, and everything that you had worked so hard to become. Love was the destroyer. But oh—a tide of longing swept through her leaving her so weak she was forced to sink onto a convenient garden bench—how sweet it was! How could something so dangerous make her feel so alive, as though she had just been declared the best prima donna in the entire world. And whatever was she going to do?

# Chapter 33

REALITY, IN THE FORM OF BRINGING THE LITTLE GIRLS down from the schoolroom to tea, brought a welcome dose of normality, pushing all soul-searching thoughts into obscurity as Grace led Laura and Beatrice into the drawing room where a tense silence greeted them.

The Dowager Marchioness sat ramrod straight in a chair next to the fireplace glaring at no one and everyone in particular while Max and his sister, ensconced in two chairs opposite, exchanged glances of mutual support.

"Really, it is too bad of Sir Digby to leave without a moment's notice. I cannot think how he came to do so without even consulting me when he knew we were out visiting." This time the glare was focused unmistakably on her son who remained impassive under its scorching intensity. Indeed, to Grace, he had the appearance of someone who had endured it so many times before that it simply did not register on his consciousness.

"And now who will escort me back to town?"

"I am sure you may have the carriage whenever you wish, and certainly you can ride in it when it goes to collect Edgefield," her daughter murmured.

"That is not the point," the Dowager snapped. "I cannot travel alone. Why think of what . . ."

"Of course we shall send servants to escort you."

"Max can do it. He will be returning to town, and he can escort me when I go to visit the Daventrys in Brighton as well since he is Lady Caroline's beau."

Henrietta's eyebrows rose nearly to her hairline as she turned to her brother.

Max shrugged. "Actually, I must leave tomorrow morning. Castlereagh has requested my presence in town immediately."

"I do not know how you think I could possibly be ready by then." If the

Dowager had been glaring before, she positively blazed with righteous indignation now.

"I had no thoughts on that score as I was under the impression that you had come for a visit with my sister—your daughter—which, naturally, I expected to be of some duration, or at least longer than a day or two."

"Why would you think I would bury myself in the country when there is so much happening in town?"

"Why indeed?"

But Max's sister was more conciliatory, though equally cynical. "I had thought you came because town was so thin of company at the moment."

"I was being metaphorical, of course. Well, I can see I shall have to direct Sally in the packing." She rose with slow dignity, then sailed regally from the room.

"Well, that was illuminating." Max did not bother to soften his sarcasm in front of the two little girls who were open-mouthed at the spectacle of adults behaving badly.

"I am sorry you are stuck with her."

"Have no fear. Our interaction will be at a minimum, for the weather promises to be fine enough for me to ride most of the way. And, once I arrive in town, I shall be too busy for her to commandeer me. Of course, she will press some poor swain into her service to escort her to the Daventry's." Max practically spat out the name as he too rose. "Now, if you will forgive me, I have some letters I must write before dinner."

"I think it is time you girls had your bath, and in the meantime, Miss Owen can play something for us." The Countess rang for Nurse and settled back in her chair, holding her cup of tea.

"And my mother thinks the country is dull," she remarked to Grace after the girls left reluctantly with their nurse, setting down her teacup and fanning herself gently with one hand. "She should know by now that life is never dull with her around. The moment she appears she has everyone at sixes and sevens. Most of the time I am spared her machinations because I am simply a woman, but Max, poor Max. She must always have a man dancing attendance on her even if it is only her son. No wonder he is with the Foreign Office. Even if he didn't live for his work, he would have joined just to get away . . . that or the East India Company." Henrietta scowled into the empty fireplace for a moment. Then she brightened. "At least he managed somehow to convince that little toad Sir Digby to leave before Castlereagh called him back. And now we shall have the place all to ourselves again and we can go on as delightfully as we were before."

Grace was not at all sure that such a thing was possible—for her at any rate. After the girls had gone up for their bath, she repaired to the pianoforte in the schoolroom, her fingers drifting idly over the keys, hoping they would fall into some soothing piece that would restore tranquility to her soul, if not rationality to her mind and heart.

It was love. She had to admit it and then ignore it. It was his energy, his quick and inquiring mind, that had first attracted her (aside from the broad shoulders, long legs, proud carriage and eyes that missed nothing), but it was the unexpected kindness to her, to Dora, to his nieces that had truly won her heart. However, she could not let that distract her from the quest that had kept her alive after her mother had died, after her father had taken to drink, after Smedley had defiled her, after she had joined Helen's establishment.

No, she would not let it. She would bid Lord Maximilian Hawkesbury a friendly good-bye in the morning, if good-byes turned out to be unavoidable, and then hope that whatever affairs had recalled him to London would keep him so occupied after she returned herself that he would forget all about her— even as she hoped he was a better man than that, a man who would not idly indulge in a flirtation one day and disappear the next.

And here was the crux of the matter; it had not felt like flirtation. It was deeper, more serious than that. Here was another problem; what did one do with serious? The answer, she knew, for people like her and everyone at Mrs. Gerrard's, was nothing. For them, serious, at least where men were concerned, did not exist. Everything else in their lives was already too serious for such a thing to be even remotely conceivable.

As it turned out, it was *not* possible to avoid saying good-bye to Max, for he sought her out in the schoolroom the next morning where she had sat the girls down for an early and extended French lesson in the hopes that she would be able to escape any personal good-bye in the general farewell to his nieces.

"Now," he rose smiling, after hugging each of the girls in turn, I must speak a moment in private with Miss Owen to . . . to give her personal instructions."

"Is it a surprise for us?" Laura wanted to know.

Max quirked a mischievous eyebrow at their teacher, "Perhaps. We shall see." He held out his arm to lead Grace into the hallway, closing the door behind them.

"And now," he gathered her into his arms, kissing her until her knees threatened to buckle underneath her, "remember this when I am no longer here." He pulled her hard against him as he captured her mouth with his, devouring hers with an intensity that left her breathless, then, releasing her, put his finger to her lips. "Not another word. Just remember it."

And then he was gone, leaving her gasping and grasping a nearby table for support as she tried to catch her breath and to slow her heart which pounded so hard it felt as though it would explode in her chest.

It was some minutes before Grace, one of Mrs. Gerrard's excruciatingly poised ladies, could regain her composure enough to return to the schoolroom where she was peppered with questions by two girls certain that their adored uncle was preparing some special treat for them. "Your uncle was merely offering suggestions as to how I might best continue your instruction in mathematics," Grace quelled them with a barefaced, albeit clever, lie.

But she could not lie to herself later that night as she lay sleepless in her bed. She missed him. What had heretofore been a restful vacation in the country now seemed dull and lacking in excitement which, if one could call living with two active little girls, a far too observant and clever hostess, and an appealing canine, unexciting, was saying a great deal about Grace Owen and her relationship with Lord Maximilian Hawkesbury.

# Chapter 34

Fortunately for Grace, diversion, in the form of a letter, arrived a few days later.

"A most impressive seal," the Countess could not help remarking as the post was delivered to them in the morning room.

Grace examined it curiously before opening it. Who would be writing to her? Yes, she had received the occasional missive form the ladies at Mrs. Gerrard's, but they were not franked. Clearly this was someone important, but who?

She examined the seal once again, then, shaking her head, slit it open and unfolded the heavy cream-colored paper. *I do hope the enclosed brings as much gratification to you as it does me. I look forward to seeing you in your element in London soon. Wrothingham.*

Her curiosity piqued even further, Grace opened the enclosure, then gasped.

"Oh dear, not bad news?" Henrietta looked up from her own correspondence.

"Nnnnno . . . it is not. It is rather good news. In fact, it is the very best," Grace replied, her eyes sparkling. "It is from a Mr. Samuel Arnold, recently resigned as the director at Drury Lane to return to the English Opera House. His lead singer is ailing, and, at the suggestion of his colleagues, Mr. Greatorex and Mr. Dance, as well as the Marquess of Wrothingham, he invites me to take her place on the evenings she is not able to perform."

One look at Grace's radiant expression as she sat staring at nothing in particular, the letter clasped in her hands, and the Countess knew her daughters' music lessons had come to an end. And she could not have been happier. No one was more deserving of such a chance at success than Grace. But what would happen to Max? The Countess, at times—more than she liked to count—found herself ignoring her own husband as she fussed over the girls and the problems and issues of everyday life. How much easier it would be for Grace to forget Max, despite the intimate looks Henrietta had recently interrupted between the two of them, when Grace had adoring audiences at her feet. And she *would* have adoring audiences at her feet. Henrietta was not a connoisseur like the Marquess of Wrothingham, but she had heard Grace sing, and she had been to the opera enough to know that Grace was a very good singer indeed. Not only that, she was beautiful, and she conveyed a wealth of emotion in her singing and her gestures that could not help but bind her audiences to her. Poor Max. Henry frowned thoughtfully. But maybe Max's urgent business in London was distracting him as well. At the very least, it had pried him from their mother's clutches—so conveniently that she occasionally wondered if her brother had engineered the entire thing.

"Well," the Countess rose and headed toward the door, "we must arrange for your journey. How fortunate the carriage has returned so you can travel in comfort." She paused in the doorway with a rueful smile. "We shall miss you, you know. *I* shall miss you. It can be frightfully dull here sometimes, and it has been delightful to have a sympathetic companion."

Grace was touched. She would miss them too. She was more grateful than Henrietta would ever know to have been treated as an equal, as a friend, not some wicked fallen woman, scorned by the likes of Lady Lavinia Harcourt and the *respectable* women of the world.

"Please don't go," the girls pleaded with flattering distress when they heard the news. "We like having you here."

"And so does Pippin," Laura clinched the argument. "Don't you Pippin?"

"Arf!" The little dog wagged his tail emphatically

"We will miss her, but we are so glad she has been asked to sing for the English Opera at the Theatre Royal in London," their mother comforted them.

"Will it have a stage and boxes and everything . . . Like Astley's?" Beatrice wondered.

"Very much like Astley's, so you can see how famous she will be," Henrietta added, smiling as two sets of eyes opened wide.

"Can we come see you, Miss Owen?"

Grace laughed. Laura was always determined not to miss out on anything. "I do not know how often or how long my engagement will be. And I seem to recall two girls who were desperate to get back to their ponies. How would Prince and Caesar feel if you went haring back to London so soon after coming home?"

How indeed? But bit by bit, the girls were reconciled to remaining at Edgefield with the promise of all the fun they would have when their father came home in the not-too-distant future. Still, it was a sad little group standing on the steps waving good-bye a few days later as the carriage pulled out of the drive.

Grace waved back, a lump in her throat. It was the closest she had ever come to having a family—a real family. Yes, she had, had her parents and the cottage, but kind though they had been to her, their devotion was all to one another, with very little time for a little girl who wanted to play shuttlecock, ride her ponies and raise the stable cat's kittens.

The melancholy clinging to her evaporated in the warm welcome she received when she arrived late in the evening to the usual gay chatter floating down the stairway and Fenwick, who unbent enough to favor her with a smile of greeting as she made her way to her bed-chamber, too crumpled and weary to face the brilliant crowd in the drawing room.

But Grace had not even removed her pelisse before Dora popped her head around the door. "Such delicious news about your singing engagement! We were so delighted when Freddy shared it with us. Now you are truly on your way."

Grace chuckled, despite her exhaustion. There was no resisting Dora's high spirits, no matter how tired one was, and Dora entered into her friends' good fortunes with as much gusto as if they were her own.

"It is a start but I am only there to take Miss Kelly's place should she feel too ill to perform."

"All it will take is one time with you before the audience to have them begging for you to be engaged permanently. I am certain of that. Now I must return to the drawing room, but I will have Rose bring you some supper." Dora whisked out the door only to pop around it again with a grin. "I am glad you are back."

Rose, too, was delighted to see her. "We all missed your music, Miss Grace. It's that lovely to hear it as we are doing our work—very peaceful, if you know what I mean."

"Why thank you, Rose." Grace sank gratefully into the chair by the small fire lit to take off the evening chill and tucked into cold chicken and a slice of meat pie with relish. It did feel like home, and she would need all the confidence that sense of belonging gave her for her meeting with Mr. Arnold the next day.

But first, she needed a good night's sleep, which was apparently not to be hers as there was a soft rap on the door not long after Rose had departed. Helen floated in. "Good. I see you've gotten something to eat." She disposed herself gracefully in the chair opposite Grace's, subjecting her to a quick searching glance. "It appears the country agreed with you. Despite the journey, you are looking refreshed. I take it that, in addition to the generous wages she offered, the Countess was good to you."

"Very good."

Helen's sharp green eyes narrowed ever so slightly. "It seems that we were not the only ones who missed your company. Lord Maximilian Hawkesbury has continued his instruction here and he has been particularly helpful to Dora and me regarding our possible investment in the new buildings being constructed in Marylebone, but after you left, he appeared a trifle distracted—almost as though his interest were elsewhere. And then he apologized for having to leave town." She tilted her head, fixing Grace with her catlike gaze, firelight dancing on her emerald earrings. "Aaaah, I thought so. Be careful, my dear. No matter how kindred our spirits might seem to be with another's, nothing but disillusion and heartbreak lie in that direction. Lord Maximilian is a most unusual man, an intelligent man, a thoughtful, and, I think, a kind man; he certainly has been so to us. But he lives in one world, and we in another, and never the twain shall meet."

Grace lifted her chin. "I know that. And my world is music which, with any luck, I can succeed in on my own."

"There's my girl." Helen rose. "Now get some sleep so that you can prove to Mr. Arnold tomorrow that you are going to be London's next sensation."

*Prove to Mr. Arnold*, Grace though as she snuggled into bed. Did everyone in the entire household know her business? Actually, it was rather comforting that they did, and that they were so eager for her to succeed in her dreams.

# Chapter 35

Anumber of the inhabitants of London's most exclusive seraglio were there to give Grace an encouraging send-off the next morning, despite the early hour and their very late night. Seeing them clustered at the top of the stairs as Fenwick held the door gave her that little extra bit of confidence. She knew she could compete with the best, but if nothing came of it, she had friends to come home to.

The theater was a hive of activity when Grace arrived. A likely young lad was sent to find the manager who appeared some minutes later looking harassed, but on seeing her, his features softened, and he welcomed her cordially enough. "Greatorex and Dance spoke very highly of your ability, and naturally, the Marquess of Wrothingham is a great admirer, but . . ." he paused to give her a measuring look which was not without humor, "it is Olivia Child's opinion that matters most to me. She says you are serious about your music, work exceptionally hard, and have an unusual rapport with an audience that some of our greatest musicians lack. A very clever woman, that one."

*And kind too*, Grace wanted to add, thinking how far she had come from those awful days when she was at the mercy of the dreadful Smedley.

"But come, I shall introduce you, and then we can begin." Mr. Arnold gestured to various musicians warming up their instruments and their voices.

"It was wonderful beyond all my imaginings," Grace confided to Dora later that evening. "To be amongst all those musicians and thinking of nothing but music."

"I am sure that things other than music will soon intrude as you get to know the various personalities," Dora, ever the pragmatist could not help cautioning, "but I am glad you are happy. Do you think you will have a chance to sing?"

"Perhaps. I met Miss Kelly, and I must say, she does not look well. In fact, she seemed almost grateful that I was there and hinted that she might need to rest next week."

"Excellent. We'll soon have you winning over adoring crowds, for once they hear you and see you, they will want no one else. This Miss Kelly, is she an attractive person?"

"Her face and figure are well enough, but she looks rather dour which may just be that she is feeling unwell."

"There you have it." Dora grinned.

"But if I am truly going to be at the theater, I cannot remain here," Grace remarked sadly looking around her elegant bed chamber. "I cannot trespass on Helen's good nature, even though I know . . ."

"Never mind that. I already have a solution."

"You do? You are such a wonder, Dora, you truly are."

"A wonder? No, and not talented like you and Juliette, but I do have a good head on my shoulders." She dug in her pocket and pulled out a letter. "This is from Juliette to you. I wrote to her, and this is her reply."

*Dear Grace, Dora has told me of your good fortune, and that you might need to find another abode. I would be most happy if you would make use of the unoccupied chambers above Maison Juliette, as I would like to think I am contributing not only to your dream, but to the improvement of London's musical scene. Alice only uses the rooms at the back of the shop so those above are all yours. Affectionately, Juliette.*

"There, you see? It is all arranged." Dora could not help looking just the slightest bit smug, nor did she bother to try.

"I say again, Dora, you are a wonder."

Grace's mind was so full of hopes and plans that evening that she hardly noticed who was in the drawing room as she took her seat at the pianoforte. As she played and sang, she could now truly picture herself on stage at the theater, and it was not just a dream. It was a true, real picture of things to come.

Grace might not have known who was in Mrs. Gerrard's drawing room, but someone else was very aware of its occupants. Max, cursing himself for arriving too late to congratulate her on the good news relayed to him by his sister, was forced to make up a fourth at the card table, though he was not likely to present much of a challenge to Helen and Lord John, already paired together, as his whole attention was on the pianoforte.

Lord John, surprised at the lukewarm nature of the game, surveyed Max discreetly over his cards and quickly came to his own conclusion as to the mediocrity of the play.

The quality only deteriorated as Max recognized that Grace was in a world of her own. She looked not only happy, but complete, and Max did not want her to be happy and complete. Well, he did, but he wanted to be the reason she was happy and complete. No, that wasn't quite it. He could not love a woman who needed a man to complete her, he just wanted it to have been Max and not Freddy who had helped her achieve her heart's desire. And yes, it would have helped if she happened to glance up, see him, and smile, but she didn't. And yes, he *did* love her. He knew that now.

He had actually known that when he returned to London and plunged back into his uncle's affairs, when he read dispatches and letters full of questions about interest on the debt owed by France, which ordinarily would have completely captured his attention, but now seemed rather lackluster. In fact, the life that had previously suited him perfectly well now seemed rather lackluster. He did not have to look far for the answer. Without Grace around, his life was flat. She was challenge, she was intelligence, she was curiosity, she was companionship, and she was love. He'd seen the understanding and compassion in her eyes as he had spoken of his parents, as he was hounded by his mother's unremitting selfishness and self-centeredness. She had made nothing of it, but simply knowing that that she saw it all and felt for him was enough to make him feel cared for—for the first time in his life.

At last the card game ended in an unsurprisingly ignominious defeat, and the music stopped as the card players rose from the table. Max was the first to reach the pianoforte.

"I understand from my sister that congratulations are in order, Miss Owen." Damn, did he have to sound so awkward and stilted, like a raw youth whose pulses were racing at the sight of his first love . . . which they were.

"Why, thank you, my lord. Naturally, I shall miss the Countess and her daughters, but, as you know, this has been my dream."

How could she respond so calmly and serenely when all he wanted to do was take her in his arms, tell her how happy he was to see her again, and kiss her breathless?

"Yes, we are all excited for her," Max jumped at the sound of Dora's voice at his shoulder, "but we are sad to see her go."

"See her go?" He knew better than to ask but he could not help himself. A quick glance into a pair of sparkling brown eyes told him that the clever Miss Barlow was up to something, for Dora never did or said anything without a very good reason behind it.

"Well, of course she cannot stay here, so Lady Adrian, with her usual kindness, has given her lodgings over Maison Juliette, which means we shall have to do without music in the evenings."

So that was it. Dora had decided to make sure he knew Grace's new address. Because she didn't think Grace would share it with him? It was a lowering thought, but Max took comfort from knowing that the redoubtable Dora was on his side.

Apparently others were on his side as well. Grace had quickly pled fatigue and gone to her chamber without giving Max another chance to speak with her so he had left with Lord John, hoping to distract himself with a discussion of Morrison's *A Concise System of Commercial Arithmetic Adapted to Modern Practice* as they made their way towards Piccadilly before pausing to go their separate ways.

"I do hope you will not take this amiss, but as a man of the cloth, I am permitted to dispense unsolicited advice," John began with the singularly disarming smile that had surprised many an unsuspecting parishioner into an unplanned confidence, "I simply wish to assure you that, while it may be extremely difficult to bring up the subject of love with the self-sufficient ladies of Mrs. Gerrard's, it is by no means impossible. Take, for example, my brother Adrian. Consider that. I bid you good evening." And with that, he was off down Piccadilly whistling to himself as Max stared after him.

Then a slow smile broke across his face. Lord John Claverton was certainly nobody's fool. Max had seen those bright observant eyes assessing him, assessing opposing players, assessing everyone, during the evenings at Mrs. Gerrard's. It wasn't assessing precisely, because there was always an abundance of sympathy in his expression, coupled with a clever mind and a wealth of experience among his parishioners. If Helen Gerrard respected the man, as she so obviously did, then Lord John was clever indeed, for no one knew more about people than the enigmatic proprietress of one of London's most exclusive establishments. So perhaps, just perhaps, Lord John Claverton knew what he was talking about.

Lord John Claverton *did* know what he was talking about. As the Rector of St. George's Hanover Square settled into his favorite chair with a glass of port in one hand and a mathematical treatise in the other, he could not help smiling as he recalled the blank expression on Lord Maximilian Hawkesbury's face as they parted. Too much the skilled diplomat to give anything away, he had kept his angular features sternly in check—no betrayal of shock or surprise there—but it was so carefully and unnaturally blank that it offered all the answer John needed.

Even before Grace had left for the country—her concert at the Countess of Edgefield's and subsequent invitation to Edgefield Park provided proof of Hawkesbury's interest—John had recognized the special understanding that existed between the two of them. It was just a glance here and there, a shared, secret smile there, but it was enough. This evening, however, Grace had seemed oblivious to Max, and he, increasingly tense, until Dora's well-timed remark, and the ensuing hurt in Max's eyes had convinced John that it was time to step in, do his Christian duty, and bring the two lovers together. Now all he could do was wait and hope. Truly, human beings were inordinately complicated; mathematics was so much simpler. John took a sip of port and opened his book.

# Chapter 36

G RACE, HOWEVER, HAD NOT BEEN *THAT* OBLIVIOUS. In reality, she had been
far too aware of Max's presence for her own comfort. The minute she entered the drawing room, she felt his presence rather than saw it, and as she
took her seat at the pianoforte, it had taken every ounce of will not to look
in his direction. She forced herself to play, knowing that eventually the music
would take over, clearing her mind and soothing her soul, cleansing it of her
complex and disturbing preoccupation with Lord Maximilian Hawkesbury.
Thank heavens, she thought later as Rose helped her out of her gown and into
her night-rail, she would soon be at Maison Juliette, away from his attractively
distracting presence.

The rush of sadness that overcame her at this bolstering thought did not
bode well for the future. She was going to have to throw herself into her new
life with such vigor there would be no time or energy, for the way her heart
and various parts of her body—moribund until now—melted at the thought
of him.

Steeled by this resolve, Grace rose early the next morning to begin packing,
after sending off a grateful letter of thanks to Juliette. With Rose's regretful help,
she was finished in time to be deposited by Mrs. Gerrard's carriage in Cork
Street before noon. Helen had insisted on the carriage despite Grace's protesta-
tion that she was on her own now. "Nonsense, you will always be one of us, and,
should things not turn out, though I am sure they will, you can be sure we will
welcome you home with open arms. At any rate, no matter what happens, do
not be a stranger to us." It seemed to Grace that the green eyes sparkled with
something deeper than irony, but Helen swept from the room too precipitately
to be sure.

Her welcome at Maison Juliette was as warm as the farewells at Mrs. Gerrard's had been, though it was only Alice, two seamstresses, and a maid, compared to the many inhabitants at Mrs. Gerrard's. "Everything is in readiness for you, the rooms aired, and a package from Lady Georgiana awaiting you on the table," Alice greeted her, adding with a shy smile, "it will be that nice to have company, even though I expect you will be out most of the time, what with rehearsing and all."

"Thank you." Grace swallowed the lump that had lodged itself in her throat as Helen's carriage had rounded the corner into Piccadilly and followed Alice upstairs.

The apartment was a good deal larger than her bedchamber and considerably less elegantly furnished, lacking the rich draperies, the satin bed hangings, and the marble fireplace, but the furniture was comfortable and of good quality. "Also supplied by Lady Georgiana from the lumber room at Claverton House when Miss Ju . . . er, Lady Adrian first moved in here," Alice volunteered.

Grace undid the parcel on the table with eager fingers. She could not remember ever having received a present from any other than her parents or those from hopeful gentlemen trying to win favor, and she forced herself to be patient as she opened the box to unwrap the paper covering the objects inside. "Oh! How kind of her." She lifted out an elegant gilt porcelain tea service decorated with landscape scenes in emerald green. For a duke's daughter, raised in luxury her entire life, Lady Georgiana Claverton had a unique sympathy for others, and an understanding of their needs born of an observant eye and an inquiring mind.

"That she is," Alice agreed. "Even before Lady Adrian was her sister-in-law, when she was just her modiste, Lady Georgiana would be over here doing what she could to help out. She claimed it was because she was bored by London life, but I think it was because, as you say, she is kind. Perhaps you would like to put it to use this very moment. I shall put the kettle on."

As she sat sipping tea from her very own tea service, contemplating her appointment with Mr. Arnold that afternoon at the theater, Grace told herself she was finally on her way, on her own, and now solely in charge of her own future. It was a bit daunting to think about, but with friends like Dora to confide in, and Olivia, who had also sent a congratulatory note, to advise her, she felt strong in their support.

Olivia had sent a note to the theater inviting her for supper after rehearsal which, though others had grumbled that it had been repetitive and exhausting, had been exhilarating for someone who had not had the opportunity of singing with other professionals. "It may grow old, but at the moment, it is still exciting," she recounted exuberantly over the snug little supper the actress had ordered for them in her lodgings.

"And what do you think of Miss Kelly?"

"She is very kind, kinder than I expected, and her range is adequate and true, but her voice is . . . is . . . well, I could call it weak."

"And she is not nearly so lovely or compelling as you are, nor can she sing nearly so well. If she is clever, she will retire to gain back her strength and leave her role in your capable hands. The public, who has seen only her in that role, will delight in someone new."

Which was precisely what happened. The next day when Grace arrived at the theater, she was eagerly accosted by the singer, or as eagerly as someone obviously in failing health could accost her. "I listened to you yesterday," Miss Kelly began, "and . . ." she was overwhelmed with a fit of coughing, "and I was agreeably surprised. Most English singers do not do justice to recitative, nor do they have the taste that Continental ones do, but you, I think, do. You have been well trained, and therefore, I can leave my role in good hands." She bowed gracefully and was gone before Grace could collect her wits well enough to respond.

Her own role! Her chance had come. Grace floated home, or she must have, because she had no memory of how she got there. She only wished she were at Mrs. Gerrard's to share her good news, but they would be busy now getting dressed for the evening. Her eye caught a gleam of gold on the table—her own tea service, and perhaps Alice might find a moment to join her.

But Alice had been busy when Grace went down to the shop, so she heated the kettle, found the tea, made up a pot and was just about to sit down and pour herself a cup when there was a rap on the door.

# Chapter 37

It was Tilly, Maison Juliette's maid of all work. "A gentleman to see you, Miss."

"A gentleman?"

"Well, several gentlemen, actually, begging you pardon for the intrusion." Max hovered behind Tilly, an almost sheepish expression on his face. Behind him, Grace could dimly see a rather bulky gentleman, perhaps two.

Her curiosity got the better of her, besides which, and despite her resolution to avoid his dangerous company, Grace could hardly turn the man away when he was calling on her.

"Again, I beg your pardon for the unexpected call, but I know you have embarked on your career, and I thought you might find this rather useful. And Randall agrees with me." He entered the sitting room and then stepped aside as two burly men shuffled in holding a long wooden box between them, followed by a lad carrying what looked like a small table which he proceeded to place on the floor near the window. The men carefully set the box down and lifted the top.

"A pianoforte," Grace gasped, hurrying over to run a reverent hand over the shining wood.

"Made by Mr. Zumpe himself. Randall assured me that his are the very best," Max replied, the anxious expression in his eyes at odds with the commanding physique that seemed to fill the room. "He does have his uses, that boy, and he expressly directed me to tell you how impressed he is by your success, also to remind you of his promise?" Max lifted an inquiring eyebrow.

"Yes. When I told him I was not a proper person for him to know, he agreed to abide by my dictates, but promised that when I went on the stage he would attend every performance. And he is entirely correct in his recommendation of

Mr. Zumpe, but how did you kn . . . how could you guess . . . what a wonderful . . . oh how very kind of you!" Grace reached out to clasp his hand, her eyes shining with the tears that would come at his extraordinary kindness and the living proof that he took her dreams as seriously as she did. In her excitement over her engagement at the theater, she had completely overlooked the fact that, for the first time in her life, she no longer had access to a musical instrument. And now here he was, taking better care of her than she was of herself.

A gratified smile chased away the anxious look as Max handed some coins to the first burly man who nodded discreetly and led the little group back down the stairs. "I was hoping it would find favor with you."

"Oh yes, oh yes. But how can I ever repay you?"

"By using it to make a singing debut that will have all of London talking," the smile turned into a grin, "as Freddy assures me you will."

"Oh, Freddy. He is a friend, and far too partial."

"He is a connoisseur, first and foremost, and he tells me that Mrs. Kelly is leaving and that you are replacing her, much to Mr. Arnold's great joy."

"How kind of Freddy to say that." She crossed the room, sat down on the stool that the boy had brought in after placing the stand, and ran her hand lightly over the keys. So Lord Maximilian had been talking to Freddy, had he, which meant he was still frequenting St. James's Square. It made her both happy that he continued to enjoy the company there without her, and slightly miffed that he continued to do so in her absence. Grace shook her head, mentally taking herself to task for such dog-in-the-mangerish thoughts. He was here after all, wasn't he? On the other hand, what did she care, whether he were or not? But oh she was glad to see him! It wasn't until she looked into those eyes so concerned with her happiness, it wasn't until she saw the twitch of his lips into that special smile, that she realized how much she had missed him.

What an extraordinary person—even more—what an extraordinary man Lord Maximilian Hawkesbury was. Other men might give her flowers or jewels, or shower her with trinkets because she was a woman . . . and, of course, they expected something in return. He gave her a pianoforte because she was a musician, and all that he expected in return was her success in her chosen career.

Her heart too full to speak, Grace turned on the stool as he stood behind her and reached up to clasp his hand and bring it to her lips. "Thank you again," she whispered against it.

Gently, ever so gently, he pulled her up to hold her in his arms as he looked deep into her eyes. "You are a rare and precious person and friend, Grace Owen, and I would do anything in my power to make you happy. I want you to know that."

She nodded slowly. It was true. He had already proven that by suggesting his sister hold the musicale that had convinced Mr. Dance and Mr. Greatorex to recommend her to Mr. Arnold. Even though it had actually been Freddy who brought them to the concert, it had been Max and his belief in her, his support for her dreams that had brought it all about.

What could she do as he looked at her so searchingly, his eyes questioning her, but reach up and kiss him? And then she was lost. His arms tightened around her, one hand sliding up to tilt her chin so he could kiss her more deeply, his lips hungry for hers, caressing them, devouring them, as though he were starving.

"Oh Grace, my darling girl."

She felt his breath warm against her throat as his lips traced her neck to her shoulder. He groaned and pulled her closer so she felt the hard length of him against her, felt every fiber of him craving her. And, most wondrous of all, she craved him too. It was more than the delicious throbbing between her legs that was desperate for him, or her breasts aching for his caress. She longed for him the way a drooping plant craved water, her entire being—body, heart, mind, soul—needed him to make her whole, and she wanted him to know it. She wanted to answer the question in his eyes, the hope in his smile. She wanted to show him that he knew her, understood her better than anyone else in the world. And she wanted to thank him by giving him the one thing she had never given anyone, never even thought of giving anyone—herself.

"Take me, Max," she whispered.

He stopped kissing her, setting her away from him, his hands on her shoulders so that his eyes could search hers, so he could be absolutely certain. "Are you sure? I do not want you to do this because you are grateful. I want to be sure you want this for yourself."

Grace could not help smiling. He looked like a little boy in his earnestness. Her heart melted. "I do."

"Ah, my love." He led her to the sofa against the wall opposite the pianoforte, pulling her down next to him as he tilted her head up to kiss him, twining his fingers in her curls, tracing teasing kisses down her throat to the fall of lace which he gently untied, leaving her neck and shoulders bare as he pushed the edges aside, his lips gentle yet tantalizing, the scrape of his jaw against the tender skin sending shudders through her body as his probing tongue pushed the muslin down to capture one taut nipple and then the other.

"Aah." Her head fell back as her entire body opened up to his kisses. One hand slid up her thigh, trailing sensuous fingers until she writhed in an ecstasy of wanting him there, assuaging a hunger she had never known before, a hunger that pulsed and throbbed through her veins until she thought she would lose her mind. "Please.

His fingers circled slowly gently, steadily, the heat building until she could bear it no more and then . . . the world exploded in exquisite, indescribable . . .

She gasped and clung to him as waves of pleasure washed over her, leaving her limp and weak with the power and wonder of it all.

He reached up with his other hand and gently cupped her head so he could look into her half-closed eyes. "My love," he breathed, "so perfect, so beautiful."

Grace leaned her head against his chest, feeling his heart beating, but she wanted more. She wanted him, the warmth of his skin against her. She tugged at his cravat, pulling him down to her and sliding her hand into his shirt, reveling in the smooth, hard planes of his chest as she kissed the square line of his jaw, nuzzling the column of his neck, tasting, inhaling the tantalizing maleness of him.

Max groaned, and she smiled a secret smile. To think that he might be as desperate for her as she was for him. But then he pulled away, a rueful smile twisting his lips. "You must take care. I want you so desperately that I have to save myself."

"What?" Grace looked up, utterly mystified.

He reddened, and her heart tugged at the change from masterful lover to awkward schoolboy. "I had not expected, well . . . I do not have anything with me . . ." she still looked confused, "to protect you from, er, any unforeseen circumstances."

Who would expect one's throat to tighten around a lump of emotion after the most shatteringly passionate experience in one's life? But it did. He was so very earnest, and so very dear. She kissed him gently on the lips. "Thank you . . . for the most wonderful . . . for being so . . . oh how can I ever thank you?"

"By telling me when I can see London's newest sensation on stage. I want to be there when everyone discovers the incredible treasure that you are. When is it to be?"

"Monday, but you are too kind to me," she smiled mistily, "always too kind."

"I want to take care of you." Max rose and pulled her to him, his kiss sealing the pledge of his words. Now I will leave you to try out the pianoforte." He paused in the doorway, "But if it does not suit, blame Randall; I had nothing to do with the selection." He grinned and was gone, leaving Grace to pull herself together as best she could.

It was some time before she made her way back to the pianoforte where her hands roamed dreamily over the keys, the lingering sensuality evoked by his fingers trickling through her fingers, capturing the precious moments for her, making an impossible dream real. It was real. Her whole body had come alive at his touch, and so had her heart. So this was what it was. Love. No wonder poets, and painters, and composers struggled to capture the uncapturable, to describe the indescribable. She was not the Grace Owen she had been before. She was transformed. And for the moment, she thrust aside the question of what that all meant to her, of whether it was a good thing or a bad thing and just reveled in the feeling.

# Chapter 38

The transformation was not a figment of Grace's imagination. The next day Dora, who had convinced Grace to join her in a quest for lavender soap, fixed her with a sly smile as they entered the elegant portal of Yardley's. "I gather the pianoforte met with your approval."

"You know?"

"Lord Max is a most diplomatic gentleman, and he would never put a lady in the awkward position of having to accept something she didn't want." Again, it was said with such a knowing look that Grace could tell those sharp eyes missed nothing, and then she confirmed it by blushing helplessly before turning to examine the blessedly distracting wares laid out before them.

Their purchases completed, they had just exited when a voice behind them exclaimed, "Miss Owen," and they turned to see Randall hurrying toward them, a packaged clutched under his arm.

"Chappell's," Grace nodded toward the package.

He laughed. "I half expected to see you there, and I must say I am surprised you have time for such an idle thing as shopping now that you have won your place on stage. My heartfelt congratulations, and Uncle Max and I are looking forward to Monday."

In the crush of people, and the hurry to get back to Maison Juliette before Grace's rehearsal, they did not see the frown on the lady behind them as they continued on down Bond Street. But Randall did see it as Lady Caroline Daventry materialized at his elbow.

"Lord Farnsworth, how delightful to see you. Does this mean you will be joining your uncle at Lady Castlereagh's soiree on Monday?"

"No, we are going to hear Miss Owen at the Theatre Royal on Monday. "You remember, she sang at my aunt's musicale."

Lady Caroline's frosty blue eyes grew even frostier. "On one would think that an evening at Lady Castlereagh's would far outweigh an evening at the opera."

Seeing that he had inadvertently made a serious blunder, Randall hastened to correct it. "But this won't be just any evening," he began apologetically before realizing he was only making things worse, "er, yes, one would think that. But I will be sure to give my uncle your regards." And ducking his head, Randall beat a hasty retreat before he could embroil himself further in what was clearly going to be an uncomfortable situation.

Randall, musical enthusiast that he was, was usually oblivious to the nuances of society and conversation, especially where women were concerned, but he did think it rather odd that the lady should be so critical of his Uncle Max's decisions. Even though he and his uncle had little in common, Randall could see that his uncle was very clever, knew a great deal about a great many things, and was not likely to make the stupid blunder that Lady Caroline implied he was making.

Still, Randall, being Randall, forgot all about the encounter the moment he got back to his chambers and began looking over the music he had just purchased.

Certainly his Uncle Max appeared not to have the slightest concern that he was missing an important social event as he and Randall made their way to the box at the Theatre Royal on the Monday evening in question. Neither one was inclined to make conversation before the curtain rose, each one being absorbed in his own thoughts. And after the curtain rose, their attention was naturally riveted on stage.

Max, gifted student that he had been, and superb sportsman, and skilled diplomat that he was, had rarely suffered an anxious moment in his life, and many of those who shared his side of the diplomatic bargaining table or sat across from him accused him of possessing no nerves at all, but as the first strains of music wafted up from the pit, he leaned forward on the edge of his chair, hands clenched at his sides. Yes, he had utmost confidence in Grace, but he wanted so desperately for everything to be perfect for her that he was as fretful as a mother watching her child taking its first steps.

At last she appeared, utterly glorious—commanding all eyes and winning all hearts as he had known she would—and he let out the breath he had not even known he was holding. Grace, as Isabel, the daughter forced into marriage by a father hungry for riches and power, was the picture of heartrending affection as she pulled the audience into her struggle between love and duty— her voice, her face, her movements all conveying the excruciating war raging within her.

Finally it was over, and the audience burst into thunderous applause. Max stole a look at Randall, searching for the connoisseur's reaction to the performance.

Feeling his uncle's eyes upon him, Randall looked up, surprised and a little touched by the question he saw in them. He nodded and smiled. "Yes indeed she was superb. The opera itself was, in my estimation, overlong and needlessly complicated, but *she* was brilliant."

"Oh, the story," Max snorted, "far too involved, and not nearly enough opportunities for Isabel to show us her character."

Randall grinned. "Precisely. But see how they call her back? She has made her mark. The reviews tomorrow will sing her praises. I know they will. Not only does she have range, purity of tone, and an extraordinary ear, she, unlike many singers, knows how to act, to move her audience with her presence as well as her music."

And then what was he to do, Max wondered. Now she belonged to the theater-going world. Would she still smile on Lord Maximilian Hawkesbury with that smile she reserved for him, or would he be just one among many admirers?

His rational mind told him that he'd always been one among her many admirers, but this was different. Those previous admirers had been after one thing, their own amusement. They didn't care about her or her hopes and dreams. Now she had stood on a brilliantly lit stage, now she had poured her heart out to everyone, with everyone hanging on her every note, her every gesture. She had seemed both alone in her power over the audience and at the same time intimate with each one of them in her appeal to their raw emotions. He was awed by her magnificence. Would he be able to know her again as a person, his own particular person, after all this?

As they rose to go, Max caught sight of Freddy, accompanied by the two men who had come with him to Henrietta's musicale making their way backstage to join the crowd of well-wishers and admirers, to fawn over her, no doubt until Grace departed for Mrs. Gerrard's where, he had learnt from Dora, she planned to share everything with her friends.

Max had no stomach for it—the conviviality, the congratulations, the excitement—not when he was gripped by an odd sense of what almost seemed like melancholy. A wave of something like loneliness washed over him. He had relished their time at Edgefield park, playing with the girls, quite simply, enjoying himself. He couldn't ever remember having done so before. And the sharing—he had never shared anything with anyone before, but time and again after Beatrice had made a clever remark and Laura had tried to outdo her, he would glance over at Grace to see his amusement reflected in her face. They were both proud of the girls, proud of what both Max and Grace had taught them and of how quickly and eagerly they learned. What could be more rewarding than that?

And now it was all gone, the cozy moments in the schoolroom, having tea with Henrietta in the drawing room as the girls competed with one another on the pianoforte, or all of them sitting in front of the fire listening to Grace play and sing for them. Max could not believe that he wanted something so mundane for himself, but suddenly he did. He wanted to come home to a place where he belonged. He had never truly believed that such a thing existed, but now that he did, he wanted it . . . and he wanted it with Grace Owen.

But her dream did not include that, and she was just beginning to realize that dream. Anyone who loved her the way he did could not do anything but rejoice with her in her success, even though it tore at his heart to do it, a heart that was also filled with happiness for her.

For the first time in his life, Max, who had thought his way out of every problem, whether it was an unfortunate hand of cards, a challenging mathematical puzzle, a risky business proposition, or the fate of the economy of a beaten nation, had no idea what to do. All he knew was that he had to see Grace as soon as he could, especially since his business in London was finished and affairs in Paris required his presence.

# CHAPTER 39

B UT THERE WAS SOMEONE ELSE WHO NEEDED TO SEE Grace Owen even more immediately. The afternoon after her triumph—even Grace allowed herself to admit that her debut on stage had been a success as evinced by the raving reviews Randall had predicted—Tilly appeared to announce that she had a visitor.

"Did the person give you a name?"

"No, ma'am. It is a lady, but not one of your friends from Mrs. Gerrard's"

"Do send her up." Since Tilly knew Olivia Childs and Lady Georgiana Claverton, who would not be caught dead in town if she could help it, Grace was left to guess who it could be, but not for long.

Tilly reappeared, breathless. "It's a Lady Caroline Daventry."

Grace had no time to respond before the pretty blond woman from the Countess of Edgefield's musicale breezed into the room. "Good day, Miss Owen. No, do not get up," Lady Caroline directed a fiercely dismissive look at Tilly who quickly backed out of the room, closing the door behind her, "this will only take a moment."

Grace couldn't imagine why the supercilious Lady Caroline would waste even a second of her precious time on someone so beneath her notice as Grace.

"I understand you are, er *acquainted* with Lord Maximilian Hawkesbury. I suppose that goes without saying since you performed at his sister's musicale."

She spat out the word *performed* as though it were some sort of disgusting menial task. "At any rate, his mother, the Dowager Marchioness of Swanton, is a very dear friend of mine. In point of fact, she lately visited us in Brighton where she happened to express her concern at your determined pursuit of his lordship."

Grace, who remembered the look of surprise on both Max's and Henrietta's faces when their mother mentioned her upcoming visit to the Daventrys, did not deign to reply. She'd been on the receiving end of *respectable* women's scorn too often to gratify them with any sort of reaction or response, and she was damned if she were going to let this intruder disrupt her carefully acquired glacial calm.

"Surely you must know how damaging any association with someone like you would be to Lord Maximilian's career, and I am certain that even someone like you has his best interests at heart."

"A musician, you mean?" Grace couldn't help herself. She knew she should have maintained a dignified silence in the face of such boldfaced calumny, but even she, accustomed as she was to scornful looks, found this a bit much to swallow.

"What Max . . . er what Hawkesbury," Lady Caroline corrected herself for what Grace could easily tell was a deliberate slip of the tongue to show the level of intimacy between her and Lord Maximilian, "needs is someone who is part of his world, someone who is on the best of terms and has close family ties with those in His Majesty's Diplomatic Service, someone who has spent her life among powerful allies in the government and can be an asset to him, not some *actress* who will simply be an embarrassment."

"*Actress*," Grace suppressed a smile at her visitor's horror that Max knew an actress, saying to herself, *that is only the half of it—if only you knew.*

Lady Caroline paused for a moment to gauge the effect of her words, which appeared to be none at all. Her delicate brow wrinkled in what almost could be called frustration, if she were passionate enough to endure such an emotion. "Surely you must know that we are affianced to one another."

Grace did *not* know that, and, furthermore, if Max were engaged to this woman, Grace was reasonably certain that Max, or Henrietta, or both of them would have mentioned it to her. "I had no idea, but forgive me, I do not understand what this has to do with me." Of course Grace, being Grace, and one of Mrs. Gerrard's ladies, had a very good idea, but she was not about to give this conniving woman an inch of advantage.

For a moment, Lady Caroline was nonplussed while Grace rejoiced inwardly; then she smiled what she undoubtedly thought was her most winning smile. "Clearly you are friendly with Lord Maximilian and therefore must want what is best for him as, I, the one who is about to be his wife, do too."

Grace remained silent, Her guest obviously expected her to draw some conclusion from all of this, which she was not about to do—well, not the conclusion Lady Caroline was rather transparently angling for. Then she smiled. "Naturally I want what is best for Lord Maximilian, but I would not *presume* to guess what that would be. He is a very clever man, and therefore, I leave it up to him to decide what is best for him."

"But surely you cannot think that any connection with you is anything but unfortunate?"

"As I just mentioned, I have infinite faith in Lord Maximilian Hawkesbury's good judgment, and therefore, I leave it entirely up to him to decide with whom he wishes to be acquainted. Now, if you excuse me, Lady Caroline, I must be off to rehearsal." Rehearsal was still some time away, but Grace had, had enough, and could think of no other way to get rid of her intruder.

"Well, I never . . ." Lady Caroline curled her lip in a way that would have done a petulant two-year-old proud, then, remembering that she was a superior being, pulled herself together, bid Grace a frigid "Good day," turned on her heel, and flounced out of the room, nearly running into Dora, who was making her way up the stairs.

"Not your usual sort of visitor," Dora remarked, stripping off her gloves and sinking into a chair. "Rather high in the instep, I would say."

"Verrrrrry. She is Lord Maximilian Hawkesbury's *affianced* come to warn me away from him in no uncertain terms."

"Did she now?" A sly smile lit up the new visitor's face. "Odd that we have not heard that he is affianced, and Helen, who knows everything about everyone, never mentioned it."

"I thought so too. Why would Lord Maximilian not refer to his betrothed, or if not he, why wouldn't his sister?"

"Because the betrothal exists in only one person's mind . . . at least I would hazard a guess, if I were a betting person." Dora was silent a moment, considering, then she grinned. "This bears some looking into. Rather amusing, don't you think?"

"Don't do it on my account," Grace replied a little too hastily, and Dora's grin, which she had quickly covered up with a discreet cough, grew wider.

"But tell me the news from St. James' Square. Of course I could not be happier than I am, doing what I am doing, but I do miss hearing how everyone is faring. And what of the Friendly Society? How is it progressing?"

"Very well indeed, and we are now thinking of investing in a building scheme in Marylebone . . . or at least I am, and Lord Maximilian is very encouraging."

"Is he? I can tell from the look in your eye that it is actually your building scheme. I am so glad he approves. That's splendid."

"He is a very kind man, isn't he? I mean, one might not have thought it at first, but he is so genuinely interested in things."

"Yes, he is," Grace smiled mistily as, avoiding Dora's eyes, she glanced over at the pianoforte. Which was why, despite her loathing for Lady Caroline Daventry and her officious, interfering ways, Grace would distance herself from Lord Maximilian Hawkesbury . . . for both their sakes.

At least telling herself that she was doing it for him made ending their friendship somewhat less painful. Doing it for herself seemed both weak and selfish, so weak and selfish that Grace could not delude herself into thinking she was doing it for the sake of her career, or that she was married to her music with no time or passion to waste on anything else. No, it was fear, pure and simple, that had already made her decide that she had to end their friendship. It was far too dangerous. Every time she saw him, all she could think of was how much she longed for his touch, for his kisses, for the chance to satisfy the hunger that consumed her to join their bodies the way their minds and spirits had melded into one another's.

Grace knew what happened when two people joined together like that: they forgot everything else but one another—so much so that when one was not there, the other ceased to exist. She was not going to do that. She was not going to destroy herself, or anyone else for love.

Sitting across from her, Dora saw it all—the longing, the struggle, the decision—and she ached for her friend. There was no such thing as that sort of happiness for Mrs. Gerrard's ladies.

But maybe there was. Dora remembered witnessing a similar struggle in Juliette, now Lady Adrian Claverton, so perhaps there was a way. And Dora was putting her money on Lord Maximilian Hawkesbury to find it, if anyone could—a very clever, determined sort of gentleman was Lord Max. Dora had infinite faith in him, and she was not one to have faith in anyone—Helen, Lord John Claverton and his brothers, and now Lord Max, as she called him privately, excepted.

# CHAPTER 40

Determined definitely described Max the next morning as he strode along Piccadilly toward Cork Street and Maison Juliette. Yes, the hour was too early for an ordinary call, but this was no ordinary call. His revelations the night of Grace's performance had convinced him that in order for him to be happy—and happiness, his or anyone else's, was not something he had considered until very recently—he must have Grace Owen in his life. And, having decided that, there was only one thing left to do—beg her to be in it. He could not analyze it, philosophize it, or agonize over it, he just had to put it to her and not worry about the consequences, because if she didn't feel as he did, well, he could not think about that.

"Lord Maximilian Hawkesbury to see you, Miss," Tilly announced as Grace sat at the pianoforte looking over music for upcoming roles.

"Oh." She rose quickly, forgetting the music in her lap which cascaded all over the floor—not the cool, calm position in which she had next hoped to encounter Max.

He leaned swiftly to pick it up, just as she bent to retrieve it, and she found herself looking directly into his eyes whose message was perfectly clear. He wanted her.

Grace tried to draw a steadying breath, but her knees were shaking, and her chest rising and falling with pent-up desire. This was not good, not when she had planned for their next conversation to be farewell.

"Grace . . . Miss Owen," he handed the sheets of music to her, his hand sending a jolt through her entire body as it touched hers. "I came . . . ah . . . to congratulate you on your success last evening." It was an utter lie, but he could not launch right into asking her to be his without some sort of preamble, and she had been stunning last night. "I mean, I was struck with awe, but you always strike me with awe." This was actually true, but he was making a complete mull of it. "I mean, Randall assured me that, despite the music's being mediocre, you were truly brilliant. I cannot believe that I am so fortunate as to be personally acquainted with such talent. I bask in your reflected glory." Worse and worse.

Grace could not help smiling. He was so earnest and so dear, and so awkward, and yes, it had been a triumph. The bouquets on the mantel and the notes Tilly kept delivering were proof that she had indeed achieved her dream, and here was someone who knew just how much that meant to her, and shared in that triumph. She could see it in his face. Freddy had been triumphant as well, but it was more the triumph of the vindication of his taste and influence than sharing in her dreams—not that Freddy didn't wholeheartedly endorse and support them, he just didn't share them the way Max did. Freddy was proud of his discovery and his successful efforts to get her on stage; Max was proud of her because he understood her drive and her dedication, what it meant to her to be accepted into the world to which she aspired—the musical world of London, and maybe, the world.

The smile transformed her face, which had been worryingly difficult to read when Max had entered, into pure joy. He could not help himself. He pulled her into his arms. "My love, I am so happy for you." He bent his head to kiss the lips that opened under his in pure blissful connection. He felt as though he had come home, as though he were known and loved and treasured as had never been in his life. A groan escaped him as he gathered her tighter to him, his precious, precious love.

"Oh Grace, my darling girl, my precious love." He smoothed a dark curl that had escaped from its bun and tilted her chin up with one hand. "Say you will be mine forever. Say you will marry me."

"Marry you!"

Max smiled at the utter shock in her voice and her expression. "Yes, marry me. Is that so surprising? I love you. I hope, I pray, that you care for me, and I want to be with you for the rest of my life. You are the closest, dearest, most wonderful friend I have had in my life."

The *friend* did it. Grace had, had impassioned words of love whispered in her ear times out of mind, meaningless words, transitory promises never meant to be filled, but no one had ever mentioned friendship as well. The man was serious—deadly serious. And her heart was breaking. It made her love him even more, and she could not do that to him, not to this dedicated, clever man who had a brilliant career ahead of him . . . unless she destroyed it by saying yes.

The most effective way to end it all would be to laugh off their friendship as the merest flirtation. That would guarantee he would never want to see her again, but she could not do it. She could not be that cruel. She loved him too much, God help her. She wanted to be with him forever too, except she knew what happened to people who believed in that dream; they were destroyed, and she would not do that to either of them.

Grace swallowed a sob, shaking her head slowly as she reached up to cradle his face with her hands. "It cannot be. You know it cannot be." It was the barest whisper. She could not manage anything else.

"No, I do not know, Grace."

She put one finger to his lips while she smoothed the wrinkles of the frown that pulled his brows together and she gathered her ragged thoughts. And here Lady Caroline had been so concerned about Grace's *association* with Max. If she only knew. Grace was not proud of that gloating thought, but it was true. Not in Graces wildest dreams would any man love her, much less marry her. How brave and generous of him, when she had nothing to offer in return. And how was she going to do what was best for him—which was to refuse him—without making him suffer?

"It is a most flattering and highly unrealistic offer, my lord," she began with a shaky laugh, "and I thank you for . . ." For what? For seeing her as a person? For thinking of her as an equal? For loving her? For making such a dramatic and foolish offer when he was the essence of intelligent practicality?

"It is *not* unrealistic. Grace, please listen to me." But Max could read the decision in her eyes, the resolute set of her lips as she straightened her shoulders. It was no use. The answer was going to be no, she did not want him. Yes it was hurting her to have to say it, but it was not her own pain that darkened her eyes, it was her concern for him that did.

"I never dreamed of such a thing. It is not possible. You do me too much honor. Ah, you laugh, but it is indeed an honor to be asked by a man like you . . ."

"I *love* you, Grace. That is all, the sum of it. I love you and I want you to be with me forever. I want to take care of you, to show you every day what you mean to me. I have to return to France now, but I will be back soon, and I want to have you to look forward to."

She smiled sadly and reached up to touch that dear, dear face. "I believe you, Max, incredible and far-fetched as it is, but I have spent far too long studying, slaving, to win a place in the musical world, and now that I have at least a foothold in it, I cannot give it up. I would no longer be the person I am if I did not hold onto that dream of being a great singer. I would no longer be the woman you say you love if I did not have that."

His heart was being torn apart, but he understood. Grace Own was not Grace Owen without her music, without that hunger, that passion, and he could not take that away from the woman he loved. "Very well," he murmured, gathering her hands into his and clasping them tightly to his chest. "You are right. I love you too much to take that from you, but if you ever change your mind, promise me you will tell me no matter where I am, no matter when it is."

His eyes bore into hers, willing her to promise him. "There will *never* be another woman for me, Grace. You are the one and only. I will always be there for you. Please promise me."

"I promise." It was the faintest of whispers.

"And I shall always be there." He pressed his lips to hers, and then was gone, leaving her to stagger to a chair and collapse into sobs.

# Chapter 41

Hat was she to do? Of course, Grace knew what she would do. She would do as she always had—after her mother's death, the assault by the wretched Smedley, her father's death—lose herself in her music. But this time it was different. All those previous things had brought pain and unhappiness to her. This time, she had brought pain and unhappiness to someone else, someone she loved. She would admit it fully now: she loved Max. She loved the way he challenged her, but showed how he appreciated her—not with trinkets and effusive compliments, but with trust and respect for her skills and talents. She loved how he had carved his own life out of nothing—ignored by his family, unappreciated by his peers. He had followed his own interests and found his way in life as she had done. In an odd way, despite their very different pasts and their very dissimilar interests, they were soulmates.

Another sob rose in Grace's throat. When had she become such a watering pot? When a vision of heaven had been dangled in front of her and she refused it. For it would be heaven to come home to Max every night, to share their days over dinner, and their nights . . . And that was another thing. Her body turned to liquid desire when she thought of the tall muscular frame, the thatch of dark hair, the intense face, the long lean fingers that had stroked her into an ecstasy she could never have conceived. She wanted more of it. She wanted more of him, and now she could never have him, never know what it was to be one with the man she loved. And why couldn't she? Because she did not want to do anything to impair his career. Because she could not risk the loss after so much heaven. She could not risk the chance that after she truly became his, she might not want anything except to be Lady Maximilian Hawkesbury, not Grace Owen, singer, who brought passion and joy to everyone who listened to her. No, she was not ready to risk losing herself, but oh how it hurt to lose him. It was almost more than she could bear.

There was another knock at the door. Grace stiffened, but before she had time to panic at the thought of Max returning, Dora popped her head around the door. "Good, you are here and," she glanced at the sheets of music that had been scattered on the floor once again during her desperate interlude with Max, "you are practicing. Are you on your way to rehearsal?"

"Nnnnooo, not . . ."

Dora shot her a sharp look. It was not like Grace to be so vague or disorganized. Her eyes were almost black with misery, and the pale skin was dead white. Something had occurred, and Dora, having come to impart the news she had to impart, could hazard a fair guess as to what it was. "You have given him his *conge*, haven't you?"

"Not precisely. He is returning to France and . . . er . . . well, yes."

"Yes, I know he is returning to France." Dora fixed her with a look that was bracing, but abundant with sympathy. "He called not long ago to give me a book, *A Concise System of Commercial Arithmetic, Adapted to Modern Practice*. It even has an *appendix containing a series of queries on bills and merchants accounts*," she added proudly, and Grace could see how much it meant to her friend—as if Grace needed proof that Lord Maximilian Hawkesbury was a kind and decent man.

"He even gave me the name and direction of someone who could help me with my Marylebone project—you know the houses I am building." Again, Dora was almost bursting with pride.

"I *do* know. Helen mentioned it when last I saw her. I must say, you are very clever, and very bold."

"As are you," Dora's warm brown eyes softened, and she laid a hand on Grace's which were twisting in her lap, "which is why you have to do this thing and you have to do it on your own. It is a lonely business being an artist of any kind—Juliette can tell you—especially starting out, but you must be on your own so you can put your whole heart into it; there will be nothing of it left for anything else. Juliette may be Lady Adrian now, but she had to forswear love at first in order to start her shop. It was the only way she could do it."

"Thank you," Grace replied huskily as she gripped Dora's hand in return. She might have just torn her own heart out, but she was not alone. She had friends, friends who understood.

"And now I have come to take you shopping. I need a new bonnet to go with a carriage dress Juliette is designing for me, and then a ride around the park because you need some fresh air. You are looking rather peaked, and you need the fresh air to make your voice as strong and true as possible. Come. Get your bonnet, and let us be off."

Dora was right. The fresh air did restore her, and the drive diverted her thoughts from the ever-present one of Max, his astounding offer, and the look on his face when she rejected it. Really, why did she keep repeating the scene in her head when she had broken off with him precisely so she would *stop* being distracted by his disturbingly attractive presence, so she could devote all her mental and emotional energy to her music?

That evening as Grace appeared on stage to thunderous applause, she felt her energy returning. Yes! This was what she was meant to do, what she was meant to be. As the song rose in her throat, she gave herself up to it, allowing it to transport her and her listeners to another world.

But Grace could not be in front of an audience all the time, and in the ensuing days, she had to work to immerse herself in her music. Fortunately, she had help. In addition to her theater appearances, she had been asked, thanks to Freddy's gentle hint to Mr. Greatorex, to sing at some of the Concerts of Ancient Music, and the Countess of Edgefield had written to several acquaintances still in town suggesting they brighten their lives in the slow season by offering a musicale featuring London's newest musical sensation, Miss Grace Owen.

In no time at all, Grace was so busy she was forced to think of nothing but music—heaven to someone who had previously had to struggle to find the time for it. But somehow, despite the success, the glowing reviews in *The Times*, *The Theatrical Journal*, and *The Morning Chronicle*, her days were flat. Yes, she was thrilled to be able to bring her special talents to the stage that she had dreamt of bringing—the inflection, the passion, the acting so lacking in other performers—and she was proud of it, glad that she had been correct in her opinions, but something was missing.

Not long ago, she had awakened with a sense of anticipation, a heightening of her senses that made colors brighter, scents more beguiling, sounds more enchanting, because there was a chance that she might see Max. His smile, the way his eyes warmed for her, made her feel more alive than she had ever dreamt she could be. She had thought that being on stage in front of hundreds of admirers would make her feel that way, but, while it was invigorating and inspiring, it just did not compare to what Lord Maximilian Hawkesbury made Grace Owen feel.

Was he discovering the same thing about her, even though he was back in his element in the midst of diplomatic discussions in Paris?

Of course, no man who had been so clearly dismissed by a woman would sink to writing her a letter, no matter how much she might secretly hope he would, but a certain visitor did reveal that, despite the miles between them, and her rejection, Lord Maximilian Hawkesbury remained concerned about her welfare.

"A Lord Farnsworth to see you, Miss," Tilly announced one morning as Grace sat practicing at the pianoforte.

"Do send him in, and would you mind bringing us some tea?" Tilly was really in the employ of Maison Juliette, but she enjoyed listening to Grace sing, and seemed to welcome any excuse to announce a visitor, in the hopes she could hear more. Grace assuaged her guilt for these services by slipping her a few coins on a regular basis and checking with Alice to see that Tilly wasn't neglecting her real duties. She also occasionally managed to secure tickets to her performances for both Tilly and Alice.

"Randall, this is a delightful surprise. How is your music coming?"

"Very well, thank you. One of my professors has hinted that he might secure a place for me—a performance, or maybe two, in the Lenten oratorios."

"Oh, Randall, this is wonderful news!" His shy smile told Grace how much it meant to him to have someone with whom he could share it, someone who could truly appreciate it. Titles and wealth were all very fine, but people like Randall and Freddy were trapped by them, unable to pursue their passions because of family expectations. Grace had seen how Freddy relaxed discussing fashion with Juliette or decoration with Helen, and Randall was the same. It reminded Grace of her own good fortune in her career, despite the hole left by Randall's uncle. She resolved to do what she could to help him achieve his dreams the way others had helped her, to show him how much she appreciated his early validation and the chance to talk about music with someone who was also longing for someone to share that sort of conversation.

"And . . ." he regarded her rather nervously, Grace thought, "I also came at the suggestion of Uncle Max . . . oh, and the Marquess of Wrothingham."

"Freddy?" She couldn't bring herself to ask about Max.

"Yes, but it was actually Max's idea. As usual, I am not explaining myself very well, am I?"

Grace shook her head and laughed at his awkwardness which she had always found endearing.

"Well, Max knew, of course, what a success you were at the opera, but, well, he's a diplomat and a businessman, so he plans for any eventuality, and private concerts can be very good for musicians' careers so he reminded the Marquess that when you performed at Henrietta's musicale that the Marquess' mother had mentioned having your perform at a musicale of her own and he suggested to me that I make sure of it by offering to accompany you. So I did, and we can perform pretty much at our convenience—the Duchess being able to command an audience whenever she issues an invitation. I realize this may be unexpected," Randall paused, smiling apologetically, "and I am only an organist, but I am competent enough at the pianoforte, and people won't be paying attention to me anyway."

"Why thank you, Randall," Grace smiled at him, "that is a lovely idea, and most kind of you.

"Don't thank me, thank Max . . . always thinking of you, you know." His brilliant blush told Grace everything she needed to know. Randall might be buried in his music and oblivious to many things, but, like his aunt, he had noticed a certain connection between Grace and his uncle. And how very amusing, and to his credit, that the uncle who had been so concerned about Grace's ruinous effect on his young nephew, was now sending that young nephew to help that ruinous woman as best he could.

"Good then, I shall tell the Marquess and his mother that we would be delighted and honored to perform at Claverton House. Now I must be off, as I have some practicing of my own to do. Let me know as soon as you have decided on the music, and when you would like to practice." He grinned. "I happen to know that you have an excellent pianoforte for me to play." And with that, he was gone, bounding down stairs in his usual ungainly fashion.

# CHAPTER 42

Nᴏᴛ ᴇᴠᴇʀʏᴏɴᴇ ᴡᴀꜱ ᴅᴇʟɪɢʜᴛᴇᴅ ᴛᴏ ʜᴇᴀʀ ᴛʜᴀᴛ Lᴏɴᴅᴏɴ'ꜱ newest musical discovery was entertaining the very top tier of the Upper Ten Thousand at the Duchess of Roxburgh's, though, in actual fact, it was her daughter who was taking care of the details as the Duchess' favorite spaniel had just delivered an unexpectedly large litter of puppies and couldn't possibly be left to handle such a momentous task on her own.

In fact, Lady Lavinia Harcourt was expressing a good deal of surprise at these details to her prospective sister-in-law not long after Randall's visit with Grace. "I am most puzzled by your choice of performer, Georgiana. I should have thought you would have chosen someone with a better reputation."

"How can you say that when Miss Owen has received such glowing reviews in all the press?"

"Oh, music," Lavinia waved one lavender gloved hand dismissively, "I am not talking about *that*."

"Then what precisely *are* you referring to?" Georgie's voice had grown dangerously quiet.

"Well, let us just say that I find it hard to believe you would invite that sort of woman into Claverton House."

"*That sort of woman* has been a music teacher and governess to the Countess of Edgefield. If she entrusts the education of her daughters to *that sort of woman*, then I certainly have no compunction about trusting our guests to her performance."

"Oh, well, the Countess of Edgefield . . ." another disparaging wave.

Georgie's eyebrows rose alarmingly. "Yes?"

"Well, she lives a few doors down from us and her daughters are perfect hoydens, not to mention that dreadful little mongrel who is a complete disgrace."

"I still fail to see the moral peril of inviting the governess of two lively girls to entertain guests here."

"Let us just say that she is no better than she should be." Lady Lavinia's mouth shut with a snap.

Georgiana regarded her curiously, then enlightenment dawned. "Do you know what? I think you have been indulging in gossip, gossip about things a lady should know nothing about." She smiled triumphantly as two unbecoming spots of red appeared on her future sister-in-law's lean cheeks. "Never fear, Lavinia, Mr. Greatorex, of your much vaunted Concert of Ancient Music felt comfortable enough to ask her to perform, and Freddy says she is also to perform with the Philharmonic Society, a group appreciated by true connoisseurs, which, he assures me, is far superior to the Concert of Ancient Music." *There, Lady Lavinia Harcourt, take that, you self-righteous prig,* Georgie gloated inwardly, happy to strike a blow, even a subtle one, at the woman who was going to make Freddy's life so joyless and miserable.

"Oh Freddy," his fiancée sniffed disdainfully, "if he paid more attention to his duties as the Marquess of Wrothingham and spent more time seeing to his estate than he does in the theater, he would know that one's place in society and one's reputation are more important than musical taste. You have been on the town a very short time, Georgiana and have no idea how precious is a woman's reputation."

"Actually, I think I have a very good idea," Georgie faced the fuming Lavinia with calm assurance, "which is why I would never indulge in salacious gossip. And if I were you, I would be proud that my husband-to-be is considered an arbiter of musical taste instead of criticizing him. Now, if you will excuse me, I must speak to Cook about arrangements for refreshments." And, holding her head high in majestic imitation of her mother, Georgie marched from the room. *There, let Lavinia think about that for a while.* Everyone knew that it was Lavinia's constant carping at poor Freddy that kept the builders at Wrothingham Abbey renovating it so it would be fit for the future Marchioness of Wrothingham, and ultimately Duchess of Roxburgh, thereby continually postponing the nuptials of the two who had been promised at birth.

Poor Freddy. Georgie, like her brothers, sympathized heartily with his plight. Any one of them would have been better suited to take on the mantle of the Dukes of Roxburgh than the softhearted, lovable Freddy who asked for nothing more than to indulge his love of the beautiful, even if it were only consulting over fashion or designing a looking glass at Maison Juliette, advising Helen on new decorations for her establishment, or promoting Grace's career among his musical friends. Well, it couldn't be helped, though all of them would be perfectly happy to help in any way they could to stave off the horrible day. Georgie, who knew full well that there had been no pressing engagement to keep Lady Lavinia from attending the Countess of Edgefield's musicale as she had claimed, was dying to see what she would do this time. The choice between swanning around as the Duchess-to-be at a function at Claverton House had to be carefully weighed against the horror of sullying her pristine reputation by consorting with *that sort of woman* who was the attraction of the evening.

Georgie could hardly wait to talk to her sister-in-law. Lavinia had no idea that Lady Adrian, though a daughter of the illustrious house of Fournoy, had once been *that sort of woman*, or, maybe, given her penchant for gossip, that was the reason for Lavinia's conspicuous absence from St. George's Hanover Square when John had joined Juliette and Adrian in holy matrimony in the presence of God, the Duke and Duchess of Roxburgh, Georgie, Freddy, the Comte and Comtesse de Fournoy and the inhabitants of Mrs. Gerrard's.

"How very amusing." Juliette rocked a sleeping Auguste in her arms the afternoon of Grace's concert. "Lady Lavinia certainly has very little to do with me, but then we are mostly in the country. Though, come to think of it, she rigorously avoids Maison Juliette, no matter how often you and your mother invite her to join you when you stop in.

Georgie grinned, "Which we do quite often, just to hear her mutter under her breath about people connected with trade. Unfortunately, it hasn't tainted us enough to make her cry off. You wouldn't think of selling the shop to Freddy, would you? Having a business establishment named House of Wrothingham might just do the trick."

Juliette laughed. "A tempting offer, but I enjoy it too much to let it go, and talented designer though he is, Freddy does not strike me as someone who would have a head for business."

"No. Too soft," Georgie agreed. "Oh well, I shall just have to keep trying, as should the rest of you. We *must* save Freddy from that harpy's clutches."

In the end, it was an *indisposition* of the Countess of Harcourt that kept Lavinia, who would never be so weak as to be indisposed herself, from attending the Duchess of Roxburgh's musicale, but she was the only one on the illustrious guest list who did not pack the drawing room at Claverton House. The double doors connecting it with the back drawing room had been thrown open to accommodate the crowd, many of whom Grace now recognized from her appearance at the Countess of Edgefield's and opera devotees to whom she had been introduced by Freddy, Mr. Arnold, and Mr. Greatorex. All in all, it was a great deal less intimidating than her first musicale, but still exciting. Smiling at Randall, she nodded, and he began to play.

The applause this time was even more enthusiastic than it had been at the Countess of Edgefield's, and both she and Randall were besieged with admirers as they stood with the Clavertons accepting congratulations, so it was some time before Grace was able to approach Lord John who stood a few feet away next to Adrian and Juliette.

"My lord?"

"Yes, *ma prima donna assoluta?*" His blue eyes twinkled conspiratorially, "I have the feeling a request is coming, and I assure you, your wish is my command."

Grace laughed. "You are far too omniscient which, I am sure, makes half of your parishioners drawn to you, and the other, sinful half, avoid you like the plague."

"Something of that order," he admitted. "Now, what can I do for you?"

"I have no idea how these things work, but surely you are on good terms with your organist."

"You mean Mr. Knyvett? He is not *my* organist, but the church's, yes."

"My accompanist, Lord Farnsworth is actually an organist. He was only playing the pianoforte tonight to help me. He is desperate to make his mark in the musical world, and if there were any chance that Mr. Knyvett might want a Sunday to himself, or . . . well . . ."

"Say no more. I am no musician, but I know enough to vouch for your accompanist's performance at the pianoforte to Mr. Knyvett. I shall mention your Lord Farnsworth when next I see him."

"It is not *my* Lord Farnsworth. Actually, he is Lord Maximilian's nephew."

"I see. Well then, I shall be sure to speak to Mr. Knyvett." And John *did* see—far more than Grace could have guessed, or would have wanted. John had noticed Max's decreasing enthusiasm for their card games and discussions at Mrs. Gerrard's, and he had at first attributed it to his upcoming departure for France and the necessary distraction of attending to all the details, but, on closer inspection, he had seen the somber expression that seemed to have taken up residence on his friend's face, not that his angular features had ever been sunny and smiling, but they had been alive and energetic, especially when a certain dark-haired singer was around.

Something must have happened to steal the happiness from that relationship, and the light from Max's eyes. Come to think of it, Grace had lost some of her sparkle as well. It was not just the physical distance between them, John had decided, but an emotional one as well, and he mourned for both of these two fine people whose feelings ran deep, but strong. This, however, the wish to help Lord Farnsworth, gave John hope that all was not over between Grace Owen and Lord Maximilian Hawkesbury, because, if it were, she would never have selected Hawkesbury's nephew as her accompanist, and she would certainly not have tried to further his career.

John's singularly sweet smile, lit up his face. "Have no fear, Miss Owen, I shall try my very best for Lord Farnsworth."

And with that, Grace was commandeered by Freddy who wanted to introduce her to the Earl of Mount Edgecumbe, "for he has been most impressed by your performances on stage and here, and if Mount Edgecumbe thinks highly of you, your success is assured." Freddy beamed.

# CHAPTER 43

J OHN DID DO HIS VERY BEST FOR RANDALL who wrote exultantly to his uncle in Paris some weeks later. *I have been studying this past month with a Mr. Knyvett who is organist at St. George's Hanover Square. He has been most kind and has taught me a great deal. Even better, he has agreed to allow me to play for several services so that he may assist his father at the Chapel Royal. It was very kind of Lord John Claverton to suggest me, but as he is no musician, I suspect that the idea was put in his head by Miss Owen during her musicale at Claverton House where she was much admired and yours truly did his best to accompany her on the pianoforte. If I am seen at St. George's Hanover Square, I feel encouraged that other engagements might arise.*

Max laid down the letter to gaze out over the embassy courtyard in Rue du Faubourg St. Honore where Castlereagh had given him a set of rooms. He never in his life would have dreamed he would be carrying on a correspondence with his nephew, not to mention the occasional missives that arrived from Laura and Beatrice, but he enjoyed them immensely. He actually enjoyed being part of a family, of being connected to people who cared enough about him to share their news, whether it was organ recitals or puppies or ponies. But this letter was more than that. This letter told him that Grace still cared . . . or, at least, that she did not wish to cut all ties with him as she so very easily could have. If she had truly wanted to eliminate him from her life, there were surely others who could have accompanied her at the musicale, and she certainly need not have gone out of her way to make Randall happy. It also made him realize that he needed to tackle the task of making his nephew happy by convincing Hubert and Almeria to let their son pursue his dream, and by encouraging Randall to show enough interest in the estate that they would feel sufficiently reassured that he would assume his duties when the time came to leave him alone now. It was simply a matter of diplomacy, and Max had never failed at helping two sides find common ground.

At least, that was what Max hoped. Upon his arrival in Paris, Max had thrown himself into working on a structure for French reparations to such an extent that even Castlereagh commented. "I know you are devoted to getting this done, Hawkesbury, but you are going to wear yourself into exhaustion, man, and then where will we be?"

Max could see the truth of his words. He was exhausted, and still had not worked hard enough to wipe Grace from his mind. He thought of her constantly, wished he could show her the sights of Paris, stroll with her in front of shop windows filled with the latest in fashion and taste, linger in cafes and watch as all the world paraded by. And when he did at last fall into bed, sleep eluded him as he remembered holding her close, feeling her heart beat, her lips respond to his, her head tilt back, eyes heavy-lidded with desire. Surely she had not completely forgotten him? Surely she must think a little about him, at least enough to wonder how he was.

Randall's letter, tenuous as the connection it offered was, gave Max hope that all was not lost, and so he put down his papers and emerged briefly into the gay world surrounding him to attend the opera. At least there he could feel Grace's spirit, even if he could not see her face. Just listening to the music and trying to imagine her opinion of the performance made him feel closer to her, and at the same time, he could be a better uncle by showing Randall his support for his chosen field as he shared with him, his own amateur impressions of the performances . Gradually Max began to attend more musical events, scouring the papers for reviews, seeking out the obvious connoisseurs as he recalled what Freddy, with his connections, had been able to do for Grace. If he could not match her talent, at least he could understand music and the musical world better and therefore appreciate her more intelligently.

It was not a world for the faint of heart. The struggle to be the best, to produce such beauty in a dependable way, demanded stamina and devotion, and the more Max learned, the more he marveled that Grace had been able to spare any time, energy, or thought for him at all. It was not like the world of diplomacy where, if one were too tired to contribute, one could stay silent hoping to appear reflective and intelligent, or one could fade into a crowd of people gathered in discussion. No, a performer in front of an audience was answerable to each and every member of that audience, even though most of them viewed the entire thing as more a social than a musical occasion.

It was at the opera where Max inadvertently ran into someone who clearly viewed attendance as the former rather than the latter. Actually, *ran into* was a misnomer, for it was obvious from the determined look in her eye that Lady

Caroline Daventry had hunted him down. He knew this because he had not been anywhere near her since he had learned of her return to Paris, and he had kept a weather eye out for her, always managing to be at the far end of a room at a function where she might be present. This time, however, he had let his attention slip and was now about to pay the price as Lady Caroline had slipped away from her mother whom he could now see engaged in deep conversation with the Duchess de Berri.

"What a pleasure to see you again, my lord. I do not believe I have spoken to you since we were last in England together."

Max bowed. There was nothing he wanted to say to her and was damned if he would validate her *together* with any sort of acknowledgement, besides which, he was reasonably sure that she had so much to chatter about that she would not even notice his silence.

"I see you are as devoted to the opera here as you were in London," she smiled slyly, "and here I thought it was one particular person there who commanded your attention rather than the music itself."

This time it was irritation, pure and simple, that kept him from responding. How on earth had she arrived at such a conclusion, and what earthly business was it of hers anyway? She must have been observing him closely, very closely indeed. The mere thought of it made his skin crawl.

"Yes," she continued, blithely oblivious to his clenched jaw, "a certain Miss Grace Owen, I believe. I warned her that a connection with you was not the thing, but would she listen to me?"

"You spoke to Miss Owen of me?" Max could not contain himself any longer.

Oblivious to his deadly undertone, his unwelcome companion shook her head in pretty dismay. "Of course, anyone who was concerned for your career and your reputation, as I am, would have spoken to her. But, would you believe it, she had the temerity to tell me that she trusted *you* to decide who you wanted as your friend. Of all . . ."

"And she was exactly right in her opinion." Max did not even bother to hide the fury in his voice, which gave even the irrepressible Lady Caroline pause. "I am quite capable of managing my career on my own behalf, thank you." And rather than strangle her then and there, Max abruptly turned and left her gazing after him open-mouthed.

By the time he had reached the street, his anger had cooled, dissipating as the implication of Grace's reply seeped into his consciousness. She hadn't rejected him because she no longer cared for him. She might not even have rejected him because she cared more about her career than she cared for him. She might even possibly, by the remotest possible chance, have rejected him because she cared about him, or his reputation, at the very least. And she was sending him a message through Lady Caroline because she recognized her for what she was, a woman determined to capture Lord Maximilian Hawkesbury as her own special prize, and Grace knew that a person like that would not be able to refrain from casting bitter aspersions on someone who was *no better than she should be*, someone who had the audacity to refuse an order from one of her betters . . . not only one of her betters, but the self-anointed darling of the British diplomatic mission in Paris.

Max chuckled—the first time he had actually, since he had last seen Grace Owen. How he wished he had been a witness to the scene. He himself had been the victim of Grace's magnificent scorn and knew what a lowering experience it could be. How delightful it was to picture Lady Caroline Daventry being taken down a peg in a similar way by his own Grace.

A burst of energy shot through him. All at once, he was ready to take on the world. The work he had accomplished through sheer dogged determination became interesting once again, and he plunged back into correspondence with the private banks the British were hoping to convince to assume the French reparation debt with all the eagerness of a young man writing his first love letter.

Despite his renewed enthusiasm, Max was ready for a change, he acknowledged to himself. Much as he enjoyed and believed in the work he was doing for Castlereagh, he had seen another way of life, a richer, less lonely existence that he had enjoyed in his sister's household, and, for the first time in his life, he craved that existence.

He was contemplating this very existence, sitting at his desk in the embassy a few days later when Lady Caroline popped in unannounced, without even a maid accompanying her. "Oh, I am glad you are in. I was just calling on Papa when I happened to look in and see you."

Max highly doubted the coincidental nature of their encounter. Lady Caroline was always well turned out, but this morning her hair was so artfully arranged under an extravagant French bonnet crowned with ostrich feathers that matched the pale canary colored spencer, gloves, and slippers, that it belied her claim to a casual encounter, besides which, there was that determined glint in her eyes.

"I am afraid you took my remarks amiss the other evening. It is just that Papa speaks so often of your diplomatic prowess, and predicts such a brilliant future for you that I get carried away in my enthusiasm. I wanted Miss Owen to understand how utterly crucial it is to your career that you move only in the highest circles where you are continually surrounded by those who can help advance you in your profession. Which is why I took such exception to her remarks about your selection of friends. She simply does not understand this sort of thing. I, on the other hand, do. I am devoted to making sure you have every opportunity to . . ."

"What Miss Owen understands," Max gritted his teeth, "is that I care more for my soul than my career, and *I* will choose those friendships that bring me pleasure, inspiration, and insight into the wider world, which is why I shall soon be going to Italy."

"Italy!" His visitor was thunderstruck

"Yes. I have been offered the secretaryship at Turin."

Lady Caroline shuddered. "But nothing is happening in Turin, and nobody who *is* anybody is in Turin."

A sardonic smile twisted his lips. "Then it is fortunate for you that you can remain in Paris. Now, if you will excuse me, I must deliver these papers to Castlereagh. I promised them to him several hours ago." Max rose, and then added, as if in afterthought, "May I escort you to your father's office?"

"That won't be necessary." Raising her chin, his unwelcome visitor flounced out of the room.

The sardonic smile expanded into a grin of unholy glee as Max gathered up his papers. Lord that had felt good. This time, he felt certain, he was well and truly free of Lady Caroline Daventry at last.

# Chapter 44

Grace glanced out the window at a dreary gray day. Rain spattered against the window, she had practiced all morning, and there was no performance of any kind to look forward to today; she was at a loss for anything to do. The weather was too nasty even to make her way over to St James' Square and the fellowship of the ladies at Mrs. Gerrard's. She almost felt like volunteering to help in the shop below, but she was no seamstress and, given Juliette's and Alice's exacting standards, she knew she would be more a hindrance than a help.

Flexing her fingers, she sighed and turned back to the pianoforte. She could always use extra practice, but her hand paused over the keys and she ran it over the smoothly polished wood instead, her eyes misting. How dear he had been to purchase this instrument for her, anticipating her need and fulfilling it before she had even recognized it herself. How she missed him, still missed him, after nearly a year.

Grace had thought that once Max had departed for Paris and she was firmly launched in her career, he would fade from her memory, but the longing for his companionship, for him—all sardonic six feet (and then some) of him—remained. Truth be told, it had actually intensified. Then too, there were the constant reminders in Henrietta , Randall, and the girls who not only kept him constantly alive, but shared news of his latest exploits, especially Randall who seemed to be on growing good terms with his uncle as they carried on a lively correspondence which Grace hoped was as gratifying to Max as it so obviously was to his nephew. She could not have cut off these friendships even if she had wanted to, for that would have meant Lord Maximilian Hawkesbury meant so much to her that even the slightest connection to him was too much for her to cope with, and Grace was not about to admit anything of the sort, even to herself.

"Gentleman to see you, Miss." Tilly was breathless from having hurried up the stairs in an effort to precede the visitor, but it was too late. Her heart recognized the tall figure behind the maid even before her consciousness did.

"Max!" The flood of joy washing over her was utterly disconcerting, not to mention demoralizing to someone who had worked so hard to need no one but herself.

"Grace!" The smile, tentative at first, broadened.

"But what are you doing here? I mean, please, do come in. I mean, I thought you were in Paris. And, Tilly, would you be so very good as to bring us some tea. And, please, my lord, do sit down."

"I am accustomed to being asked to explain myself, so I shall, in good time, but first, things first," he chuckled, digging deep into the pocket of his greatcoat to pull out a letter and hand it to her. "As to my presence, I have come to deliver this letter."

"But it is addressed to me."

"Which is why I am delivering it to you."

"That is *not* what I meant, silly man." Happiness was making her giddy.

"I know." He smiled down at her with an expression in his eyes that made her heart stop and her knees go weak. Drawing a deep breath, she opened the letter with hands that shook ever so slightly. Really, who would have thought one person could have such an effect on her? She glanced curiously at the signature. "Davidde Banderali? But why would he write to me?"

"Read it and see."

Grace sank down in her chair, her eyes fixed on the letter. One hand rose to her throat. "Good heavens! He is offering to take me on as his student. But how . . .?" She looked up in wonderment. "I know you are very clever, but the Conservatory of Milan? How did you know I . . ." Grace could not go on. It was all too inconceivable that a career diplomat would know how much studying in Italy would mean to her, would mean to her career.

"I cannot claim all the credit for myself." His tone was deprecatory as he took a seat opposite her, but his smile was proud and happy. 'You have often told me that no one is truly a successful opera singer until one has trained in Italy. Once I had determined on that, I called in Randall who asked Signor Lanza who he would recommend, and then I relied on him and Freddy to arrange for recommendations from Mr. Greatorex and Mr. Arnold, who, by the way, all seem to have become quite friendly with my nephew; you wouldn't happen to know about, would you?" He raised a knowing eyebrow. "And then, of course, there were the glowing newspaper reviews I assembled myself."

"And you arranged for all that to be sent to Signor Banderali?"

"No," the smile grew broader, "I went to see him myself."

Grace could not speak. It was all so overwhelming. He cared enough to do all that for her. Tears stung her eyes as she struggled for words as Max rose from his chair to clasp her hands in his as he knelt at her feet.

"I love you, Grace. I told you that before, and I told you I would always be there for you, and I wanted to show you that I am."

"Too kind . . ." she whispered. "I do not deserve . . . and after I sent you away so . . ." her voice trailed off.

"Lady Caroline told me." The smile had vanished entirely now and his face was grim.

"She told you she had called on me?" Grace was aghast. What sort of woman would admit to such a thing?

"She did, the infernal meddling . . ." he caught himself with an ironic half laugh. "Little did she know she was bringing me far greater happiness than I could have hoped for. She was irritated to no end that you refused to interfere in my affairs, that you were irrationally confident in my ability to choose my own friends. But you did interfere in my life, Grace. The moment I saw you I was lost." He grinned. "Antagonistic as that meeting was, I knew I'd met my match. And then you interfered again by breaking off with me for my own good, for the good of my reputation and my career."

Max reached up to cup her chin, forcing her to look directly into his eyes. 'Please tell me you did it a little bit because you care for me in addition to caring for your own career."

The tears spilled over. "I saw that I had hurt you, and it broke my heart. I had never caused anyone pain ever before, especially someone I loved, but I thought it would be best," she whispered, "for both of us."

"But it was not for the best, was it?" He rose, pulling her to her feet and into his arms. "I missed you desperately, and, I think, I hope . . . I realize I am pressing . . . but you *did* seem glad to see me just now."

She hung her head. "I was. Oh so glad."

"Then smile, and kiss me."

His lips came down on hers, and the world felt right again. Yes, she had missed him, oh how she'd missed him. He explored her mouth slowly, completely, as he pulled her against him, one hand sliding up to tangle in her hair and tilt her head so he could drink more deeply as his other hand drifted down her back to her hips to pull to him so she could feel just how much he wanted her.

"Excu . . ." Tilly tried to back out before they were aware of her presence, but, hampered by the laden tea tray, she was forced to give in and set it on the table next to Grace's chair. "Excuse me," she me, she muttered again before retreating red-faced.

"Perhaps it's as well we were interrupted," Max led Grace to her chair and resumed his seat, "because I do have more to say than I love you."

"You do?" Grace couldn't imagine what it could be, but then, she had never imagined she would be invited to be a student of Davidde Banderali, nor could she imagine Max visiting Signore Banderali.

"Yes." He drew a deep breath. "I asked you once to be my wife and you refused for reasons that made some sense at the time, I will admit, but now, I think . . . I hope, after the combined efforts of Randall and Freddy, that you will be studying in Milan so that if you marry the British Secretary in Turin—despite its distance from Milan, for after all what is a few days journey where love is involved—you will not be threatening your career or mine. Yes, we might not be together constantly, but we won't be condemned to being apart."

Grace gazed at him open-mouthed. "You gave up Paris for Turin? Even I, unfamiliar as I am with world affairs, know that Turin is not the center of international diplomacy. And what about the upcoming conference at Aix-la-Chapelle?"

Max grinned. So she *had been* paying attention to what he was doing. "I can still correspond with Castlereagh, if he needs me, and this is an actual post for me, not just assisting or advising. What do you think?"

He had done this for her, to prove to her how much he understood and respected her, how much he cared. "I think," Grace's voice grew husky as, once again, her eyes filled with tears, "I think you are the dearest, cleverest man . . . er . . . person, I have ever known."

"Even cleverer than Helen?"

She nodded solemnly. "Even cleverer than Helen."

He let out the breath he hadn't even realized he had been holding, but there was one more hurdle. "And will you marry me?"

"And I will marry you," she barely managed before she was pulled into his arms and kissed until she was nearly senseless, but not too senseless to look into those eyes shining with love and tenderness. It was all going to be right. They could love one another without losing themselves, and together, they would be so much stronger and happier than either one of them had dared to dream

# EPILOGUE

"**I**S MY BOW TIED WELL ENOUGH? Is it straight?" Beatrice frowned as she strained to look over her shoulder at the bow in question.

"It is lovely, dear, now stop worrying." The Countess of Edgefield patted her daughter's head.

"Besides, no one will be looking at you." Her sister offered scant comfort. "They'll be looking at Miss Owen. *She* is the bride."

"I know that." Beatrice turned her frown from the bow to her irritating sister. "But I want everything to be perfect for her."

"Come girls." Their mother shepherded them and their flower-filled baskets into the chapel at Edgefield Park where a small, but select company was gathered to witness the joining in holy matrimony of Miss Grace Owen and Lord Maximilian Hawkesbury by the Reverend Lord John Claverton. The groom's family, minus the Dowager Duchess of Swanton, sat in the front row on one side of the church, Randall having convinced Hubert and Almeria, after much discussion, that they owed it to Max for having guided Randall through a London season, to bestir themselves to attend his wedding. Randall, of course, was in his favorite seat in front of the small and ancient organ determined to give the performance of his life.

On the other side of the aisle, clustered various Clavertons, though, once again, oddly enough, Lady Lavinia's mother had been stricken ill enough to demand her daughter's attention. Also present were the Comte and Comtesse de Fournoy, the ladies of Mrs. Gerrard's, Messieurs Arnold and Greatorex, and Dance, and Olivia Childs.

Freddy, as the longest and most enthusiastic supporter of London's—soon to be Europe's—musical sensation, beamingly escorted the bride down the aisle to where John and Max, beaming even more than Freddy, stood waiting.

Olivia turned to Helen, her own face alight with a happy smile. "You have done very well with your ladies, Helen. Who would have thought? Two careers launched, and two marriages to two peers in two years."

"And yet, I did my best to make them independent and self-sufficient regardless of marriage."

"But not regardless of love."

The all-seeing green eyes twinkled merrily, but the smile remained as enigmatic as ever. "Clearly not."

# Bibliography

ALL AUTHORS OF HISTORICAL FICTION STRIVE to immerse their readers in the period by making the historical details accurate. I may be biased, but to my mind, authors of Regency novels are particularly devoted to this ideal, going down rabbit holes of research until they forget what century they live in. For those readers who would like to know more, I share my own sources with you in this bibliography.

I also like to make my heroes and heroines believable as well as unusual so try to find real-life counterparts who prove that the lives I am constructing could actually have been lived. *Mistress of Music*, the story of an opera singer marrying into the aristocracy does have an example in the life of Catherine Stephens, a well-known singer who became Countess of Essex. The career of Lord Maximilian Hawkesbury is somewhat modeled on that of Lord Stuart de Rothsay

GENERAL BACKGROUND ON THE REGENCY PERIOD

*Letters of Dorothea, Princess Lieven To Her Brother* 1813-1834 edited by Lionel G. Robinson, London, Longmans Green & Company, 1902

*The True History of Tom and Jerry or Life in London From the Start to the Finish With a Key to the Persons and Places, Together With a Vocabulary and Glossary of the Flash and Slang Terms Occurring in the Course of the Work* by Charles Heidley (includes selections from Pierce Egan's work), London, Reeves and Turner, 1888

*The Regency Reference Book* compiled by Dee Hendrickson, n.d.

*What Jane Austen Age and Charles Dickens Knew: From Fox Hunting to Whist—the Facts of Daily Life in 19th-Century England* by Daniel Pool, New York, Simon & Schuster, 1993

*Daily Life in 18th-Century England* by Kirsten Olsen, Westport, CT, Greenwood Press, 1999

*The Regency Companion* by Sharon H. Laudermilk & Teresa L. Hamlin, New York, Garland Publishing, 1989

*The Family, Sex and Marriage in England 1500-1800* by Lawrence Stone, New York, Harper & Row, 1977

*An Elegant Madness: High Society in Regency England* (rev. ed) by Venetia Murray, New York, Penguin, 1990

*The Gentleman's Daughter: Women's Lives in Georgian England* by Amanda Vickery, New Haven, Yale University Press, 1988

*The Writer's Guide to Everyday Life in Regency and Victorian England From 1811-1901* by Kristine Hughes, Cincinnati, OH, Writer's Digest Books, 1998

*Jane Austen: the World of Her Novels* by Deidre Le Faye, New York, Harry N. Abrams, 2005

*Jane Austen: Selected Letters 1796-1817*, (R.W. Chapman, ed., introduction by Marilyn Butler), Oxford, Oxford University Press, 1985

*The Prince of Pleasure and His Regency* by J.B. Priestley, New York, Harper & Row, 1969

*The Reminiscences of Captain Gronow Being Anecdotes of the Camp Court, Clubs & Society 1810-1860* by Rees Howell Gronow (abridged and with an introduction by John Raymond), New York, Viking Press, 1964

*A Portrait of Jane Austen* by David Cecil, New York, Hill and Wang, 1978

*Mrs. Hurst Dancing and Other Scenes from Regency Life 1812-1823 watercolors* by Diana Sperling, text by Gordon Mingay, London, Victor Gollancz, Ltd. 1981

*A History of the English People in the Nineteenth Century, vol. I England in 1815, vol II The Liberal Awakening 1815-1830* by Elie Halevy (translated from the French by E. I. Watkin, London, Ernest Benn Limited, 2nd. Rev. ed., 1949

*The Diary of Frances Lady Shelley 1787-1817* by Frances Lady Shelley, edited by her grandson Richard Edgcumbe, New York, Charles Scribner's Sons, 1912

*The Squire and His Relations* by Esme Wingfield Stratford, London, Cassell and Company, Ltd, 1955

*English Social History: a Survey of Six Centuries Chaucer to Queen Victoria* (ch. XV Cobbett's England 1793-1832 I, ch.XVI Cobbett's England II) by G.M. Trevelyan, London, Longmans, Green and Co., 2nd ed., 1946

*Life in Georgian England* by E.N. Williams, New York, G.P. Putnam's Sons, 1912

*Jane Austen's Town and Country Style* by Susan Watkins, New York, Rizzoli, 1991

*The Regency Years* by Robert M. Morrison, New York, W.W. Norton, 2019

*The Memoirs of Harriette Wilson* by Harriette Wilson, London, John Joseph Stockdale, 1825

*Mad and Bad Real Heroines of the Regency* by Bea Koch, New York, Grand Central, 2020

*Repository of Arts, Literature, Fashions, Manufactures, & etc.* by Rudolph Ackermann various appropriate years

*La Belle Assemblee* various appropriate years

*The Times* (London) various appropriate years

*The Edinburgh Review* various appropriate years

*Blackwood's Edinburgh Magazine* various appropriate years

## COSMETICS

*Georgians at Home* by Elizabeth Burton, Longmans, 1967 (chapter 8)

## COURTESANS AND SERAGLIOS

*London's Sinful Secret* by Dan Cruickshank, New York, St. Martin's Press, 2009

*The Memoirs of Harriette Wilson* by Harriette Wilson, London, John Joseph Stockdale, 1825

## ECONOMY/FINANCE

*Growth and Fluctuation of the British Economy 1790-1850* by Arthur D. Gayer, Oxford, Clarendon Press, 1953

*The London Stock Exchange: its History and Functions* by Victor Morgan, William Arthur Thomas, New York, St. Martin's Press, 1962

## EDUCATION

*A Plan for the Conduct of Female Education in Boarding Schools* by Erasmus Darwin, New York, Johnson Reprint Company, 1968

*A Governess in the Age of Jane Austen: the Journals and Letters of Agnes Porter* by Agnes Porter and Joanna Martin (ed.), London, Hambledon Press, 1998

*English Popular Education 1780-1970* by David Wardle, Cambridge, Cambridge University Press 1970

*Four Hundred Years of English Education* by W.H.G. Armytage, Cambridge, Cambridge University Press, 1964

*Review by Sidney Smith of Advice to Young Ladies on the Improvement of the Mind* by Thomas Broadhurst, 1808 in The Edinburgh Review, vol. XV, no. XXX, Jan., 1810

## FASHION

*English Costume of the Nineteenth Century* by James Laver, London, A. and C. Black Ltd. 1929

*Western World Costume* (Chapter 15 "Transition Period 1789-1813) by Carolyn G. Bradley, New York, Appleton Century Crofts, 1954

*The Cut of Women's Clothes 1600-1930* by Norah Waugh, New York, Faber & Faber Ltd. 1968

*Fashions in Hair: the First Five Thousand Years* by Richard Corson, New York, Hillary House Publishers, 1971

*Fashions in Hair: the First Five Thousand Years* by Richard Corson, New York, Hillary House Publishers, 1971

*Georgians at Home* by Elizabeth Burton, Longmans, 1967 (chapter 8)

*The Mode in Costume* (chapter 36 English Fashions 1790-1830) by R. Turner Wilcox, New York, Charles Scribner's Sons, 1948

*Costume In Detail 1790-1930* (Chapter 2, 1800-1835) by Nancy Bradfield, New York, Costume & Fashion Press, 1997

*Repository of Arts, Literature, Fashions, Manufactures, & etc.* by Rudolph Ackermann various appropriate years

*La Belle Assemblee* various appropriate years

**FOOD**

*The Art of Dining: a history of cooking and eating* by Sara Paston-Williams, London, National Trust 1993

**FURNITURE**

*The Regency Period (The Connoisseur Period Guides)* by E.T. Joy, New York, Reynal and Company, 1958

"*The Roots of Regency Taste*" by John Cornforth, Country Life, April 25, 1991

**HAIR**

*Fashions in Hair: the First Five Thousand Years* by Richard Corson, New York, Hillary House Publishers, 1971

**HORSES AND CARRIAGES**

*The English Carriage* by Hugh McCausland, London, The Batchworth Press, 1948

*Illustrated Book of the Horse: (Thoroughbred, Half-Bred, Cart-Bred) Saddle and Harness, British and Foreign, with Hints on Horsemanship; the Management of the Stable; Breeding; Breaking and Training for the Road, the Park, and the Field* by S. Sidney. Originally published 1875, Reprint by Wilshire Book Company, No. Hollywood CA, 1972

**HOUSEKEEPING**

*The House Servant's Directory* by Robert Roberts, Armonk, NY, M. E. Sharpe, 1998

*The Gentleman's Daughter: Women's Lives in Georgian England* by Amanda Vickery, New Haven, Yale University Press, 1988

*Home Comfort: a History of Domestic Arrangements* (in association with the National Trust) by Christina Hardyment, Chicago, Academy Chicago Publishers, 1992

## LANGUAGE AND SLANG

*The True History of Tom and Jerry or Life in London From the Start to the Finish With a Key to the Persons and Places, Together With a Vocabulary and Glossary of the Flash and Slang Terms Occurring in the Course of the Work* by Charles Heidley (includes selections from Pierce Egan's work), London, Reeves and Turner, 1888

*A Dictionary of Slang and Unconventional English* by Eric Partridge, New York, Macmillan Publishing Company, 1984 (8th ed.)

*A Regency Lexicon*, compiled by Dee Hendrickson n.d.

*The Regency Reference Book* compiled by Dee Hendrickson, n.d.

*What Jane Austen Age and Charles Dickens Knew: From Fox Hunting to Whist— the Facts of Daily Life in 19th-Century England* by Daniel Pool, New York, Simon & Schuster, 1993

*The Memoirs of James Hardy Vaux: including his Vocabulary of the Flash Language* by James Hardy Vaux, edited by Noel McLachlan, London, Heinemann, 1964

## LETTERS AND MEMOIRS

*Letters of Dorothea, Princess Lieven To Her Brother 1813-1834* edited by Lionel G. Robinson, London, Longmans Green & Company, 1902

*Jane Austen: Selected Letters 1796-1817* (R.W. Chapman, ed., introduction by Marilyn Butler), Oxford, Oxford University Press, 1985

*The Reminiscences of Captain Gronow Being Anecdotes of the Camp Court, Clubs & Society 1810-1860* by Rees Howell Gronow (abridged and with an introduction by John Raymond), New York, Viking Press, 1964

*Mrs. Hurst Dancing and Other Scenes from Regency Life 1812-1823* watercolors by Diana Sperling, text by Gordon Mingay, London, Victor Gollancz, Ltd. 1981

*The Diary of Frances Lady Shelley 1787-1817* by Frances Lady Shelley, edited by her grandson Richard Edgcumbe, New York, Charles Scribner's Sons, 1912

The Diary of Fanny Burney by Frances Burney d'Arblay, edited by Lewis Gibbs, New York, Dutton, 1966

*The Creevey Papers: a Selection from the Correspondence and Diaries of the Late Thomas Creevey* by Thomas Creevey, edited by the Right Hon. Sir Herbert Maxwell, London, John Murray, 1933

*The Memoirs of Harriette Wilson* by Harriette Wilson, London, John Joseph Stockdale, 1825

## LONDON

*Old and New London: A Narrative of its People, History, and Places (Vol. IV "Westminster and the Western Suburbs")* by Edward Walford, London, Cassell Petter &Galpin 1880

*The London Encyclopedia* edited by Ben Weinreb and Christopher Hibbert, Bethesda, MD, Adler & Adler Publishers, INC. 1986

*Romantic London* by Ralph Nevill, London, Cassell & Company, Ltd., 1928

*London Past and Present: a Dictionary of its History, Associations, and Traditions* (3 vol.) by Henry B. Wheatley, London, John Murray 1891, reissued by Singing Tree Press, Detroit MI 1968

## MARRIAGE

*The Statutes at Large From the Twentieth Year of the Reign of King George the Second to the Thirtieth Year of the Reign of King George the Second to Which is Prefixed a Table of the Titles of all the Public and Private Statues during that Time Cap. XXXIII An Act for the Preventing of Clandestine Marriages,* Volume the Seventh, London, Mark Basket Printer to the King's Most Excellent Majesty, Henry Woodfall and William Strahan Law Printers to the King's Most Excellent Majesty, MDXCCLXIV

## SERVANTS

*The House Servant's Directory* by Robert Roberts, Armonk, NY, M. E. Sharpe, 1998

*The Gentleman's Daughter: Women's Lives in Georgian England* by Amanda Vickery, New Haven, Yale University Press, 1988

## MUSIC

*Memoirs of Mrs. Billington From Her Birth* by Mrs. Billington, London, James Ridgeway, 1792

*The Careers of British Musicians: 1750-1852* by Deborah Rohr, Cambridge, Cambridge University Press, 2001

*Fashionable Arts: Opera and Elite Culture in London* by Jennifer Hall-Witt, 1780-1880 (Becoming Modern: New Nineteenth Century Studies), New Hampshire, 2007

*Musical Reminiscences of the Earl of Mount Edgecumbe: Containing an Account of the Italian Opera in England from 1775-1834,* New York, Da Capo Press 1973

*Five Centuries of Women Singers* by Isabelle Emerson, Music Reference Collection Number 88, Westport CT, Praeger, 2005

*Opera in London: Views of the Press 1785-1830* by Theodore Fenner, Carbondale IL, Southern Illinois University Press, 1994

*A Selection of Instrumental and Vocal Tutors and Treatises Engered at Stationers' Hall from 1789-1818* by Albert R. Rice, The Galpin Society Journal, vol.41 (Oct., 1988) p16-23

*Musical Memoirs: An Account of the General State of Music in England from the First Commemoration of Handel in 1784 to the Year 1830* by W.T. Parke, New York, Da Capo Press, 1970


**FINANCE/ANNUITY**

*The Early History of the Annuity*, by Edwin W. Kopf Proceedings of the Casualty Actuarial Society,1926-1927, Vol. XIII, p225-266


**DIPLOMATS/DIPLOMACY**

*The British Diplomatic Service 1815-1914* by Raymond A. Jones, Waterloo ONT, Wilfrid Laurier University Press, 1983

*Correspondance Diplomatique du Comte Pozzo Di Borgo et du Comte de Nesselrode*, by Charles-Andre Pozzo di Borgo, comte; comte de Nesselrode, Paris Calmann-Levy, 1890-1897 (Annee 1817)

*Lord Stuart De Rothsay* by Robert Franklin, Sussex England, Book Guild Publishing, 2007

EVEN BEFORE STUDYING EIGHTEENTH-CENTURY LITERATURE in graduate school, Evelyn Richardson decided she would have preferred to have lived in England between 1775 and 1830. Now living outside of Boston, she enjoys access to the primary sources that allow her to explore the details of the period and immerse herself in the same journals her heroines enjoyed which for her, as a longtime reference librarian, is the best of all possible worlds.